ENLIGHTENMENT

THE ENLIGHTENMENT SERIES
BOOK 1

NICOLE JAMES KELLEY

5 PRINCE PUBLISHING
5PRINCEBOOKS.COM

Digital ISBN: 978-1-63112-416-7

Print ISBN: 978-1-63112-417-4

Cover design by Marianne Nowicki

First Edition F07212025

For more information about this title, visit: www.5princebooks.com

To my husband, Nathan.
This book was made possible thanks to your unwavering support.

ACKNOWLEDGMENTS

Thanks to Bernadette Soehner for making my publishing dream possible. From the moment you heard my pitch, you have proven to be supportive, kind, and professional. Your encouragement and mentorship have made the publishing process everything I dreamed it would be.

To Cate Byers, thank you for your wit and knowledge. I could not imagine a better editor. You can untangle even the most complex of my "thought knots" and weave it into something beautiful.

To Wyoming Writers, Inc. for providing opportunities to connect with authors, agents, and publishers. The writing community you've helped cultivate in Wyoming and beyond has brought many previously untold stories to the public.

Thank you to my family. To my husband, Nathan, who supported me through every step of my writing journey. To my parents, Tim and Karen James, who always encouraged me to find my passion and instilled in me the work ethic to chase my dreams. I would not be the person I am today without your guidance. To my sisters, Jennifer James and Tracie Binkerd, who helped me organize my thoughts into something others might enjoy. Thank you to my nieces, Izabel and MacKenzie, who prove that the future is bright with women like them leading the way.

Many thanks to you, the person reading this book. I hope you enjoy reading it as much as I enjoyed writing it. You have made my dreams come true.

ENLIGHTENMENT

1

MAYDAY

Hawk watched the image of her face in the dingy metal walls and was grateful her reflection was her only companion tonight. Her feet padded softly against the floor, but otherwise the hallway was silent. She rushed onward, her eyes darting toward every surface looking for any sign of movement in the corridor. Now was no time for prying eyes, and lately it seemed everybody knew her every move.

She reached the end of the hallway and placed a hand on the door. As the door slid to the side, Hawk lifted her arm to block the rays of the blinding blue light. She took hesitant steps forward, her eyes cast down toward the floor.

Soon she was staring through a grating panel. A glow shone up through the metal grid allowing Hawk to see clearly the emptiness below. The door made a soft whoosh as it closed behind her. Hawk narrowed her eyes and extended her hand while taking one final step forward. Her hand hit a metal railing, which she gripped tightly as she slowly lifted her head.

Finally, her eyes adjusted and she could see the beauty before her. The blue orb glowed behind thick glass. Its surface seemed to roll upon itself in varying shades of blue and black.

The bubbling blue hues meant Hawk never got the same view twice, no matter how often she came to look at it. Ironically, its nature of constant change felt like the most stable part of her life.

Hawk sat with her legs crossed, gazing at the blue mass in front of her. The sphere was taller than even the tallest of men, and yet it looked dwarfed in the massive space provided for it. The surface swirled and rolled until Hawk's mind finally released its burden and she could no longer recall what emotional turmoil had brought her to this secluded wonderland.

She blinked the color from her eyes and began to rise when a familiar whoosh came from the doorway opposite her. Hawk jumped to her feet and backed away. Before she could turn, her eyes fell upon a green-eyed gaze. Hawk froze for a fraction of a second before stepping toward the door only a few paces away.

"Hawk! Wait!"

His deep voice bounced in the near-empty space. Hawk paused.

"Not tonight." She said just loud enough to reach him. She had come to clear her head and prepare for the stresses the next day was sure to bring. There was no room for anyone else.

He nodded in understanding and watched as she walked away.

Hawk fleetingly wondered if he was looking for her, or seeking his own solitude. She looked backward toward the door, then hastened her pace.

The universe for Hawk Larson was simultaneously as vast as space itself, and as restrictive as a prison cell. On some days, life seemed as though it could be forced to fit in a desk drawer, haphazardly tossed away with all the other forgotten junk. Today was one of those days.

Hawk stared at the radio in front of her. She wanted to look elsewhere, but there was nowhere to look. Hawk would usually welcome someone to talk to during this type of situation, but her present company was far from appreciated.

Rowan Sheridan was supposed to be training her. So far, he'd done very little to suggest he knew anything of importance, let alone that he was capable of teaching anyone. Still, there was nothing else to look at in the shabby communications room besides him.

First, Hawk looked to the table, then slowly lifted her eyes toward the seat back on the bench across from her. She hoped if Rowan noticed, he would think she was merely taking in her surroundings. When Hawk finally moved her eyes to the left, it was like glancing into a high-powered light. The intensity of his blue eyes caught her off guard.

She quickly flitted her eyes back to the radio before bouncing them back to Rowan. His gaze hadn't moved at all. He was watching, and he wanted her to know. He was brave. Cocky even. Hawk wished she had continued inspecting the wood grain of the table.

She tried to focus on the static emitting from the radio until she felt her face redden as if his stare were burning her. "Do you have to do that?" she finally snapped.

"Do what?" he asked innocently, adjusting his position to face her fully.

"Watch me." She turned to look at him, and his intensity seemed to have lessened with the rise of Hawk's words. "You're always watching me."

"Where would you rather I look?" He bared his teeth in a genuine smile that was even more dangerous than his gaze.

Hawk refused to look away this time. "I don't know.

Anywhere. It's bad enough that I'm stuck in this room with nothing except you and this ancient radio. The least you could do is leave me alone."

"If I'm not mistaken, you were the one who started talking to me," he smirked.

Hawk sighed heavily. "Yeah, today."

Three days ago, Hawk had started to fall asleep with one elbow propped upon the table and her hand holding her face above the hard surface. The other hand lay lazily in front of her on the tabletop. She had awoken with a start when she felt Rowan's fingertips graze her once-relaxed hand. No matter how bored, she never came close to falling asleep again. It didn't seem to help, however. Just yesterday, Rowan had actually moved from his side of the bench to sit next to her. He moved closer and closer until she finally relocated to the bench that he had previously been occupying, like a slow-motion game of tag.

"You need to stop."

Rowan's head slammed backward as if he had been slapped. "Stop what? Being friendly?"

"You know what I mean."

Rowan remained silent for a while, but nodded his head as if to say, *Message received.*

When he did speak, it was to change the subject. "Why do you hate this so much, anyway?" His eyes pointed toward the radio that sat between them. "I mean, it's probably the easiest job you're going to get under these circumstances."

"That's the problem." Hawk looked at her folded hands that had settled in her lap. When she finally found her words, she spoke barely louder than a whisper. "I'm better than this." Rowan arched an eyebrow in confusion, so she continued. "I'm trying to be a junior diplomat and instead, I'm stuck in this room with a radio that's only had static and audio tests pour through it for over four hundred years."

Rowan smiled mockingly, "Hey, it's an important job. I'm doing it, remember? And I'm a junior diplomat."

Hawk rolled her eyes. "You're my babysitter. We all know that *peer mentor* is code for *council spy*. You're only here to tell the Council if I'm good enough to be one of you."

"If that's what you think, then why are you making this so difficult for me?" His smirk widened as his smile and eyes worked together to aim all his charm at an unwilling target.

Hawk countered with her best glare and simultaneous frown. "I'm talented, Rowan. I'm not getting any position based on..." She shook her head as if to shake off the words she longed to say and finished with a more professional version. "I earn what I get."

This time Rowan looked away first with an expression of, what Hawk hoped was, shame. Hawk continued to stare at the radio. She imagined the pops and pulsations coming through to be a hidden code. Every once in a while, Hawk thought she heard a beep or even a human voice behind all the usual pops and scratches, but when she looked up, Rowan seemed as if he hadn't noticed. Hawk settled back into her seat, resigning to another three hours of the usual.

"You could bring a book you know," Rowan broke the silence.

"Huh?" Hawk had been focusing so intently on the sputtering hisses that she hadn't heard his words.

"A book. You could read while we're here. I usually do."

"I've never seen you read." Hawk thought back to their first day together. He had brought a bag, but never took anything out of it.

"Well, I've been hoping you'd talk to me," he shrugged apologetically. For the first time, Hawk thought she saw some pink creep up his cheeks.

"You mean you were trying to bore me into a conversation?"

Hawk tried to sound as if she were joking, but truthfully, she was a bit offended he had tried to trick her.

"Something like that," he shrugged again. "Look, Hawk I—"

Hawk held up a hand suddenly and cut him off. "Shhh!"

He ignored her and pressed on, "I just want to say—"

"Shhh!" she hissed again. "There's something there."

Hawk leaned in to hear the radio better. There was the beep again, but louder. It was long and piercing. She was certain of it this time. Rowan turned a dial and the clicks and hisses became much louder, filling Hawk's mind with confusion on top of what only seconds ago had been certainty.

"Did you hear that?" She studied Rowan's face for recognition.

His eyebrows pulled together in concentration. "That could be anything," still, he leaned in to listen closer, "is that a voice?" His voice quavered as he asked.

"I think it is, but what's it saying?" She turned the dial even further until it was so loud the static filled the small room.

"I still can't tell," he raised his voice to be heard over the crackling and popping.

They listened for a few more minutes, certain a voice was there, hiding behind the static, until Rowan turned down the volume.

"Why'd you do that?" Hawk reached for the knob, but Rowan reached out to stop her. "Something was there, I'm sure of it."

"Me too," Rowan said matter-of-factly, "I'm calling her."

Hawk inhaled a deep breath as she eagerly watched him punch in a code on his wrist transmitter. When the transmitter buzzed in response his wide eyes met hers. "She's on her way."

"Here? Now?"

"Right now."

Hawk sat back on her seat unsure if her legs would support

her weight any longer. She was finally going to meet Loris Goring

Hawk had seen Loris Goring many times during her lifetime but had never spoken with the woman, finding her intimidating, to say the least. Diplomat Goring was a woman of power and everybody knew it. She oozed confidence. Goring didn't merely receive respect. She *demanded* it by every word, every movement, and every action she took.

Technically, Diplomat Goring was no more powerful than any other Senior Council member, yet nobody made a move on the Council without her approval. The Council contained eleven senior diplomats, each with their own handpicked successor. Loris Goring was well known for her accomplishments as a junior diplomat to Gabbro Higgins.

Diplomat Higgins was ill for over a decade prior to his death. Although he officially remained in a position of power until the end, it was widely speculated that Goring had actually been in control of his position, and vote, for at least four years. With his recent death, Loris Goring had risen to power in an official capacity and was now looking for a junior diplomat of her own.

This was Hawk's ultimate goal: to become a junior diplomat under Loris Goring. Hawk had been selected as a candidate with nine other hopefuls. Each candidate for the junior diplomat position worked with a peer mentor, one of the junior diplomats already accepted by the Council. The ultimate decision would come from Senior Diplomat Loris Goring herself. If selected, Hawk would be trained as the successor to the most influential person local humanity had ever known.

Loris Goring swept into the room in a fashion befitting her stature. The door slid to the side in a silent, sweeping motion while Diplomat Goring's shoes hit the floor with a deep, hollow finality that made Hawk feel as if her whole adventure was coming to an abrupt end.

Although they had expected her, the haste with which she arrived caught Rowan and Hawk by surprise. The pair stood when they heard the first thud of her shoe approaching the table. Hawk's eyes were drawn toward the woman's face in search of approval. She found none. Diplomat Goring's eyes were fixed upon the radio sitting on the table. When she did speak, it was aimed at Rowan.

"What did you hear?" She spoke in a quick tone, bordering on hostile. Hawk winced slightly and looked toward Rowan to see his reaction. To Hawk's surprise, he seemed just as he usually did, as if this were a normal way to be spoken to by the senior diplomat.

"There was a voice, ma'am," he turned to her in a casual way as if they were friends, but the formality of his tone told a different story.

"And a beep. A long tone really," Hawk added.

The diplomat turned to look at her for the first time as if she had just now noticed Hawk was in the room. She turned her attention back to Rowan. "A voice? What did it say?"

"We couldn't tell. Hawk heard it first," he gestured toward Hawk. "It's still there, I think. It's mixed with the static, but it's there." He reached forward and increased the volume.

She listened for less than thirty seconds before she waved him off. "We'll never hear it from here."

Rowan quickly quieted the radio. "What can we do? How can we hear it?"

Goring started to walk toward the door. "There's a better radio in the helm and a crew that can help pick up the signal. We'll go there," she waved her arm as if instructing Rowan to follow. Hawk took a few hesitant steps before stopping.

"Er, did you want me to stay here then?" She questioned with an eyebrow pointing high toward the ceiling.

Diplomat Goring stopped a few steps from the door and responded without so much as turning her head. "Why would you do that? The action's going to be in the helm."

She continued her brisk exit and Hawk took a few running steps to catch up. Where the senior diplomat's shoes made a deep thud as they hit the floor, Hawk's made a mild squeak as if a small rodent were pursuing them. She continued to follow, determined to stay with the woman she so admired.

The path was unfamiliar to Hawk. She tried to memorize the route in case she was ever asked to return. Left. Pass two corridors. Right. Forward until hitting a wall. Right again... The turns and doorways started to blur together until, finally, they reached what must be their destination, because both Rowan and Diplomat Goring stopped.

Hawk, who was only one step behind, immediately noticed the impressive speed with which Goring began pressing buttons. She hit a series of keys and then stood stone-still as a bluish beam of light flitted over her, appearing to spend extra time on her face. When the light disappeared, a green glow shone around the doorway while the door slid open.

Goring entered first, but Rowan stood behind. "After you," he made eye contact with Hawk as he nodded toward the entrance.

Hawk stepped forward expecting to be in the thus-far-unknown beauty of the helm, but she was not. Instead, she was in a very small, empty room with a door on the opposite side. It was exactly the opposite of what she desired most to see. Hawk attempted to hide her disappointment by focusing her attention on the new doorway.

As the entry door slid shut behind them, Goring had already approached a keypad next to the opposite door and was hastily typing a series of numbers. Hawk wasn't sure exactly how long the code was but noticed it was quite lengthy. After Goring was finished, she again stood and waited for the scan to read over her body. The now-familiar green lighting appeared around the door. Rowan stepped behind Hawk to indicate that she could once again enter before him.

Hawk attempted to follow Diplomat Goring with the speed that she had exhibited earlier but found herself unable to do so. Hawk gasped as she entered the helm with hesitant, dazed steps. She had never seen so many levers, buttons, and screens in one place, but that was not what stood out most.

In front of her was an expansive window that opened to the stars. Ahead of her, thousands of bright orbs filled her view. Some disappeared behind the ship as it pushed onward. Others seemed to stand in place ahead of her. Hawk had never seen anything like it. She heard others speaking near her but was unsure of what they were saying. It was as if she were suspended in a bubble outside the helm, removed from the voices, floating with the stars.

She felt a gentle hand on her shoulder that caused the bubble to pop, dropping her back into reality. Rowan's voice whispered in her ear, "You'll have time to take it all in later. Right now, we have a job to do."

Hawk nodded and blinked a few times to regain her composure. Rowan nudged her forward gently, and she moved in the direction in which Diplomat Goring had headed. She watched as the woman stepped up into an area toward the starboard side. Although many people bustled around the helm, this platform was empty.

The area itself was separated by a waist-high partition with two entrances, one toward the port side and the other toward the navigation center in the front of the helm. There were no buttons or levers that Hawk could see, although there was a small speaker built into the center of the table. It appeared to be a conference area.

Hawk approached the nearest entrance. Rowan followed closely behind her as if he were trying to ensure that she did not become distracted by the view once again. When she finally reached the platform, Hawk did her best to ignore the stars and instead focused her attention on Diplomat Goring and the table in front of her. Goring stood facing the navigation center and soon began shouting orders.

"We need sound here, and headphones." Hawk wasn't sure who she was speaking to, but her words appeared to produce a great deal of movement. Soon, Rowan was handed three pairs of headphones that he immediately plugged into the jacks positioned around the outer edge of the table.

Hawk accepted her pair and placed them over her ears. The clicks and electric buzz resounded through the earpieces. She pulled them away quickly before gingerly placing one ear close to the earpiece.

"Check to see if there's anything out there." Again, the order was to no one in particular, but Hawk was certain it would be followed.

A timid voice responded from a nearby station. "We're picking up a signal, but it's very weak." Hawk saw a young woman hitting buttons in quick succession.

"We're not getting it!" Goring snapped back.

"I'm almost there," the woman responded with a voice that displayed little confidence.

It started slowly, but soon Hawk could hear a voice breaking through the white noise. She placed the headphones over her ears and began listening intently.

At first, only a few unrecognizable words could be heard. "We need this clearer," Goring barked.

The young woman's fingers seemed to move even faster. "Stop!" Rowan hollered. "That's it."

Mayday. Mayday. This is Seeker. *We are in distress. Does anybody copy?*

Hawk nearly fell from her seat as the voice continued. *Is anyone there? Repeat, this is* Seeker. *We are in distress. Does anybody copy?* The man's voice fell silent, and Hawk was left with only the sound of her own heaving breathing.

"Did that say *Seeker?*" Rowan questioned, before Diplomat Goring quieted him with a glance.

The voice continued. *Nobody's coming. This is pointless. I can't believe we are still doing this,* he let out an exasperated sigh followed by silence. The voice returned abruptly in a panicked yell, as if the man had reached his breaking point. *MAYDAY! CAN ANYBODY HEAR ME!* Hawk jumped and pulled the headphones away from her ears, startled by the sudden increase in volume.

She carefully brought the earpiece back toward her ears and heard a scraping sound followed by grunts and thumps. Soon a new voice sounded through the speaker. This time a woman's voice resounded with the same original message repeating again and again. *This is* Seeker. *We are in distress.*

The ship began to shake around them. "Get this turbulence under control!" Goring shouted. Despite multiple people jumping into action, the shaking continued, and with it, the static started to creep in, first softly, and soon so strongly that the voice could no longer be heard. The ship gave a final, violent jolt that caused Hawk to slide a few inches in her seat.

"We're losing it!" Goring was looking straight at the nervous-looking woman whose fingers continued to blur with speed as she pressed buttons.

"It's not working," the young woman finally stated flatly,

"we've lost the signal." She looked up, a mixture of sadness and fear on her face.

Goring did not acknowledge the helm worker in any way. Instead, she took off her headphones and laid them on the table in front of her. Rowan and Hawk did the same.

Hawk could not hold back any longer. "What did I just hear?" Her eyes first met Rowan's and then Diplomat Goring's. "What just happened?"

She waited for an answer but was only greeted with more silence.

2

MIRROR, MIRROR

Hawk once again found herself rushing to keep up with Loris Goring and Rowan Sheridan as they swept through the halls. "Where are we going?" She managed to ask as they turned a corner.

"Conference room," Rowan grunted.

Hawk nodded even though she knew nobody was watching. "And what are we doing in the conference room?"

Diplomat Goring answered quickly, as if there was no time for discussion. "Having a conference."

Hawk looked toward Rowan for more information, but he provided none. He stared forward with the occasional glance toward the senior diplomat he walked beside.

Hawk slowed slightly to follow a step behind. She was certain she would learn more by listening to their conversation than by forcing her own involvement.

"Did you call for Ural yet?" Diplomat Goring asked him without turning her head.

"As soon as we left, I sent him a message. He said he'd contact the rest of the Council," Rowan spoke clearly despite moving at a brisk pace.

"Excellent. They'll be waiting for us then?"

"Hopefully. Or arriving shortly after."

Hawk felt as if she were going to hyperventilate. *The whole council.* She had been nervous enough meeting only Loris Goring, now she was going to see *the whole council!*

Just then a tall man with hair a color that resembled a rusted bolt came full speed around the corner. Without missing a beat, he began walking side by side with the senior diplomat.

"What's happening? All Rowan told me was that it's urgent." He sounded slightly out of breath. The whiskers below his nose quivered with each breath.

"It is urgent," Loris did not elaborate. "You've contacted the others?"

"They're on their way." The tall man did not ask any more questions. Hawk continued to follow. She studied the way that Rowan stood to the right and half a step behind the new arrival: Ural Ambrose, a senior diplomat on the *Enlightenment* Council, and Rowan's mentor.

Hawk knew where they were heading. Although she had never set foot in the official Council's Conference Room, she knew exactly where it was located. The halls themselves seemed to brighten as they approached.

Finally, they stood on the outside of an expansive door. Hawk took a moment to memorize her surroundings. The waiting area outside the conference room was metallic, like all of *Enlightenment.* However, this area was polished to a luster whereas much of *Enlightenment* had fallen into a dingy state. This was a location of great prestige and was therefore treated with greater care. The cushions on the chairs had clearly been recently re-stuffed to allow a comfortable wait. Not that they would be waiting.

Loris Goring was first to approach. There were no keypads or scanners like Hawk had seen earlier. Instead, the door resembled an oversized version of the entry to her living quarters.

"Loris Goring, requesting entrance for official Council business."

The door slid to the side to reveal a large rectangular table in the center of the room that was surrounded by plush, red upholstered chairs. Diplomat Goring immediately walked toward the head of the table. Rowan and Ural stopped midway along the table and sat in what were clearly their usual spots. Hawk stood awkwardly, unsure of where guests should sit.

"Hawk, you can sit here for now." Diplomat Goring gestured to a seat that had been pulled away from the table and was situated behind the senior diplomat's seat. Hawk nodded and hastened her way to the seat that was deemed appropriate. When she sat, Hawk could hardly believe the softness of the cushion. She had rarely been in such comfort, even in her own living quarters.

The room was shockingly quiet as the other diplomats trickled in. Most senior diplomats arrived with their protégés. Hawk took note that the junior diplomats appeared to always sit to the right of their mentor. She eyed the empty spot to the right of Loris Goring and noted that the chair she was in must have been intended for that spot but had been pulled away to accommodate her lesser status as a guest. She longed to push the seat into its usual spot and take her coveted position around the table. But for now, she would sit against the wall. Watching.

In a matter of minutes, every seat was filled. Hawk watched as all eyes examined Loris at the head of the table. "Thank you all for coming on such short notice." She paused while the other council members shifted uncomfortably in their seats. "We have a situation that requires discussion immediately."

Loris nodded toward Rowan and Diplomat Ambrose.

Rowan handed his mentor a small chip. The whole room watched as he stood and placed the chip inside a slot in the center of the table and then looked toward Loris for instructions.

"Play it." Loris commanded. Before the words had fully left her mouth, he had already pushed a button and the familiar static filled the room. When the voice began speaking, one man stood from his seat with such haste his chair fell backwards and hit the floor with a loud clatter. Hawk blinked at the loud sound, but nobody else seemed to notice it. They were all fully engrossed in the voice coming from the center of the table.

At the peak of the message, when the man began to yell, no less than three of the diplomats sitting around the table held up a hand in front of their mouths in complete shock. The message was one-sided. Hawk could still hear the orders being yelled toward the helm crew, but the rest of the Council could only hear the shrieks and pleas from the crew in *Seeker*.

The message ended just as abruptly as Hawk had remembered. She sat still as her chest rose and fell with deep breaths. Loris waited for what seemed like an eternity before she spoke to the rest of the Council.

"This transmission was just picked up."

"By whom? Who received this message?" a small man at the opposite end of the table asked.

Loris looked toward Rowan, who looked toward Hawk. Hawk cleared her throat causing all eyes to turn in her direction. "We did." She kept her eyes fixed on the junior diplomat at the center of the table. "Rowan and I did."

Loris continued. "It was picked up faintly during standard radio monitoring. Upon receiving notice that a possible frequency was intercepted, we continued monitoring in the helm and recorded the message that you all just heard."

"Is this all that there is? Did you make contact?" Ural

Ambrose was sweating profusely in his seat, but his voice was clear.

Loris took a deep breath before continuing. "There wasn't enough time before the signal was lost."

"Can we regain contact?" Diplomat Ambrose continued to question.

"That's what we're here to discuss." Loris' eyes searched the faces of her fellow councilors. "Do we want to seek out contact?"

Hawk was certain she looked like a confused child. Her mouth was agape with complete shock at what she was hearing. How could they even consider ignoring the message?

Nobody spoke as eyes darted around the table looking for a brave soul who dared to voice an opinion. Nobody did until Loris offered her own. "If this is *Seeker*, these people are our own. They are from Earth just like us. We can't abandon them."

Voices around the table rose to a heightened urgency in agreement. "Then it's settled. I will talk to the helm crew immediately. We'll alter course if necessary and attempt to make two-way contact." The woman smiled for such a fraction of a second that Hawk wasn't sure if anyone else had seen it.

A few council members began to stand but Diplomat Goring's voice stopped them. "We still have one more matter to discuss." The councilors settled themselves back into their seats.

"We have an unexpected guest with us today." All eyes turned to Hawk. "Ms. Larson was present for the initial detection of the message and subsequent recording. She is the only non-council member to have access to this information. We need to remedy that situation."

Hawk squirmed uncomfortably in her chair. "I'm not going to tell anyone if that's what you're thinking."

Loris Goring smiled the first full smile Hawk had ever

witnessed upon her face. "I know you won't tell anybody, dear. You're one of us now. Welcome to the *Enlightenment* Council, Junior Diplomat Hawk Larson."

The rest of the meeting had been a blur for Hawk. She had heard words and shook hands, but she wasn't sure if she had even responded to the declaration of her receiving a prestigious position on the ship. Hawk knew as she walked away in a haze that she was supposed to continue with her usual affairs that evening.

Hawk walked without any real knowledge of where she intended to go until she found herself in Wing 5. She shook her head as if waking from sleepwalking when she discovered she stood outside the familiar metallic door marked as room 51132. "Hawk Larson requesting entrance." The door did not immediately move. Hawk heard the recognizable hum as she knew her image and voice were both in the process of being analyzed. The door swiftly slid to the side to allow entry.

Hawk entered the room while assessing the scene in front of her. She had already cleared the bed which was now folded neatly into the wall. In its place sat a small, cozy couch. Its tan color fit in with the muted colors in the rest of the room. Hawk picked up the objects that were scattered on the floor from the turbulence while she headed toward the far side of the room. She kneeled next to the couch and dislodged a small, cut away portion of the wall's paneling. The private storage area was one of her favorite features of the living quarters, but it was not unique. All rooms were equipped in a similar fashion. Hawk's hand hovered over a lockbox which took up the majority of the storage area but then reached her hand for the leather-bound case sitting next to it, exhaling sharply as her fingers reached the cool material.

"Time." Hawk wasn't sure how much time had passed during the meeting or how long she had wandered the halls in a daze. The time flashed against the wall, 4:23 p.m. Hawk was due for her next ship duty at 5:00. She had time. Not much, but enough to satisfy her need.

Hawk opened the case to reveal a thick file folder filled with neatly stacked papers containing hand-written notes and drawings. She had meticulously collected and sorted everything she thought might be useful in her pursuit of a junior diplomat position. These were notes from her classes and past experiences that Hawk thought might come in handy. She had been planning her acquisition of the position for years.

Being a junior diplomat required an expert level knowledge about Earth and her spacecraft home, *Enlightenment*. It would also mean knowing the basics about Onsella, the planet to which they were heading. She was not expected to be a specialist in this area, but communication skills, and knowledge of the Onsellans' involvement in the *Enlightenment* Project were a must.

Hawk thumbed through the papers until she found the one she was looking for. She gazed down at a hand-drawn image of a glowing, blue, spherical object hovering in a clear dome. A large metallic cylinder, looking much like a needle, extended from the gleaming orb and led to the clear dome until it finally connected to a metallic tube that ran outward away from the ball of blue light. The tube spiraled downward before connecting with a massive control panel. This was the key to *Enlightenment*'s survival, the power source that enabled the ship to move: Blue Vigor.

Hawk had studied Blue Vigor intensely for years. She found the process fascinating, but not nearly as fascinating as she found Earth. Knowledge about her home planet had become like a drug to Hawk. She was in constant search of more facts and information. Hawk was certain she was one of the most educated souls on the ship about both Blue Vigor and Earth, despite her age.

She stared at her reflection in the mirror above her dresser. Hawk's shaking hands still clung to the folder as the sketch of Blue Vigor flitted to the floor. She closed her eyes tightly attempting to chase away the tears that she knew were hiding just behind her lids. When she opened them, Hawk saw the redness in her cheeks and puffiness around her eyes that told a very different story than the one she tried to tell herself.

"You earned this." She said flatly to the reflection staring back at her.

She lifted the folder in her hands as more of her meticulously organized documents fell to the floor. "I earned this."

Hawk left the room feeling utterly unprepared for her shift as Energy Production Manager. There was always someone present in the Energy Production Room, but her job was more complicated. Blue Vigor had been brought from Onsella itself. The power it emitted was great enough to move the ship through space. Extracting the power and harnessing the energy, however, was much more complex. The ship needed to produce its own energy to do so. This energy was created by the citizens of *Enlightenment*. Hawk was one of several in charge of overseeing how this happened. With her position as Energy Production Manager, Hawk saw to it that every citizen contributed their part.

Each citizen of *Enlightenment* was required to participate a minimum of one hour per day in the Energy Production Room. Most people referred to the area as a gym. Treadmills, stationary bikes, stair climbers and other equipment were all hooked into the power grid. The power produced by the equipment was used for the non-essential functions of the ship such as lighting, door operations and visual imaging. More importantly, it was used to extract the energy from the Onsellan force known as Blue Vigor.

Hawk's job was to check to see who had not yet contributed their hour of production time. Most people came around the same time each day to be sure they didn't miss their required contribution. It became part of their daily routine. Hawk always completed her time after her shift as EPM.

She would be working with Everest today. He was one of her favorite people to work with. Although, "people" was not exactly accurate. All beings in *Enlightenment* were referred to as "people", but Everest wasn't human. He was Onsellan. Everest was taller than most humans. He had very little hair on his head but had facial hair. His skin had a light bluish tint that was lighter than most Onsellans. His body was very much like a human's body with the exception of his tail. Hawk barely noticed it anymore. It was long and blue, like the rest of his skin. It usually laid over his shoulder like a scarf. It only moved when he was especially animated in his talking. Some Onsellans used their tails more than others. Everest was not very excitable and, therefore, his tail sat limp most of the time. Like all Onsellans aboard *Enlightenment,* his primary language was English. He would, on occasion, speak in Onsellan with Hawk, but only to keep the language alive.

When Hawk arrived at the EPR, Everest was already at work. "Not too many today, it looks like." Everest didn't even look up from the screen in front of him that displayed the names of those still requiring their hour. Most people were able to complete their contribution before 5:00 p.m. when Hawk's shift began.

Few people were allowed exceptions from the contribution. Adults who had been declared medically unable were not required to do so. However, this was a difficult status to achieve. An adult who had injured a leg, for instance, would still be cleared to use a rowing machine. Elderly adults might be cleared for walking the treadmill rather than jogging and exerting themselves too fully. Indeed, to be exempt from Energy Production was a rarity and usually a temporary situation when issued. Even children were required to participate after reaching the age of eight. *Enlightenment* needed as much energy as could possibly be achieved.

Thirty-seven names were on the list today, Hawk's and Everest's included. "Ok, well let's send out the reminders." Hawk quickly typed in a code only known by herself and a handful of other EPMs. Reminders would appear on the cabin walls and on the wrist transmitters of anyone not yet meeting their production requirements.

Hawk had the ability to take her own name off the list, but she never did so. She didn't want anyone accusing her of abusing power. Something that would become even more important now that she actually *had* power. The thought of her recent addition to the junior diplomats fluttered in her chest.

Once Hawk sent the notification, all those who had received it were required to acknowledge the message and set an appointment to come in. Hawk and Everest were charged with the task of finding those who did not respond within thirty minutes of the initial message. It was Hawk's least favorite part of the job. It was rare that a person did not respond. Everybody knew their duties in *Enlightenment*.

Immediately after sending the message, Hawk felt the familiar buzz of her wrist transmitter. She didn't even glance at it before she clicked to a screen to schedule her own energy production time. She knew that the flashing red message in her room would fade now that her contribution time was scheduled. Everest did the same.

Hawk noticed his catlike eyes shift uncomfortably in her direction. Everest was over two decades Hawk's senior. He was closer to the age of her parents than herself. He was an outspoken, calm man, but not a nosy one. She could always count on Everest for a good conversation, but tonight was different. He sat quietly tossing occasional glances her way. Finally, Hawk could take no more. "Just ask, Everest. I know you're curious."

He sighed heavily as if relieved. His tail gave a subtle twitch. "Ok. How're things going with your trial run? Are you the next big name on this ship?" He kept his voice level low and showed little excitement although the twitch of his tail told Hawk otherwise.

She smiled to herself before looking up. "It's been an eventful few days." *More like few hours.* "Nothing really big to talk about yet." Hawk wished she could tell him the truth, but the warning to tell no one was one of the few things she remembered being said to her as she left the conference room.

"What will you do if you get it? I mean, as far as your positions go. Most diplomats don't take on jobs that are so people-heavy." Everest sounded nervous while his eyes pointed to the contributors in the EPR.

All citizens of *Enlightenment* were required to work a minimum of three jobs. Hawk had selected roles of teacher, horticulturist, and energy production manager. All people applied and were interviewed for positions they were interested in. Hawk was fortunate enough to be assigned the three occupations of her choice. Now that she was a junior diplomat, she would be required to resign from one position and replace it with her new career. Even diplomats were required to work three positions.

"Are you asking me if I would leave this position?" Hawk couldn't help but tease. "You really can't live without me, can you?"

"Who would want to?" Everest played along. "People like you don't come along every day." Hawk laughed until she realized he was being sincere.

"I wouldn't leave this job, Everest. Somebody needs to keep you in line." Even as she said it, she felt guilty.

"Good." Everest said nothing else about it. It was clear he had pushed his comfort zone past its limit.

Hawk smiled at him and turned her attention to the screen in front of her. It had been only ten minutes since she had sent the reminder notification and already twenty-four people had responded. "Here's hoping we don't have to go searching for anyone today."

Everest responded with a grunt. *Now that's the Everest I know.* He was never shy about expressing his feelings, but he didn't feel the need to fill an enjoyable quiet with babble. Hawk smiled to herself.

Hawk had told Everest she would keep her job as EPM; however, she wasn't entirely sure if that was true. Most council members chose research or office jobs as their second and third positions. Being in the public eye so much of the time left diplomats open to persuasion. Some had tried to keep their public service positions but usually ended up switching after having too many run-ins with angry or overly enthusiastic citizens.

Hawk wasn't aware of how much time had gone by until Everest nudged her back to reality. "It's time for physical reminders."

"How many today?" Hawk asked the question while she was already looking toward the screen.

Everest sounded smug and mischievous as he answered. "Two. I bet I know which one you're picking."

Two names appeared on the screen in front of her, but Hawk's eyes were only fixed on one.

Loris Goring.

3

A BUMPY LANDING

Hawk stared at the screen, blinking in disbelief. Loris Goring?

"Ah, yeah. I guess my choice should be pretty obvious, right?" Hawk laughed a forced giggle that was meant to show excitement but really exuded nervousness.

Everest lowered his chin and peered at Hawk over his glasses. "I thought you'd be thrilled to see your new boss. Was she that intimidating?"

Hawk gulped, knowing that he was attempting to joke with her, but his attempt at humor resembled reality too closely for her to laugh. "No. No, not at all. I just... It can't be a coincidence that her name is on this list *today*. I've been working as EPM for six months and she has never once appeared on this list. Have you ever seen her need a physical reminder?"

Everest shrugged. "No. I can't say that I have."

"Exactly, and you've been here what? Thirty years?"

"Hey now, don't make me seem any older than I am. It's only been twenty-eight years thank you very much." He mock-frowned at Hawk in a way that said he wasn't really angry.

"Sorry." Hawk smiled back. "But really, why today?"

Everest shrugged the *I don't know* shrug as he jotted down information for his physical reminder. "Well, good luck with that. I'm off to see Mrs. Jenkins. Again."

Mrs. Jenkins usually required a physical reminder at least once a week. "Ok. See you in a few." Hawk wrote down the information for Loris Goring with trembling hands. She knew this was why Everest left so quickly. He was allowing her a few moments to compose herself and she couldn't be more grateful.

Wings 4, 5 and 6 were used for living quarters. Diplomat Goring was in Wing 6. As Hawk entered the wing and approached the room, questions flooded her mind. What should she say? Should she give the normal reminder? How does someone—anyone—demand anything of Loris Goring? Did Diplomat Goring plan on this or was it really a coincidence? What if she was injured? Why else wouldn't Diplomat Goring complete her energy contribution? She probably wasn't even in her room. Why else would she not respond to the reminder?

When Hawk finally reached room 68187, she took a deep breath and rang the door alarm. The door opened almost immediately. There she was, perched on elegant heels that caused her to tower inches above an average woman's height. Her usual, confident smile beamed down on Hawk. "I was hoping you would be the one to come. Please, come in." She waved a steady arm as if presenting the room as a piece of art.

"Er, ah, ok?" Hawk winced at her own response. Why did that sound like a question? *Come on Hawk. Get it together*.

Diplomat Goring continued, "You seem surprised to be here. May I ask why?" As she spoke, she moved toward the sofa. Before Hawk could respond, the diplomat was patting the seat next to her as if to say, *This is where you will sit*.

"I never imagined I would be in your quarters. I certainly never imagined I would be here for something like a required physical reminder for your contribution time." Hawk said this while positioning herself in the assigned seat. She tried to make it sound playful but wasn't confident that she succeeded.

When she looked up, she noticed the diplomat was pursing her lips tightly, one eyebrow arched toward the ceiling. Now this was the look Hawk was expecting from Loris Goring. "You don't really need a reminder, do you?" Hawk probed.

"No. I don't."

"Then why am I here?"

That brought a smile to Loris Goring's face. "Direct. I like that." She paused for a moment and studied Hawk's face as if to memorize it. "I couldn't pass up the opportunity to meet you in a less professional setting. I'm not sure that we got off to the best start." Her eyes studied Hawk from head to toe when she finished speaking.

Hawk flinched as if hit by the words. She finally organized her thoughts. "I suppose not." She glanced up and felt that she may have said the wrong thing. "I mean, it was pretty stressful and all. I guess you did what you had to do."

The diplomat chuckled softly under her breath as she reached for a cup of tea that Hawk hadn't noticed until then. She motioned for Hawk to do the same. "Hawk, I don't want you to be confused about what happened today. I wouldn't have offered you the position unless I knew you were the right person for it."

Hawk stared at the tea she now clung to with both hands.

"I meet with the high-level professors each year. I find it is the easiest way to stay informed about the youth on the ship. You were top of your class every year. You were a shoo-in for any position on the ship, but you selected teaching, EPM, and horticulturist. Those aren't exactly high-status jobs for someone with your capabilities."

Hawk continued staring at the yellowish liquid.

"So I asked myself, why would this girl, this exceptional girl, limit herself to these positions?"

Hawk looked up, unsure again if it was her turn to speak. It wasn't. "At first I thought you lacked confidence. However, after watching you and hearing others speak of you, I realized that this was far from the case. You take on everything with great enthusiasm and never seem to doubt yourself. Then, I realized what it was."

Hawk leaned in. Diplomat Goring had a way of drawing her in and, in truth, Hawk didn't know why she had selected those positions or what it was that others saw in her. She felt as though a great secret was about to be revealed.

"Passion. You pursue only what interests you and you do it with uninhibited passion. Most people live their entire lives just skating through on what is easy to them, but you don't. Whether or not it is a challenge, in fact, *especially* if it is a challenge, you embrace it. You, my dear, have passion. I like that." She smiled smugly after saying this as if she had solved a great puzzle.

Hawk felt instant disappointment. Of course she was passionate. She became consumed with things she found of interest. Didn't everybody? Why did that make her special? At any rate, she was relieved that this impressed the diplomat.

Hawk tried to sound enthusiastic but mostly came off sounding squeaky. "I guess I've always enjoyed a challenge." It was a true statement but nothing that warranted the reaction that was expected of her. The older woman smiled, satisfied with Hawk's performance.

The two sat in silence for a moment, unsure of what to do next. "Well, I guess I should do what I came here for. When do you plan to complete your energy contribution? I'm sure you already have that planned out, but I *do* need to document a time." She indicated toward her wrist monitor and prepared to type in the information.

The diplomat's smile fell. "Oh, Hawk, I thought you would have figured it out by now. I've already completed my contribution. I changed the log." Hawk let out a soft gasp. She had never heard of anybody changing a log before. She didn't even know it could be done. "Well, more accurately, I had someone else change the log for me."

Hawk shook her head slightly as she tried to understand but found herself unable to do so. "Why would you do that? You could have just asked to meet with me. I wouldn't have refused."

"Of course you wouldn't have refused, but what's the fun in that?"

A game. That's what this was. Maybe even a test. Perhaps she was hoping to discover if Hawk would come or if she would send her co-worker and avoid the situation all together.

"Right, but I still need to schedule a time."

Diplomat Goring actually laughed at this. "It's already been taken care of. When you return to your station you will find the log accurately displaying my contribution. I always arrive at 5:30 in the morning. It's a great way to start one's day."

Hawk placed the tea back on the table and looked toward her hands which she folded together in her lap. "I see."

"I appreciate you stopping by. Your commitment to your work is admirable. We will continue our work in the morning. Remember, as far as the rest of *Enlightenment* is concerned, you're still vying for the position. I'll be watching you and will notify you when it's safe to tell others." She said this with a wink as she placed her hand on Hawk's shoulder indicating that it was time for Hawk to leave.

Hawk rose from the seat as she began to make her way to the exit with Loris Goring's hand guiding the way. "Thank you, Diplomat Goring. I don't know what to say." By this time, she had reached the exit and was now standing in the hallway looking back into the diplomat's quarters.

"Please, call me Loris."

"Ok, Loris." The door slid shut leaving Hawk to stare at her own warped, metallic reflection against the outside of the door.

When Hawk returned to the EPR, Everest had already arrived. His head slowly lifted as his eyes turned away from his computer monitor. His smile and twitching tail said it all even if he wouldn't. He had been waiting for her.

"So, what was the excuse from Mrs. Jenkins today?" Hawk breezed by him, ignoring his gaze.

Everest mimicked the older woman's raspy voice. "I got so caught up in my reading that I must have forgotten. You know how interesting these stories can be." His voice returned to his normal tone. "It's strange how she *always* forgets and doesn't feel her transmitter vibrate, don't you think?"

"She's an old lady. She's lonely. I think she likes knowing that somebody will come looking for her every day." Hawk didn't mind giving the old woman reminders. She thought it was sweet in a forced-kindness kind of way. Hawk suspected that the woman didn't have much else to look forward to.

Everest chuckled, "Yeah, you're probably right about that. Today she told me all about the difficulties of toilet training her youngest son." He mimicked an old-lady voice once more. "It was a mere fifty-four years ago."

Hawk played along, "Oh yes, my dear Lynx just couldn't get his aim quite right. I spent more time cleaning the floor that year than I did sleeping." Mrs. Jenkins always spoke of her two sons in the past tense, as if they were no longer a part of her life.

"I think we've spent too much time with sweet old Albemarle Jenkins. She really does mean well." Everest said fondly. "So, I trust that your reminder was a little more eventful?" Everest's full attention was on Hawk. He even swiveled his chair to fully face her.

"Hmm? No, not really. It was just a glitch in the system. She already completed her contribution." Hawk pulled up the log for the day. "See, it's already fixed." Hawk felt bad lying to Everest, but she wasn't entirely sure how she felt about it herself. She didn't need another voice telling her how to feel.

"A glitch? In the system? I believe that about as much as I believe that Loris Goring forgot to participate in her energy contribution today. What's really going on here, Hawk?" He gave her a look of fatherly concern mixed with the tone of chastising a young child.

Hawk shifted uncomfortably in her seat. "Nothing. Could we drop it? Please?"

Everest looked momentarily affronted. "Yeah. Yeah sure. You're the boss. Or at least, you will be soon." His playful-friend look was back.

"I don't know about that." Except she did. Hawk looked away at her computer screen quickly. Her face was a give-away. Bluffing was never her strong suit, and if Everest's watchful eye was any indication, he was well-aware of her inability to lie.

Hawk was grateful when her shift was over and she could finally complete her own energy contribution. It was the time of day that she looked forward to most. Her machine of choice, the treadmill, was calling her name. It was the only time when Hawk felt truly free.

Before she knew it, she was lost in her thoughts. Actually, only one thought. Loris Goring. *Loris*. Was she really supposed to call her *Loris*? It felt awkward, even in her mind. *Loris*. She reached to adjust the incline and hastened her pace. The conveyor belt was not moving near as fast as her mind and she needed more of a distraction.

Why would *Loris* trick her into coming to her room? Did she mean it when she said that Hawk deserved the job? Was that only *Loris'* opinion or did the Council agree? Somehow Hawk had the impression that they were one and the same. *Loris* spoke for the Council.

Could she really keep calling her *Loris*? Maybe the more she thought it, the more normal it would feel. *Loris*. Once more, she forced her feet to move a little faster against the machine.

How had she manipulated the contribution log? Hawk wouldn't even remove *herself* from the reminder list, but *Loris* had somehow altered logs just to have a private conversation. She increased the incline.

What had she meant by, "I'll be watching you." Was that a threat or a compliment?

Speed, up.

Who had she been talking to? What professor was serving as *Loris'* spy? Was there more than one? Who should Hawk add to the list of watchers?

Incline, up.

What about the way she led her around the room?

Speed, up.

Hawk had felt like a show dog being paraded around the ring like the videos she had seen of such events taking place on Earth. Was this how *Loris* treated everybody? Like they needed to be managed?

Incline, up.

Hawk couldn't speak for the rest of the Council, but she knew that she was not going to be a puppet for one voice.

Speed, up.

She was her own person with her own ideas and she wasn't going to allow anybody to silence her opinions.

Speed, up, up, up.

"Hey, hey! What are you doing there? You're going to hurt yourself!" Before Hawk could respond, a strong arm reached from her left and began punching buttons on the screen in front of her.

Speed, down, down, down.

She jumped to stand on the sides of the machine as her gaze met his. Caspian. Of course. "I—I guess I was just..." Hawk gasped for air. She hadn't realized how fast she had been going. Nonetheless, what gave him to right to barge into her thoughts? She took in a deep breath and matched his gaze with a glare. "And Caspian swoops in to save the day." She said this with so much disdain that Caspian took a step backward.

Caspian was known for "saving the day." He was a medic-in-training. He had already been trained in first aid, infections, pathogens, IVs, wound care, and was now even studying basic surgical techniques.

He was, at least until earlier that day, the most confusing part of Hawk's life. They had known each other since they had started attending classes at the age of three. They were born in the same quarter of the year and, therefore, attended classes together. Now at the age of seventeen, Hawk had known Caspian for over fourteen years. Caspian was one of only two people whom Hawk considered to be a close friend.

Hawk thought of Caspian's sister, Lark. Her only other friend on the ship. Hawk couldn't imagine a life without the two by her side. They had both become so intertwined with who Hawk was that she felt as if they were part of her. Much of who she had become was tethered to Lark and Caspian's desire for Hawk's happiness.

Hawk looked at Caspian again. *A friend.* She reminded herself as she resisted the urge to apologize for her comment. *Just a friend.* Hawk had told herself this every day for the past few years, and at times, reminded Caspian of this fact when he got too close. No matter how Hawk imagined the future, she couldn't see it without both Lark and Caspian in it. If she lost Caspian, she feared that she would lose Lark too. That would be everybody she cared about that wasn't an immediate relative and, honestly, Hawk was far closer with both friends than she was to any family member. If she messed things up with Caspian, she felt as if she would lose everything. It was better for everyone if he stayed a friend and a friend only.

Caspian shook his head. "I'm sorry, but I know you. Something's wrong and you're going to end up hurting yourself if you keep that up." He pointed to the machine, his expression softening. "Do you want to talk about it?" He had moved away and was now on the treadmill next to her. He was jogging at a slow, conversational pace. Hawk matched his pace and began running again.

"No, Caspian. Actually, I would like to talk about anything but *it*. Tell me about your day please, and make it eventful even if it wasn't."

"How did I know that would be your answer?"

Hawk turned her head so that Caspian wouldn't see her smile. "Well, on with it then. Anything exciting?"

"Oh, you know, the glamorous life of a medic." Caspian smiled but Hawk never saw. She kept her eyes forward.

"You never talk about your work. Why is that?" This time she turned her head to see his face. She wasn't sure how he would take this question.

Caspian turned his head towards hers and met her eyes. "It's complicated. What I do is..." He trailed off. "When you become junior diplomat, you'll understand." He said this with such unexpected earnestness that Hawk caught herself becoming lost in his eyes. She felt her feet stumble beneath her.

In the same instant, the ship began to shake, while flashing red lights burst into life around her.

Hawk's feet slipped as she attempted to stay upright but failed. First, she slammed into the left guard rail and then, just as quickly, the right. She was already falling as forces from the turbulence threw her off the treadmill and to the ground.

Caspian was beside her within seconds. He had stayed upright through the initial onset of turbulence but had no plans to ride it out. He threw himself to the floor in front of Hawk. She lay curled in the fetal position cradling her lower ribs on her right side where she had struck the treadmill. He faced her with eyes that pleaded for her to say something.

"Hawk!" He yelled over the sounds of the alarm. "Hawk! Are you hurt?"

Hawk tried to speak but was unable to catch her breath. She began to nod but knew that this wasn't helpful. Caspian wouldn't be able to see a nod through the continued shaking of the ship. She wasn't sure herself how badly she was hurt.

Caspian crawled toward her, concern evident in his eyes as he laid his hand on hers. The floor still jumped in all directions, as did Hawk's crumpled body. Caspian lifted himself above her and laid his body across hers in an effort to hold her steady against the floor. It helped, but her body still shook back and forth despite his protective efforts.

The ship continued to bounce through space, but the violence of it lessened. After what felt like an eternity, Hawk was able to speak in staggered breaths. "I'm ok. Just a little winded." She couldn't see his face, but she felt his body become less tense around her.

Once the shaking completely subsided, Hawk lay still, gasping for breath beneath Caspian's body. Finally, she began to move and pushed with her arms against Caspian's chest. "I'm ok. You can get up now." He didn't move. "Caspian? Are you ok?"

"Hmm? Yeah. Yes." He lifted himself up but slid his hands up to her shoulders looking at her with concern as he helped maneuver her into a seated position. "Are *you* ok?"

"I'm fine. I just lost my balance." It wasn't a lie, but it wasn't exactly truthful either. The shakes were only part of the reason she fell. "I'm fine. Really."

Caspian's eyes shifted downward, examining her. When his eyes reached her rib cage, he stopped. "You're holding your ribs."

"Well, yeah. I hit them on the treadmill arm when I fell." Hawk tried to shrug off his hands but found them unyielding, either because he didn't get the hint or chose to ignore it.

When his hands did move, they covered hers. "I need to see if they're broken."

"I'm fine I just need to..."

He cut her off. "Hawk, you need to move your hands."

Their eyes met once again but this time with stubborn intensity set on both faces. Finally, she lowered her arms and his hands sprang into gentle action. "Take a deep breath. Does this hurt?" He said this while pushing lightly on the area.

Hawk winced. "No. I'm fine." She stared at his hands hoping he wouldn't check again.

"Liar. I saw that. You're not fine."

Hawk instantly felt defensive. She hated the effect he had on her. "Well of course it's going to hurt. I just smashed myself against a treadmill and a gym floor. What did you expect? I just need to work it off." She began to stand but was immediately hindered by his grasp on her arm.

"Hawk." His stern voice called for her attention. She looked up to see that his gaze had never left her face. The red alarm lights continued to flash around them. Hawk wasn't sure if the red on his cheeks was from fear, exerted energy, or frustration that she wouldn't take him seriously. "Hawk, you may have broken some ribs. You cannot just '*work this off*.'"

"You know, I liked you a lot more before you became a medic," she quipped.

He held back a smile. "All the same, I'm not going to let you continue with your contribution."

"You don't have the authority to provide medical leave. I'm fine."

"This is coming from your friend, not your doctor. I'm donating my time. How much time did you have left?"

Hawk frowned. "That's none of your business. I'm fine. Really." Hawk shoved him away as she rose to her feet. Despite her best efforts, she couldn't hide the pain on her face.

"Look Hawk, you know this is going to happen. Look around. You know all the EPMs on duty. Nobody is going to let you continue if they know there's already someone willing to donate contribution time. So, you can tell me how much time you have left and report it to Fox over there or I can talk to Fox myself. It's your call."

In that moment, Hawk hated him. He already knew her decision. He always did. There was no way that she would allow this to look like she was forced. She was going to report the donation to an EPM on duty and let it appear to be *her* choice. At least Caspian gave her that small piece of dignity.

"I had twenty-six minutes left," she hissed.

"There. Was that so hard? I'm going to page Lark to walk you back to your room." He said with a smug, *I told you so* smile.

"No. I've got it."

Caspian opened his mouth but didn't get a chance to argue before she continued.

"Look, you've already gotten your way. I admit that contribution might be a little much for me right now, but I am more than capable of walking myself to my quarters without assistance. I can take care of myself."

She turned quickly to walk away from him. A decision made in haste that she instantly regretted but wouldn't show. She imagined his shocked expression fading away behind her as she briskly walked toward Fox and then out the door. She managed to keep up the facade until she exited the EPR. Once out of view, her walk immediately changed to the shuffling gait of the badly injured.

4

BLACK AND BLUE

Half an hour later, when the buzzer in her room indicated a visitor, Hawk knew immediately who it would be. She looked up to see Lark's face projected on the inside of the door, a frown cutting deep into her delicate features. Hawk forced herself to sit upright on the side of her bed, took a few pained breaths and mentally prepared herself for the whirlwind of emotion she knew was coming. "Allow entrance."

Lark careened in, already talking in quick bursts. "Why didn't you notify me right away? Are you kidding me, Hawk?"

"I—"

"No. You don't get to defend yourself here." She pointed a finger in Hawk's face. "I get that he was there and all, so I understand that I couldn't be the *first* one to find out, but to be told by Fox. *Fox!* Yeah, that's right. Caspian sent *Fox* to deliver a message to me. Do you have any idea what it's like to hear that your *best friend* is injured? From your *ex*?"

Hawk instantly felt guilty for not sending Lark a message. She should have known that Caspian would take matters into his own hands. However, it wasn't really her fault that Fox was Lark's ex. Lark had a history with several young men on board and the EPMs were usually her type: athletic with matching egos. "I'm sorry." Hawk said weakly as she looked at the floor regretfully.

"You should have sent me a notification as soon as you got back to the room. Right then! You didn't even send any notifications, did you?" She didn't wait for a response. "Does your mom know? We need to send her a message, right now."

"We don't need to do that. It's really not that bad. Caspian is blowing this way out of proportion." Hawk felt panic when Lark mentioned her mother. She didn't want her parents to worry.

Lark arched an eyebrow giving a look that Hawk knew was dangerously menacing. "Oh really? Catch!" She picked up a small wooden box from Hawk's dresser and launched it in a slow, underhand toss.

Hawk winced as she raised her hands to catch the box. Too slow. It smacked her in the forearm before falling to the ground and spilling the few pieces of jewelry Hawk possessed onto the cold, white floor.

Lark stared at the spilled contents. Her lip twitched a little before she stated, "I'm sure you're right. Caspian is always overreacting." Her voice was thick with sarcasm. She stood with her arms crossed over her chest, leaning against the wall next to Hawk's dresser, an ominous scowl on her face.

Hawk matched her expression. Finally, she broke the frigid silence. "So, are you going to help me pick this stuff up or what?"

Silently, Lark left her perch and began picking up the items. Hawk leaned forward to help. "Stop," Lark barked in her direction. Hawk did. Not because Lark told her to, but because Hawk was certain she couldn't reach the floor anyway.

After all the items were back in their hiding spot, Lark sat next to Hawk on the bed. At last, Hawk spoke. "I'm sorry. I should have told you right away."

"Yes, you should have." Lark snapped before leaping to her friend's side, putting her arm around Hawk and pulling her in close. "I was so worried. I don't know what I would do without you."

"I know. I'm sorry." Hawk rolled her eyes behind her friend's back. She had expected this type of reaction, but it didn't mean that she thought it appropriate for a little banged up rib.

"What happened exactly? All I know is that you fell off the treadmill during the shakes." Lark wiped at her tear-filled eyes.

Hawk explained to her friend what had happened without giving too many details about Caspian's role in the events.

"How bad does it look?" Lark asked after Hawk was done explaining.

"Honestly, I'm afraid to look."

"Ok then. I'll look. Pull up your shirt."

Hawk groaned but didn't argue. She slowly pulled at the hem of her shirt until it sat just below her bra, her head turned away. Hawk was about to ask what it looked like, but Lark was already reacting.

"Wow! That's gnarly!" she said in a loud voice.

"Is it that bad?" Hawk kept her eyes shut tightly.

Lark's fingers lightly traced the outline of Hawk's ribs. "You need to see for yourself, Hawk. I can't describe it."

Hawk opened one eye to begin with as she slowly turned her head to look downward. She opened both eyes as a last resort to inspect the area. She could see blotches of red under her skin but could not see how far it reached. Hawk stood to face her mirror in an attempt to get a better look. The red blotches crept up her right side starting around waist level in patchy groups that grew closer together as they climbed her body, with the most concentrated area beginning at the bottom of her rib cage. They stretched around her back slightly and wrapped nearly to her front midline.

Hawk inhaled sharply and felt needle-like pains as she did so. She sat back down. "At least in a few days I will have a blue ribcage. I've always thought I would look good with an Onsellan skin tone." She smiled to herself but refused to laugh, certain laughter would hurt.

"Caspian said he would come by after he was finished with his contribution. You should really let him look at it."

"I'll go to the infirmary in the morning." Hawk laid back in her bed, curled on her left side.

"Just see what Caspian says. You might need to go tonight."

Hawk grunted but said little more for several minutes. Lark usually preferred arguing, rather than agreeing, with her brother. Hawk knew if Lark was already prepared to stand with Caspian on the issue, she didn't stand a chance of winning the argument.

The buzzer sounded, announcing the arrival of Caspian. Just as Hawk suspected, he insisted on walking her to the infirmary for an x-ray. She didn't resist, this time. After over an hour of pained breathing, she knew that he was right. Lark watched closely, but didn't say anything. When Hawk entered the hallway, she discovered a wheelchair sitting by her door. "Where did this come from?"

Caspian shrugged. "I picked it up on my way here. You can walk if you want."

"No, I think I'll sit down." She felt the need to defend herself. "I *could* walk, but I'm pretty slow." Hawk sat down gingerly and with a hint of indignation. Lark reached out to help Hawk lower herself, but pulled away when Hawk glared back and quickly dismissed herself, leaving Caspian and Hawk alone.

. . .

Caspian pushed her through the almost vacant hallways. Most people had settled in for the night. Once they arrived at the infirmary, Caspian volunteered to run the machine despite not being on duty. Getting medical treatment in *Enlightenment* was not difficult. Sometimes people were required to wait for medics to arrive, but because Hawk was with Caspian, there was no wait time necessary. Hawk gave her name to a cheery woman who ran the record system for medical treatment. Once she had typed in the proper information, Hawk was escorted down a passageway marked Radiology.

Hawk was brought to a small room with a large machine inside. Caspian handed her a paper-thin gown that tied in the back and instructed her to put it on. Hawk stared for a moment with fear in her eyes. "Don't worry. I won't look." He offered her a hand to help her from the chair. She ignored it. He shrugged and then turned his body to face the opposite wall, taking a few steps away from her.

When Hawk lifted her shirt, she let out a small sigh. "Do you need help?" Caspian asked while continuing to look at the wall awkwardly.

"No, I'm fine," she gasped. It was a slow process, but Hawk was able to remove her shirt and bra. The gown, however, proved to be more difficult. She was able to get her arms inside but couldn't tie the back closed. Hawk straightened the gown to make sure she was covered. "Caspian, could you come tie the back for me?"

Caspian was behind her in an instant already pulling at the edges of the gown. Hawk could feel the heat of his breath on her neck as he knotted the strings quickly without saying a word.

Caspian pointed to a screen next to the far wall and instructed her where to stand. She did so and Caspian moved beside her, gently pushing her shoulders to guide her into the exact position needed. He then disappeared behind her. She could hear him moving things but could not see what they were. Soon he was next to her again asking her to turn so her back was against the screen. Again, he helped guide her by leaning in and lightly holding her shoulders. This time their faces were inches apart. Caspian didn't seem to notice. He watched marks on the floor and screen, focused on the task of medical imaging, but Hawk was all too aware of his close proximity.

It didn't take Caspian long to complete the x-rays once he began. He helped to untie the gown's back, but then disappeared into an adjoining room while Hawk rid herself of the lightweight gown and redressed herself. She finished and sat in silence, waiting to hear the footsteps that would signify Caspian's return.

When he finally arrived, he was smiling. "I have good news! They aren't completely broken, but they are cracked, so you still need to be careful. It won't take as long to heal."

"That's good, I guess." Hawk wasn't sure that she liked the idea of cracked ribs any more than she liked the idea of broken ribs.

"You will need to take deep breaths whenever you think about it though. When ribs take a hit like that, people tend to take shallow breaths to avoid the pain, and then you're at risk for pneumonia. We don't want that." He was still smiling. Hawk looked away.

"No, I don't want that." Hawk had heard of people getting pneumonia in *Enlightenment*. She'd seen it as an EPM. It usually meant they were on medical leave for several weeks and unable to make energy contributions, but they didn't seem like themselves for even longer.

Caspian handed her a small, oval shaped, white pill. "This will help with the pain tonight so you can sleep. You can have two per day if you need them. It's already updated in your medical file so stop by the infirmary whenever you are ready for another one."

Medicine was rarely used in *Enlightenment*. A doctor's approval was required to receive medication and it was only distributed on an as-needed basis. Hawk had read stories of people on Earth receiving full bottles of medicine that they could take to their homes. Many pills were never taken or were used in excess. She had always thought it to be incredibly wasteful. However, she knew that cities and towns were much larger than *Enlightenment*. It would have been difficult for people on Earth to have access to medicines if the people had to retrieve them from a medicine bank every day. The concept of unlimited mobility was fascinating to Hawk, even if now she only cared to move to the bed within her living quarters.

When Hawk awoke the next morning, she did not feel rested. Even with the medicine, she had barely slept. Hawk was not immediately sure what had awoken her. At first she thought it was the pain from her newly-injured ribs, but doubted this after a quick glance around the room. She first set her eyes upon the door, fearing that Lark or Caspian had come to check on her. She was relieved to see that nobody's image was projected on the door. She was still alone.

Continuing to skim the room, Hawk squinted through the dim light. There was nothing noticeably out of place. She rolled gingerly to her left side and hit a button on the head board. The lights around her began to slowly illuminate the room.

"Stop," Hawk said through a yawn. The lights halted their increasing brightness while the room was still faintly lit.

Hawk continued her appraisal of the room. The closet was

closed tight. All furniture remained in their original spots. In fact, to anyone but Hawk the room would have appeared to be in its usual state of what she called "orderly disarray." However, Hawk knew differently.

The papers on her desk that were once neatly stacked, in her opinion, in several small piles now merged into one jumbled heap. As she continued her assessment, she also noted that the picture frames on her dresser were no longer neatly turned to allow Hawk a clear view of the images from lying in the bed. No. These frames were now angled slightly to the left.

Hawk stared openly at the disheveled dresser top until she suddenly heard a familiar hum that seemed to rise from the floor itself. She rolled her eyes and grumbled, "Not again." Hawk launched herself onto her stomach—an action she instantly regretted when the pain shot through her side—and grabbed for a pillow. She thrust the cushioning over her head as she tightly held the sides down over her ears. Despite the makeshift buffer, she could still hear the sound of rattling and she felt her bed shift in small, quick jerks beneath her. She held onto the pillow tightly with gritted teeth while trying to will away the pain.

She concentrated on the sounds around her. In her mind's eye, Hawk could see the frames bouncing and shifting in the turbulence. She could hear a soft, *bump thump, bump thump* and knew her mirror had finally shaken free of its bottom restraint. It was now only secured at the top and struck the wall with each jerk.

As the shuddering began to subside, Hawk gently lifted herself into a sitting position. "Time," she said, apparently to no one. Soft green numbers appeared on each of the four walls. 5:34 a.m. Hawk sighed to herself, knowing there was no returning to sleep now. She gingerly stepped onto the cold metallic floor only to find herself immediately pulling away with a flinch.

Where did that area rug slide to now? Taking as deep a breath as she could muster, she hurriedly placed both feet on the frigid surface and shuffled to the dresser, opening the top drawer. This was a well-established routine by now. She grabbed a pair of slippers and dropped the pair to the ground with practiced precision. The slippers landed face up in front of her already moving feet. As she stepped into the lush, warm slippers, she continued her quest, moving with purpose.

"Lavatory," she rushed the word, but the results were as expected. The wall in front of her slid to the side as she hurried inside knowing that the shower would already be activating itself in preparation. For the first minute, the water would start at forty degrees Celsius and would gradually heat until reaching forty-two degrees. The perfect hot shower, at least according to Hawk.

Hawk leaned against the wall while the jet of warm water cascaded over her. *At least I have an extra half hour today. I guess the shakes aren't always a bad thing.* She stood in the stream of hot water for several minutes unwilling to move and knowing she had excess time to waste.

When Hawk finished her overly lengthy shower, she returned to her bedroom immediately moving toward the opposite wall. "Closet," she muttered while shuffling across the room, a task usually requiring only three long steps to navigate the entire length of the room. The oval door showing the closet's location slid to the side to show a vast array of clothing. Despite the closet opening being scarcely four feet in diameter, the selection extended far beyond her closet. In fact, this was not merely *her* collection of clothing but rather a collection of clothing for all women of the same approximate size who lived in *Enlightenment.*

Hawk looked at the selection in front of her. Presently she had an assortment of skirts partnered with floral print tops. Not at all something she wanted to be seen in. "Pants, tan." The closet door quickly slid to the shut position. Hawk could hear a faint swish of movement while she stood waiting. The door again slid to the side. This time a collection of outfits partnered with tan and khaki-colored pants was presented in front of her. She turned her attention toward the tops partnered with them. Her eyes were drawn to a red button-up. *Red. A color of power,* she thought. Today, she felt that she would need any advantage she could get.

An irritable Hawk was on her way to the cafeteria when Lark found her in the hallway.

"There you are! I was beginning to think you were going to skip breakfast or something." Lark was as bubbly as ever. She stood a full head shorter than Hawk. Her dark brown hair was cut short and curled around her face. She was petite, dark, and gorgeous. Hawk always felt like a cumbersome, pale giant when she stood next to her. Now with her injury, she imagined that she looked like a slouching ogre.

Hawk knew she was well-liked by most anyone she met, but as far as she cared, there were few on the ship that gained her interest. Lark was one of them. Lark walked by her side the entire way without even mentioning the slow pace. Hawk was appreciative that her friend did not feel the need to bruise her already suffering ego.

To the casual observer, Lark seemed a perky pixie of a girl with little more than the next social gathering to occupy her thoughts. She loved the social aspects of *Enlightenment*. She could be a ditsy schoolgirl type one minute, and then shock you the next with undeniable genius. Hawk tended to prefer solitude, but rarely was able to achieve it when Lark was around. Although they differed greatly in both personality and appearance, neither girl had ever been as close with another human being as they were with one another.

When they arrived, Hawk chose her favorite breakfast food: French toast. Once seated, Lark began talking as if the day hadn't begun with pain or a slow meander down a long hallway.

"You look nice today. Junior diplomat training looks like it suits you." Lark had a tendency to wrap her compliments into casual conversation.

Hawk blushed. "Oh, I had some extra time was all. The shakes woke me up early today." Hawk tried to skim over the fact that even with the better part of an hour extra at her disposal she still was running late due to a combination of her slowed gait and her increased nerves. She had spent several minutes fussing over her long, dark hair and attempting to perfect her make-up which seemed to make her look even paler somehow. She had fidgeted with her eye make-up in an attempt to make her blue eyes look more vibrant but eventually gave up, deciding that a dull blue was truer to her normal appearance anyway.

Finally, Hawk had sat blankly on the bed staring at her reflection in the wobbling mirror, willing herself to continue. She knew that she should move, but rather than getting a head start on the day, she allowed herself a few brief moments to be paralyzed with fear. She would never again get a first day as a junior diplomat. Even worse, it remained a secret from those she cared for the most. Secrets were exhausting.

Hawk shook her head to clear her thoughts. "I need to eat fast. I have to put a work order in to secure my mirror. The bottom shook loose."

"It was only a matter of time before yours did. Remember what happened to mine last week?" Lark frowned at the memory of her mirror smashing to the ground. The turbulence had been getting progressively worse.

"The shakes could be a good thing. The ship has to adjust more often as we get closer. Some people are even saying we are within a year of landing." Hawk had said similar things often to her friend. Today though, she knew the reason for the increased turbulence, and although it did involve adjustments in the course, it had nothing to do with Onsella.

Lark rolled her eyes. "Sure. I'll believe that when I see it."

Hawk couldn't blame Lark for her skepticism. They had heard it before. In fact, her mother had heard it before. Even her grandmother had heard similar tales. The truth was nobody really knew how far away they were from their destination. They wouldn't know until they were close enough to make contact. But Hawk *knew* she would see Onsella. She had no way of knowing when, but she knew she would. Lark was content to stay in *Enlightenment* for her entire life, but Hawk had always aspired for more. Maybe that was a foolish dream, but she needed to believe there was more to her life than living in what was essentially a moving city.

"You *will* see it." Hawk gave a confident smile.

"Yeah. Sure. Hey, when will you be finished with all this internship nonsense? We all know you're getting the position."

Hawk nearly choked on her French toast from swallowing too quickly. "Soon?" She said it as if it were a question and instantly regretted it.

"I know that look. Do you know something I don't?" Lark was on the edge of her seat. Hawk continued chewing her food. "If you know something, you can't keep me waiting. You *have* to tell me." Lark shook with anticipation.

Hawk swallowed. "I don't know anything, and even *if I did,* I wouldn't be able to tell you anything so..."

"So that's it then! You're in!" She threw up her hands in celebration.

"Shhh! No, really. It's nothing." Hawk rushed the words and motioned with her hands for Lark to calm down. "I mean it, Lark."

Lark leaned in and whispered, "I knew you would get it." She smiled smugly as the ship began to shake slightly. Hawk frowned to show her disapproval at the continuing conversation.

Lark immediately changed topics. "Maybe once you're in-the-know, you can explain what's going on with all this turbulence. It's never been like this before. It's getting serious."

"Oh, trust me, I know." Hawk motioned toward her ribs.

Lark pointed her fork at Hawk. "You should ask Everest. Isn't he a mechanic?"

"I think so. Do you think he could tell me anything?" Hawk hadn't even considered talking to Everest. Of course, until she had been injured, she had only considered the shakes to be a mild inconvenience.

Lark shrugged, "Maybe he can't, but it's worth asking. If the ship isn't working properly, I would like to know. I've got a lot to do before I die, and I need to know if I should speed things up." Lark's eyes brazenly followed the path of a tall, muscular young man whom she had been watching for the past week.

"Lark!" Hawk hit her friend playfully in the arm.

"What? You're honestly going to tell me that you don't have your eye on anyone special?"

"No?" Hawk's eyes briefly flashed toward Caspian as he approached their table.

"There is! I knew it. Spill it. Who's the guy?" Lark leaned in closely.

"It's nothing really. Can we drop it already?"

Caspian sat down next to his sister. "What are we

dropping?" He questioned Hawk but she wasn't quick enough to respond before Lark jumped in.

"Hawk has a secret crush she won't tell me about."

"Does she now?" His eyes shifted swiftly to Hawk's, smugness and jealousy battling for position on his features.

Hawk's throat suddenly felt dry. She took a big drink of water before speaking. "Lark doesn't know what she's talking about." Hawk sent a light kick in Lark's direction that hit her friend in the shin. "She wants a wingman while she goes to talk to Jasper over there."

"Ow! Well why not? He has a cute friend and you haven't had a date in ages." Lark rubbed her leg while she spoke.

"I'm not interested."

"Suit yourself. I'm going to go make a friend." Lark winked at Hawk as she scooped up her tray and promptly walked towards Jasper's table with a too-sweet smile spread across her face.

An awkward silence fell in her absence.

"The French toast is good today." Hawk offered.

"Hmm...? Yes." The silence began again. "How do you feel?"

"Like I was trampled by the hog herd." Hawk smiled meekly. "But I'm ok."

Caspian reached for his pocket and took a deep breath as if preparing himself to do something very unpleasant. "Last night after you were back in your room, I went to see my supervisor. I showed him your scans and he agreed that you will heal much quicker if you take a break from exercising." He produced a piece of paper and laid it in front of Hawk.

She reached for the parchment and began reading. "I have two weeks' rest followed by fifty percent reduction in energy production time for an additional four weeks." Hawk wasn't entirely sure how she felt about this. "Is all of this really necessary?"

"Yes. It is." Caspian spoke matter-of-factly.

"Then thank you." There was no point arguing. After her painful night and slow morning, Hawk knew now she was badly injured. Enjoying her contribution time didn't change the fact that she wasn't able to do so. Hawk suddenly thought of his body wrapped protectively around hers after the treadmill fall the evening before. Pink started to creep up her cheeks.

"You're on funeral preparation today, aren't you?" Hawk decided a change in subject was the best course of action.

"Yeah, I am. I'm preparing Mr. Davis today. We are launching him tomorrow." Caspian had a grim expression with his lips pressed into a thin line.

"I know it's always hard for you to launch them." Hawk started to reach out to touch his arm, a comforting gesture that she thought better of and never completed.

"This one shouldn't be too bad. He was eighty-seven. His family is ready to let him go. I always liked Mr. Davis. His stories about the medicine in *Enlightenment* were always inspiring. Did you know that it was only fifty years ago when the Council decided to differentiate between veterinarians and medics?" Caspian continued eating his breakfast as if all was normal, but Hawk knew he felt differently. Flint Davis had been one of his favorite trainers. Today, he would say goodbye to the man who had first seen Caspian's potential.

One of Caspian's jobs was preparation of the body and launching of the deceased into space. Funerals were not a big affair in *Enlightenment*. Only immediate family attended. The body was cleaned, dressed, and positioned into a cloth body bag before the family arrived. The bag was left open if requested for viewing. They were allowed to say a few words if desired and aided in loading the body into the portal. A family member was allowed to push the button that would release the body into space.

This time, Hawk did not stop herself. She reached across the table and touched Caspian's arm. "If you want to talk about it, I'm here."

Caspian stopped eating. "Thanks, but I'm ok."

He didn't say more. Hawk knew that they probably wouldn't discuss it again. Caspian rarely talked about his problems. Caspian didn't say much to her outside of basic conversations and joking. They had fun together and that was enough for both Caspian and Hawk.

"What's going on with you today?" Caspian asked innocently.

"I think I have an interview for the junior diplomat position." Hawk tried her hardest to avoid making eye contact with Caspian when she said it.

"You think you do? How could you not know?" He sounded aggravated.

"It's complicated." She looked up but only for a moment. Hawk didn't trust her face to not give away more than she intended. Caspian could always read her expressions. She usually viewed his perceptiveness as a good quality, but not now that she was keeping a secret.

"Is that why you were running so hard last night before I came in?"

"Yeah, part of it." She crossed her arms in front of herself protectively when her thoughts once again turned to the night before.

Caspian reached across the table and unexpectedly ran the back of his hand along her fingertips. "You'll do great. Good luck."

5

PICTURE PERFECT

Hawk made use of the overstuffed chairs that sat outside the conference room. She sunk into the chair feeling as if she were sitting on a cloud, but the feeling was short-lived, remembering why she was there.

Breathe. You'll get through this, Hawk assured herself as she fidgeted with the hem of her blouse. She suddenly realized the danger of wrinkling the fabric and instead turned her attention toward the arms of the chair. Even the arms were cushioned and comfortable. Hawk rubbed a hand across the fabric before finally settling on fighting her nerves by tapping the arm of the chair rhythmically with her fingers.

The door slid open. A man dressed in a slim pin striped suit stepped out. Hawk caught herself gaping at the man and quickly shut her mouth which had inadvertently fallen open with shock. Suits of such quality were difficult to come by. Clothing of such value was reserved for Council members and worn only for special occasions. Hawk looked down at her own state of dress. She had felt so confident about her selection this morning, but now felt far too insignificant to be receiving such an important position. Clearly, she wasn't even capable of picking out an appropriate outfit. The feeling of inadequacy only intensified as Hawk followed the well-dressed man into the room. All members of the Council were dressed in equally impressive attire. Hawk was certain this had probably been the case the day before as well, but she was only now calm enough to notice.

Hawk's eyes were instantly drawn to the head of the long conference table. Diplomat Loris Goring stood when Hawk entered. Her naturally tan skin and dark hair shone under the fluorescent lights. Her smile seemed sincere but awkward on a face with such robust features. Hawk couldn't imagine that such a powerful woman could possibly be considering her as anything similar to an equal.

Hawk stood awkwardly in the doorway for a moment, deciding what to do next. When Diplomat Goring began to approach her, Hawk moved forward to meet her with a handshake. She grasped the woman's hand firmly before turning her attention to the others at the table. Each member of the committee introduced themselves as they shook her hand in greeting. Hawk recognized them all.

Hawk turned her attention toward the "hot seat" placed at the end of the long conference table opposite of Loris Goring. She dreaded the thought of sitting in such a position. All eyes would be on her; her every move would be analyzed. *Time to shine, Hawk.* A voice sounding eerily similar to Lark's echoed in her head and somehow it made Hawk feel stronger as she took her seat.

The formality of the whole situation seemed out of place, considering her encounters with the council the previous day. Hawk wondered idly to herself if she should still call the woman Loris in such a setting.

After a few awkward seconds, Hawk decided she was supposed to speak. She started with an awkwardly forced laugh that mimicked the absurdity of the situation. She glanced around the room while offering a timid wave of the hand. "Hello again *Enlightenment* Council. I'm hoping today will be less eventful than yesterday. Or maybe more eventful? I'm not sure what to hope for here."

Diplomat Goring smiled approvingly.

Hawk continued, "I guess I'm a little confused what all of this is about."

Loris smiled again as if to say once more that she appreciated the direct approach. "Hawk, really this is just a formality. The Council normally narrows down the field of candidates and interviews the strongest contenders at the end of the internship. Of course, you've already been selected as our next junior diplomat, but we still need to keep up appearances. We're meeting with two of the other candidates today to not arouse any suspicion. They'll go through the official process, but for you we want this meeting to be an opportunity to get to know you better."

Hawk stared in disbelief. "You mean all current junior diplomats were interviewed before they were offered a position?" She stared around the room and searched the faces of the other diplomats. "But not me?"

Loris cleared her throat before answering, "The circumstances for this situation do not require an interview."

Hawk met her gaze and refused to look away. "I think they do. Interview me."

In her peripheral vision, Hawk noticed the other diplomats shifting uncomfortably in their seats. Still, she did not drop her gaze from Loris' eyes.

"Hawk, that really isn't necessary."

"I think it is. If I measure up to these other candidates today, I will gladly take on the job. But if they turn out to be better than me, I will step aside." She heard grumbling from the sides of the table but still stared forward. "I won't tell a soul about what I've heard and what happened if that's the case. You have the interview questions ready for the other candidates, so what exactly is the problem here?"

Nobody spoke so she continued. "Loris, this is not a situation where you should settle. You need the best right now. If that's not me, I shouldn't be here. Interview me," she paused a moment before adding, "please."

Loris nodded in agreement. "Ok." She turned her head, finally ending the stare-down by directing her attention toward the other diplomats. "Let's get started then."

Hawk smiled in her victory while the other diplomats fumbled with the devices in front of them in an attempt to access the interview questions.

She expected to be nervous, and to some degree she was. Still, she had the feeling that she had already accomplished the most difficult task of earning the interview in the first place. As the interview continued, she spoke with more confidence and moved with less tension.

As Hawk watched Diplomat Goring, she noticed the others at the table doing the same. It was as though they, too, were looking for approval. Hawk had to suppress a smile when Ural Ambrose glanced toward the head of the table and then returned his gaze to Hawk with an expression now an exact copy of the senior diplomat he obviously admired.

The interview was tedious. Questions were reworded and some were even repeated word for word several minutes after being originally asked. Hawk wondered if this was to test her answers' consistency or if they were giving her a second chance to answer in a better way. She couldn't be sure. Many questions concerned her knowledge about Earth and the ship. Some questions concerned policy, ship regulations, and, just as she had suspected, Blue Vigor.

Hawk felt confident but drained when she emerged from the interview room. She had attempted to keep her energy up while in the room, but now she suddenly felt as though her legs were weighted. Hawk forced herself to walk upright with a confident stride until turning the next corner. Once out of sight from the conference room, she quietly leaned against the wall and closed her eyes. Unable to walk another step, she slid down to the floor using the wall as a brace for her back. She wasn't sure if she was relieved, overwhelmed, or tired. Although the reality was that she was likely all three.

"Hawk, are you ok?"

Hawk felt a tender touch on her shoulder as she opened her eyes to see the familiar green-eyed gaze of Caspian. His emerald eyes shone brightly in stark contrast to his dark skin.

How long have I been resting here? Hawk thought to herself as she tried to shrug his hand from her shoulder. Comforting or not, his touch wasn't welcome. Or else it was *too* welcome. Either way, she didn't like the feeling.

"I'm fine." Hawk's voice was weak. She couldn't be sure if it was because of her exhaustion or the shock of seeing Caspian. "What are you doing here?"

She squinted past him at the bright lights coming in from the imitation windows behind him. The windows that lined the hallways were not typical windows that showed the viewer items behind the glass. Instead, they showed scenes that mimicked locations on Earth. *Enlightenment* showed images from Wyoming, in the United States. A location selected for its scenery and varying weather patterns. Now at midmorning in what would be a summer month, the lights shone brightly behind Caspian.

Caspian's face began to redden, "Oh, I was just..." He smiled, "You caught me. I could try to make up some excuse for being here, but truthfully, I was looking for you."

"For me? Why would you do that?" She began to pull herself up from the floor, ignoring the helping hand he offered despite the pain she felt in her ribcage.

He pulled his hand back and shrugged, "I knew you were nervous, and you were gone for over two hours. I thought maybe something had happened."

Hawk perked up at this. "Two hours? Has it really been that long?" She knew it had *felt* like forever, but news that it had taken that much time was still surprising.

"Is everything ok? You don't look so good." Caspian looked concerned and Hawk found her defenses melting.

Hawk began to walk toward her room knowing Caspian would continue the conversation as they walked. "I'm ok. Really. It was just exhausting. Nothing could have prepared me for that, but I think I did pretty well. Diplomat Goring likes me. I think."

Caspian shuddered. "Goring gives me the creeps."

"*Diplomat* Goring." Hawk corrected. "Why?" She had heard this sentiment before from others in *Enlightenment*, but she wasn't sure of the reasoning behind it.

"I don't know. She's so, you know... I don't know what it is about her, she's *too much* for me." Caspian tried to pass this off as a matter of insignificance.

Hawk immediately found herself becoming defensive. "*Too much?* She's amazing! How could you ever get too much confidence and security? The woman practically rules *Enlightenment*!"

"Whoa! I didn't mean to strike a nerve there." He stepped back while holding his hands in front of him in mock surrender. "I'm just saying, she's amazing at what she does but it's a little weird to think you could actually be her protégé, you know? Now with you having the possibility of being so close to her, it's made me think more about her. I'm sure the idea will grow on me once you get the job."

Hawk smiled to herself. "If I get the job."

Caspian stopped walking and lightly grasped Hawk's arm so that she was now facing him. "When." Hawk couldn't move. "*When* you get the job, Hawk. You've earned this." His eyes pierced hers.

Hawk forced a laugh. She wouldn't allow herself to take his sincerity to heart. "Ok. *When* I get the job, I will expect you to keep those kinds of comments to yourself. I like her, and I don't want anything to mess this up. Got it?"

Caspian smiled back. "Got it." He too let out a soft chuckle as if this had all been a game.

If this has all been a game, Hawk thought to herself, then Caspian definitely won that round.

Hawk's feet echoed from the metallic walls as she rushed through the corridor. The small lockbox she held in her hand bounced feverishly with each frantic step. Glancing upward toward the ceiling, the familiar pale green numbers were lit; 10:23 a.m. Her pace hastened as she raced past door after silvery door until finally reaching her destination. The interview had made her run behind her usual schedule.

Room 376 looked no different from any other on the outside, but Hawk knew what awaited her. Hawk took a nervous moment to straighten her blouse and flatten her wispy hair. Taking a deep breath, she pasted on a smile and stepped into the room ahead.

"Good morning class!" Hawk beamed at the room of eleven-year-olds sitting in front of her. She had been teaching various classes from the time that she was fifteen. Now two years later, the nerves still got her when she entered a classroom. Hawk loved teaching and was always eager to do best by her students.

Just like me to be nervous for a room full of children. Her thoughts echoed in her mind. *I just interviewed for a life changing position and I can't even pull it together for a group of well-behaved kids that I see three times a week. I don't stand a chance.* Hawk pushed the doubt from her mind as she continued.

For all her nerves, Hawk never showed it. The children never suspected their teacher of any trepidation. Her love for the subject always shone through any anxieties she may have had. Today would be no different.

Teaching was by far Hawk's favorite job aboard the ship. She knew that the position would be difficult to keep if she was allowed to continue her work as a junior diplomat, but she couldn't imagine life in *Enlightenment* without teaching.

"First, I would like you all to take out your journals. Today we are starting with five minutes of free writing. Feel free to tell me about anything at all that interests you."

A young red-headed girl with a long braid down her back raised her hand instantly.

"Yes, Coral?" Hawk didn't even need to look at the child's face to know who had a question. Coral always wanted reassurance.

"Can I write about Onsella? I want to make a story about what it might be like." The girl sounded as though she had an idea in mind.

"Of course you may. Remember, free writing is pretty open as long as you keep it classroom appropriate."

Hawk didn't always start the day with a free write, but on days she was running behind, she took advantage of the time. She quickly glanced at the clock displayed on the back wall before turning her attention to the box still clutched in her hands. Hawk hurriedly walked to her desk, carefully placing the container in front of her. She then reached into the top drawer and pulled out a box containing several white cloth gloves. Hawk glanced at the class in front of her. Nobody was watching. She was relieved. She wanted this to be a surprise.

After quietly pulling the gloves onto her shaking hands, she reached to her neck and pulled a necklace from beneath her shirt. A small key dangled from the golden chain. As she put the key into the lock, she took a deep breath before revealing the contents of the box: a stack of like-new, glossy photographs. She paused a moment at this, eyes transfixed on the top photo.

She knew the image by heart. It was one of her favorites. She even had a similar photo, presumably taken on the same day, that resided on her dresser. A waterfall. Niagara Falls to be exact. The one on her dresser was slightly different, displaying a couple she knew to be her ancestors from eighteen generations in the past, the last of her family to live on Earth. The photo was taken 442 years prior. The year her family made the choice to participate in *The Enlightenment Project*. The year Hawk was guaranteed to never see her home planet. To never *have* a home planet.

Hawk continued to prepare herself for the upcoming lesson. She looked to the wall again for the time. Free write was due to be over, and with it, her prep time.

"Place your journals back in your class packs. I have something extra special planned for today." She held up the stack of photographs in her gloved hands.

The class raised their eyes. Upon spotting the photographs, many students gasped while others openly smiled with delight. Hawk knew the feeling.

"Over the next two classes, you will each get to touch, study and research twenty different photographs from Earth. Each photograph comes with its own small pamphlet describing the photograph, and a small book with greater scientific details. But first things first. Put on a pair of protective gloves."

Hawk handed the box of white gloves to the front row and indicated for it to be passed around.

"These photographs are very old. They must be handled with extreme care." The class didn't argue. They all sat in their seats eager to put on the gloves and get their hands on the photographs. "You will have ten minutes with each photograph before passing it to the left for the next person. You are required to write down in your notebooks a minimum of five pieces of information you learned and found interesting about each image. Remember to use complete sentences."

As the students came forward to retrieve their photographs, Hawk stepped slightly to the left of the desk and quietly began placing the directions on the front wall. "Memo. Wall 1. Be careful/handle with care. Next. Ten minutes per photograph. Next. Minimum of five facts per photograph in notebook. Complete." As she spoke, the words appeared at the front of the class, this time in blue lettering.

Hawk watched as the excitement spread over the faces of her students. Photographs from Earth were a rarity. Sure, a person could find copies in textbooks, but to have an actual photo that was taken and printed while still on the planet was quite rare indeed. She allowed a few extra minutes for the first photograph to allow for the excitement in the room to subside enough to allow real work to be done.

Hawk moved around the room helping where needed, like normal. However, this time she had an ulterior motive. The photographs had been passed down from generations of family members, but she rarely saw the stored photos. She feared their deterioration too greatly to feed her curiosities. Instead, she displayed only her favorite five photos, all pictures of nature, on her dresser in frames.

Seeing such a variety of photographs from all over the world was overwhelming, even for her. These were images of ghosts from a world that none known to *Enlightenment* had witnessed. Pictures of majestic redwoods, bulky elephants, winding rivers, glossy cars, towering skyscrapers... these were all tales to those who had never experienced them. Even more ghostly were the faces peering back at them. Although the focus of the lesson was the images in the background, Hawk couldn't help but feel connected to the people in the images.

Hawk watched as the students circulated the photographs. Today, her class would view half of the photos. They would not be attending class with her again until two days from now. Earth Education classes were some of the favorites provided for the children of *Enlightenment*. Her class took place from 10:30 to 12:30 three times a week on Mondays, Wednesdays and Fridays.

As the time wound down, Hawk had nearly half an hour left. She did what she usually did at the end of class: review.

"Ok class. Who can tell me how we came to be in *Enlightenment*?" Several hands shot into the air. "Coal." Hawk called on a small, brown-haired boy in the front row.

The boy launched into an explanation. "In 2053 a ship from Onsella came to our planet. They brought with them new technology that allowed the people of Earth to travel to their home planet. In exchange for the Onsellans' technology, Earthlings agreed to allow Onsellans to live in peace on Earth. The goal of the Onsellans was to reach out to other planets and to bring people from other planets to their world; Onsellans wanted to spread knowledge about the universe and learn from the planets they found—"

"What a great start!" Hawk cut him off. "Let's give someone else a chance to tell us more. Who can tell me more? Aspen."

"It took eighty-five years before the people of Earth were

able to sustain the Onsellans' technology. They sent two ships before *Enlightenment*. *Revealer* launched in February of 2138 and *Seeker* launched in May of 2139." She paused for a moment before continuing her explanation in a hushed voice. "Nobody knows what happened to them."

Hawk cleared her throat awkwardly before continuing. "And who can tell me when *Enlightenment* launched from Earth and who was in *Enlightenment* at that time?"

This question caused pause. The children were young in appearance, but very wise. They had attended school five days a week for ten hours a day from the time they were three years old. They knew the information. It had been ingrained in their brains from a young age. Only now were they old enough to understand the magnitude of the information they had known for so long. They were without a planet.

Only one boy braved to answer the question. He didn't need to raise his hand. "*Enlightenment* launched on March 22nd in 2142. It took more than a year to get enough humans and Onsellans to volunteer."

"Thank you, Reed. At the time of departure, *Enlightenment* had 9467 human beings on board and 3359 Onsellans." Hawk said aloud but did not say all of the details that weighed on her mind.

Maximum capacity for *Enlightenment* was ruled to be 15,000. It had been decided to keep capacity slightly lower than the maximum upon launch. The stated reason was to allow the ship to function with abundance, but the real reason for being under capacity was the lack of interest.

Humans didn't want to leave their home planet. Most who had the desire to leave had already been selected for *Revealer* and *Seeker*. Onsellans had heard the tales from their parents and knew of the long journey. Most had decided to make Earth a permanent home. Those who did leave, left out of a duty for their future generations to see Onsella, their home planet.

Hawk continued, "Many feared leaving Earth, and others didn't believe the trip to Onsella could be made at all. Most volunteers were regular civilians. Some did it for adventure, others because they had nothing left for them on Earth. Some of the volunteers were scientists. They were given positions of high regard in *Enlightenment*. They taught all the citizens how to keep the ship operational and how to sustain life within the ship. A small council was formed to make the laws for the ship; that council is still formed today, keeping *Enlightenment* operational for all these 441 years that we have been in space."

Nobody talked for several seconds that felt more like minutes to Hawk. Finally, a girl in the back raised her hand. "Do you think we will see Onsella, Ms. Larson?"

Hawk looked pensive for a moment before beginning to speak, "I think..." but she did not get to finish her thought. The floor felt as though it had fallen beneath her. Soon the floor met her feet again, but Hawk found no relief as she and the children were tossed to the right and then the left. The wall that once showed instructions now flashed red as a piercing siren began to sound. Something was wrong with the ship.

6

FLASHING RED

"Quick, under your desks!" Hawk shouted above the siren. All desks were secured to the floor. They had practiced severe turbulence drills regularly, but the procedure for a real event was rarely needed.

The children all clambered to get under the desks, fighting the forces that attempted to push and pull them away. Hawk grabbed hold of her own desk but refused to crawl beneath until she saw all her students were safely positioned under theirs. Once positioned under the desk, she held onto the desk's leg. Each jolt produced greater fear as Hawk struggled to remain calm.

The turbulence lasted less than one minute, but felt much longer. Hawk waited only a few seconds before scrambling out from her hiding place, crawling on hands and knees toward the children who were still taking cover.

"Is everyone all right?" Hawk said breathlessly while a piercing pain shot through her ribs. She attempted to steady her legs enough to stand.

The children did not immediately crawl from their protection. Some began to move, others remained under their desks breathing hard and still holding onto the desk legs. All the chairs lay toppled. Papers were scattered on the floor. The lockbox containing the photographs lay sideways in the back of the room. Nothing except the desks remained in their original positions.

As more children began to move from underneath the desks, Hawk began checking for injuries. The most severe injury belonged to a child who had a small laceration above his eye from a chair that had hit him when he was crawling toward safety at the onset of the shakes.

Although the audible distress signal had subsided, the room still flashed red around them, which suggested that the ship had not been entirely cleared as safe. The class remained in the room until the flashing lights stopped and a voice boomed from all around them. The man sounded out of breath but confident, "The ship is fully functional. Please resume your regular activities."

The children walked from the room in stunned silence heading toward their next destination. Most were headed for the cafeteria but a queasy Hawk suspected that a few would opt out of lunch today.

The only student Hawk didn't release was Alder, the boy who had suffered the cut near his left eyebrow. She walked him to the infirmary to be examined. This was in the opposite direction from the cafeteria, in Wing 2. Hawk didn't think the injury to be serious, but she wanted to play it safe and get the boy examined by a medical professional.

As she reached for the door belonging to a room marked *Lacerations,* the door abruptly slid to the side, allowing its occupant to exit. Hawk inhaled sharply upon seeing who it was. Caspian. He turned to face her and she noticed the look of astonishment on his face.

"I didn't know you were working this specialty today."

Hawk smiled sweetly to cover her shock and excitement at seeing him.

Caspian didn't cover his shock quite as gracefully. He managed to stutter out in obvious confusion and surprise, "Yeah. I finished with Mr. Davis and headed here. Running stitches and butterfly bandages today. What are you doing here? Are you hurt?" He eyed her ribs suspiciously.

"Alder bumped his head during the turbulence. I wanted to get him looked at if you wouldn't mind." She motioned to the boy standing next to her who was pressing a cloth tightly to the area above his eye. The cloth had once been white but was becoming increasingly more scarlet the longer Alder held it.

For the first time Caspian noticed the boy standing beside Hawk. "Oh, of course. Come on in." He stepped to the side to allow the pair entrance.

Hawk shook her head. "I can't stay. I've got horticulture today." She started to turn away and then remembered to add, "I've already paged his parents and they've given permission. His dad will be here in a few minutes to check up on things."

Caspian's smile shifted into the serious expression expected of a medic in training. "Don't worry, I will take care of Alder. You just focus on yourself right now." Caspian eyes lingered on her ribs making Hawk squirm uncomfortably. He pulled his eyes back up to meet hers and added softly, "Be careful. Take it easy today." He cleared his throat before adding jovially, "Give all the difficult tasks to my sister. She deserves it anyway."

Hawk couldn't help but smile as she turned away.

Hawk loved her horticulture shifts. It was a peaceful job that required little thought on her part, which was a nice change of pace compared to her other positions. But the best part about horticulture was Lark. They worked together in an exceptionally large section near the rear of the ship known as "The Farm."

The Farm was where agriculture took place on the ship. Horticulture was located on the port side while animal husbandry was located to the starboard side. The center area connecting the two was a mix of both. The area was used as a grazing field that allowed for the much-needed mobility for animals. The Farm used grow lamp panels and vitamin D bulbs rather than the usual mix of traditional light bulbs and a few vitamin D bulbs that were utilized throughout the rest of *Enlightenment*.

Lark worked both sides of The Farm. She enjoyed the animals more than anything. Although Lark would never admit it, Hawk thought that she had selected horticulture only because Hawk had. Many people worked both animal husbandry and horticulture. The two jobs worked closely enough together that it made sense; however, Lark didn't seem to view it that way. She seemed to view her horticulturist's duties as a social time whenever she worked with Hawk. They had arranged it so that they worked together twice a week.

Hawk had read stories of people from Earth having gardening as a hobby, and she could see why. She imagined her job to be similar to such an activity. Unlike Earth, this was far from being merely a hobby. The job was extremely important to *Enlightenment*. Hawk planted, harvested and pollinated the plants that provided food for animals and humans alike. Additionally, the plants helped to break down the carbon dioxide exhaled by the humans and animals into breathable oxygen. The energy from Blue Vigor could also be used to break apart the carbon dioxide, but the plants had proven to be much more efficient.

"I hope we get to see these served fresh tomorrow. I'm

getting sick of cobblers and pies." Lark looked over her shoulder before sneakily popping a small strawberry into her mouth. "I like them better just the way they are." She forced the words around the berry before beginning to chew. The plants were kept in stacked planters that contained layers of soil that had been enriched to optimize production. Unlike Earth, soil was rotated rather than the rotation of the plants themselves. The plants grew in levels extending from the floor to the ceiling.

Lighting was always a challenge. Without the sun rising and setting, it was up to lighting experts to create a sun-like state in The Farm. Although the alterations in lighting was mostly for aesthetics in the rest of *Enlightenment*, it was of utmost important for the plants and animals. The strawberry plants were kept toward an upper level and the lighting was adjusted to have a partial shade effect. Lark stood on an elevated platform to harvest the fruit.

"I hear the sugar and wheat flour production is up. I guess that means more sweet doughs for us." Hawk was on a floor level. The supervisor was concerned about Hawk's balance with her injury and she had not been cleared to stand on the narrow platforms.

Hawk worked pollinating the squash and zucchini plants. She used a small brush to collect pollen and spread it to other flowers. In the early years of *Enlightenment*, beekeepers practiced apiculture to provide pollinators. However, the hives started to die out almost immediately. Within 50 years of travel, the bees had all perished. The duty fell to horticulture specialists from that time on. Hawk had read, and even watched documentaries, about bees on Earth. She was especially interested in the idea of honey. Sugar was made from sugar beets on the ship. Hawk imagined that the taste would be similar.

Pollinating was easy work for her usually. Today, however,

Hawk found it to be a challenge. She kneeled through most of the activity and had to reach out to find the right flowers. She found herself wincing often, even with her pain medication. Despite the pain, she never mentioned anything to her friend standing above her.

Hawk was about to suggest they sabotage the sugar beet production to get rid of the sweet dough increase they had both grown bored of when she felt the transmitter buzz on her wrist. She glanced at the screen, frowning.

Lark looked down. "What is it?"

"I'm being called in front of the Council."

"Am I missing something? Why is that a bad thing?" Lark continued harvesting berries.

"It's not. It's just—it says I'm excused from horticulture duties today." Hawk continued to scowl at her wrist.

"You need to go right now?" Lark looked down at Hawk's face. "Go! Get your good news! We can meet up this afternoon."

Hawk lifted herself slowly from the ground. "Meet you in C after your duty?"

Lark nodded in agreement.

Hawk hurried out of The Farm in such a rush that she didn't even notice the man standing by the exit. He had to call her name three times before she noticed. "Hawk Larson. I'm here to take you to the council," he said, sounding very official considering they had just shared the biggest moment of *Enlightenment*'s recent history together the night before.

"Is this the work of a junior diplomat then?" Hawk asked with what she hoped was a joking tone. "Fetching candidates and escorting them to meetings?"

Rowan laughed. She smiled back as she felt her heart start beating again. "I can see why Loris would be interested in you.

You have the same spunk that she does." His official tone had vanished.

Hawk's eyes sized up the well-dressed and well-formed man standing in front of her and suddenly felt inadequate again. "Do I have time to change?" She motioned towards the dirt patches on her shirt and knees.

"I'm afraid not. The Council is very busy today, as you know." He noticed the look of alarm on Hawk's face. "Don't worry. They know that you were in The Farm. They made sure to tell me that you were to be brought as I found you. No time for anything else." He looked Hawk up and down before quickly turning his eyes away as if catching himself doing something inappropriate.

Hawk looked toward the floor, a discreet smile on her lips. She looked up to meet his gaze before speaking. "Let's go then."

He walked past her and motioned for her to join him as he passed. They were soon walking silently side by side in as swift a gait as Hawk was able. In little time, they reached the same conference area where she had interviewed only hours before.

"Are you ready?" He spoke for the first time since they had begun walking. He sounded concerned. She hadn't expected this.

Hawk felt instantly unnerved. *What does he mean am I ready? Why does he sound so worried? Does he know something I don't?* Hawk took a deep breath and pushed all the doubt from her mind. She stood up a little straighter and rubbed her dirt-clad hands over her grimy pants before saying only, "Yes."

Hawk felt her pulse quicken when Rowan hit the admittance button. Her fear started to subside as the sound of laughter overtook the sound of her pounding heart that had been echoing within her ear canal. As the door continued to open, Hawk saw where the laughter was coming from. A group of well-dressed men and women were standing at the far end of a long table. They all seemed to be crowded around the woman who stood at the head of the table. Loris Goring.

Loris stopped laughing but continued to smile warmly when Hawk entered. The others that stood with her did the same. "Hawk!" Loris chuckled softly as she yelled the name out gleefully. "Come in! We're happy you were able to come on such short notice." She waved her hand toward a seat that was positioned to her right. "Have a seat. We have a lot to talk about."

Hawk looked down at her smudged jeans and hands. She glanced back at Rowan as the door closed behind her. He said nothing, but his gaze said it all. He knew they would be working together soon and he could not hide his delight.

Hawk continued to step forward unsure of how to proceed. If she acted hesitant that might show a waver in the confidence that she had tried so hard to project. If she was not apologetic for her appearance, would she appear as a slob?

Fortunately, Diplomat Ambrose came to her rescue. "Don't worry my dear. Rowan had just left from his energy contribution when we met with him last year. A little dirt is far from the worst thing that has ever been brought into this room. Hell, just last week I brought in a bag full of rotten fruit!" Hawk walked more briskly now toward her seat.

Loris continued to smile. She positioned herself to face either her fellow diplomats or Hawk with a slight turn of her head. "Of course, that was for a discussion about food waste and the need to vary food production." She turned her attention fully to Hawk now. Although she continued to smile, her face showed that it was time for business. The others in the room quickly sat in their seats.

"Hawk, I see no reason to beat around the bush." She leaned forward in her seat. "We would like you to come work for us as a junior diplomat. Do you accept?"

Hawk took in a sharp inhale. She had expected this but had not given much thought as to what she would say. Her eyes narrowed suspiciously as she looked toward her leader.

Loris held up her hands as if in surrender. "You were the best person for the job. Hands down. You earned this."

With Loris' reassurance, Hawk finally found her voice. "Of course I accept. It's all I've ever wanted."

"I had a feeling you would say that. We need to discuss your schedule and work assignments. You must begin right away. Have you decided which position you will be forfeiting?"

Hawk felt ashamed. She should have had an answer for this question already. "Not exactly."

"I know it is a very difficult decision. For now, you can have restricted hours from the EPR and The Farm until you decide. Will a week be sufficient?"

"Yes. I'm sure that will be enough." Hawk lied. She wasn't sure at all. She loved all her positions. That's why she had selected them.

"Ok then. You are to be excused from all duties tonight and tomorrow evening while we sort out some things. Plan on working late with us. We will, of course, excuse you from your morning teaching assignment as well. On Thursday you will be excused from horticulture to continue your training at 10:00 in the morning. Does that work for you?" Loris was now typing notes on the handheld screen in front of her. She arched an eyebrow in Hawk's direction but did not look up.

Hawk was certain that there was only one correct answer for that question. "Yes, thank you. I'm really looking forward to working with you. What time should I start tonight?"

Loris looked up now with the same warm smile on her face. Hawk wasn't sure if the smile was genuine or not. It appeared to be sincere but hadn't moved from her face since she had sat down. "We will meet at 10:00 tonight in the helm. It will be a late night. I think we will work well together. I wish I had more time to talk but we have several meetings today. You are excused from the remainder of horticulture duty today. You are free to tell anybody you want so long as the news stays relatively private until tonight. We will be making the public announcement tonight at 6:00."

"Tonight?" Hawk's mind was racing. "If it's all the same to you I think I would rather keep my EPM shift tonight." Hawk couldn't imagine the thought of being with a crowd when the news broke. "I would still make the 10:00 meeting in the helm."

Loris nodded with apparent understanding. "If that's your choice then so be it. We will see you tonight."

Hawk breathed a sigh of relief. "Ok. Thank you again, Diplomat Goring." She corrected herself after seeing the look on her mentor's face. "Loris. Thank you, Loris."

"You are more than welcome. Please, do not feel the need to thank me. You've earned this, Hawk. We are all looking forward to working with you." The others around the table smiled and nodded in agreement. With that, Loris stood up and began walking toward the door. Hawk stood as well with Loris' hand on her shoulder, guiding her.

"You are an impressive woman." She lowered her voice now that they were at the door. Hawk smiled meekly, unsure of how to reply. Fortunately, Loris continued talking and spared her of any attempt. "Your EPM shift ends at eight tonight, is that right?"

Hawk nodded.

"Feel free to say no, but I would like you to join me tonight in my quarters after you're finished with your EPM shift. I know that you've been given a medical clearance from contribution for the night and we could go to the helm together afterwards."

Hawk was taken aback and unsure how to respond.

Loris was opening the door now. "It's not official Council business. I want to get to know you a little better."

Hawk stepped through the doorway. "Of course." Hawk matched the smile that was aimed at her. "I think that's a great idea."

"I will see you then." She closed the door behind her.

Hawk turned around in a daze. Although she couldn't be sure, she was fairly certain she saw a familiar blond-haired figure disappear around the corner as she turned to walk away. Had Rowan been listening at the door?

7

INVISIBLE

Hawk knew that it was her responsibility to tell those closest to her before the formal announcement. There wasn't much time. Her EPM shift would begin in a few hours. She made a list in her mind of the people she needed to tell: her parents, Lark, Everest, and, most importantly, Caspian. He *had* to know.

Neither of her parents would be working so she thought they would be easy enough to find. It helped that they were always together when they weren't at work. They needed to know first.

Hawk imagined what her parents' reactions might be. She knew they would be excited of course. However, Hawk worried about how it would change their lives. Family members of diplomats were often the sounding boards for frustrated citizens. It seemed people would rather talk to the family than a diplomat. She never understood why, but it was what always happened.

She imagined her parents defending the actions of the Council. They were endlessly supportive. What would their lives become now that they would constantly hear complaints about their daughter's choices?

Hawk headed toward their living quarters. She pushed the button for admittance and was quickly answered by the door sliding open. Her mother was standing in the doorway. "What's going on? I could tell it was something big as soon as I saw your projection."

Hawk's dad was soon by his wife's side. "Well, let her in, Poppy! She can't give us the news standing in the hallway, can she? Come in, come in!" He waved her in enthusiastically.

Her parents' quarters were slightly bigger than her own. The larger the family, the larger the quarters. After Hawk had moved out at age fifteen, her parents had been moved to a smaller room. Citizens of *Enlightenment* entered the workforce and received their private living quarters when they turned fifteen. They were allowed to live with another person at age twenty if they decided cohabitation fit them better than independent living. Hawk still had three years before that became an option.

Even though they had only lived there for the last couple of years, it was home to Hawk. Her parents positioned themselves on the couch. Despite having more than enough room, they still sat close together. Hawk sat opposite her parents on a small chair that was pushed against the wall. She pulled the chair over to sit closer to her family. They looked at her expectantly.

Her father, Onyx, spoke first. "Well? Are you just going to sit there or are you going to tell us what happened?" His tone was jovial.

Hawk took a deep breath. "I got it." She didn't feel that anything more needed to be said. By the looks on their faces, they understood.

"You got it?" Poppy started this as a question, but it quickly moved to that of a statement, and then a victory yell. "You got it. You got it!" She was on her feet now, grabbing for Hawk's hands and pulling her into a hug.

Onyx was not far behind his wife. He embraced the pair with a giant bear-hug. "I never had any doubts, kiddo! You were made for that job. That Loris Goring, she's a smart gal. She knows a good thing when she sees it." His hug tightened around the pair.

Hawk was squished snugly between her two parents. She knew that others might feel trapped, but to her, this was heaven. Her parents were her biggest comfort. Hawk didn't talk to them every day, but they were the ones that she could always count on.

Hawk stood in their arms for several seconds until the couple began to sway back and forth as if rocking her. "I got it! I got it!" She began to rise slightly, forcing her parents to jump in excitement with her, something she instantly regretted as a pain jolted in her ribs. She broke free from the embrace, while her parents jumped for joy around her, hand-in-hand. When she reached for their hands, they stopped jumping but did not sit down.

"When do you start?" her mother asked excitedly.

"Tonight. We meet in the helm."

"The helm?" her dad questioned. "What are you going to do in there? Fly the ship?"

"No, that can't be right. They have pilots for that," her mom reasoned.

"I'm not sure." Hawk tried to shrug off the question. "I didn't really ask." She felt guilt build in the pit of her stomach and wished she hadn't mentioned the helm.

She found herself feeling more nervous and slightly less excited when she left her parents. However, she knew that her next stop would only build excitement. Lark's horticulture shift had ended ten minutes before.

She found her friend in Commons Area C, just as they had planned. She was still wearing her dirty clothes from The Farm.

Hawk knew that Lark must be really eager to hear from her if she hadn't even gone back to her room to change. Lark was usually very particular about her appearance in public.

Lark was sitting on a plush sofa in their usual spot. The walls were covered with images of tree branches with orange and red leaves. The ceiling above was also painted to look like autumn leaves. Having only seen photos of the season, the place was the closest the women had ever come to experiencing it.

Lark waved enthusiastically as soon as she spotted her. Hawk shook her head good naturedly. Today, she wanted to feel invisible. It was probably her last few hours to enjoy such a feeling. Of course, Lark wouldn't make that easy.

Hawk sat down next to her friend. Lark looked at her in anticipation. Hawk prepared herself. She began to speak softly. "You can't get too excited. It's not going to be announced until tonight."

A joyful screech emitted from the tiny girl before she quickly clamped her own hands over her mouth to silence herself. Lark breathed heavily through her nose with wide eyes peering over her hands in excitement.

Hawk continued. "I start to—" Before she could finish, Lark had leaped across the couch and wrapped her arms around her friend.

"I can't believe it! I mean, of course I *can* believe it. I *knew* you would get it. I just... Wow! Hawk!" Lark was talking so fast that Hawk was certain she was one of the few people who would be able to understand her.

"Shhh! Not so loud!" Hawk hushed her friend while hugging her.

Lark pulled away gently but kept her hands on Hawk's shoulders. Tears shone in her dark almond eyes. "I'm so happy for you." She said in earnest while looking at Hawk full in the face.

"I'm happy for me too." Was all that Hawk could manage, "I can't really believe it myself."

"We should celebrate! Why don't we get a group together tonight and go to Haven?" Lark referred to the area of *Enlightenment* that specialized in dancing and music, The Haven Club. "Jasper's band is going to play tonight."

"Jasper has a band? Are they any good?" There were a few bands on the ship but Hawk usually preferred recorded music from Earth. The musicians at Haven never seemed to have the same talent and they certainly lacked the equipment that bands from Earth had used.

Lark shrugged. "I don't know if they *sound good* but I'm sure they will *look* good." A sly smile spread across her face.

Hawk laughed. "I'm sorry I'll miss that. I've actually got a meeting tonight so I can't go."

"I thought you wouldn't start until tomorrow?" Lark pouted in disapproval.

"No, tonight. Diplomat Goring, Loris I mean, invited me to her place to visit tonight. I couldn't say no." Hawk tried to sound calm but was certain she wasn't fooling anyone.

"*Loris*? Did she tell you to call her that?" Lark looked amused.

Hawk attempted to hide her own amusement. "Yes. As a matter of fact, she did."

"But Diplomat Goring rolls off the tongue, doesn't it?" Lark joked. "Why would she want to ruin your fun?"

"Maybe she wanted me to shorten it for practical reasons. You know, it takes much longer to say *Diplomat Goring* than *Loris*."

"That's true. I'm sure she will expect you to suck-up often. It would take too long to say, 'Yes, Madame Diplomat. At your service Diplomat Goring, whatever you wish." Lark mimicked an uptight voice.

"Perhaps she should have asked me to call her 'Your Highness' then? Maybe that's what she wanted to discuss tonight. It looks like we've solved that mystery." Hawk couldn't help but feel less nervous with Lark. Lark always knew how to put her at ease. She glanced at the numbers displayed on the far wall and wished time would slow down.

"I've already talked to my parents, and I will see Everest tonight before the announcement. I need to tell your brother before tonight. Do you want to go with me to tell him?"

Lark beamed. "How about he joins us? I know he would want to hear it right away and maybe *this* could be our celebration if you can't go out to celebrate tonight." Lark quickly paged her brother via her wrist transmitter. The message read, *Commons Area C. We need you. Now.*

Caspian arrived a few short moments later, panting for breath. "You got it?" He managed to force out.

Hawk nodded.

"I knew it! Junior diplomat!" He threw his fist into the air in victory.

"Shhh!" Lark and Hawk both corrected him while grabbing an arm each and pulling him to sit in the middle seat of the couch.

"The announcement isn't being made until tonight." Lark explained.

He turned to look at Hawk. "And you don't want any extra attention until you have to."

Hawk nodded. Caspian always understood.

"Well then, let's enjoy the few hours you have left as a commoner." He flashed a smile in her direction. "So, what do you want to do with your little time left of blending in?"

"I just want to do *this*." Hawk didn't want to celebrate. She didn't want to tell the world. She wanted to be *her* for a little while longer. Before she was to become *Junior Diplomat Hawk*

Larson, she wanted some time with her closest friends to just be *Hawk.* And nothing more.

———

Hawk didn't want to leave her friends, but she was grateful she would be working in the EPR when the announcement was made. At least she could stay hidden in a room with only Everest for a little while. The work of a junior diplomat was what she had always wanted. The public nature of the job was another thing entirely. Hawk wasn't sure if she would ever be able to blend into a crowd again.

Her shift began at 5:00. She had one more hour until her whole life was going to change. Hawk took her place in the EPR next to Everest. She had already decided that she would wait until just before the scheduled announcement time to tell him. She didn't want to spend the last hour of her regular life answering questions. Hawk only hoped that she would be finished with today's physical reminders before the announcement was made.

Everest was his usual self when Hawk arrived. He was more concerned about her ribs than anything. Hawk assured him that she was fine despite the medical restrictions. "You know how protective Caspian can be over his friends."

Everest smiled, "Somehow, I imagine he's even more protective over you. Still, I know those clearances aren't just handed out. You need to be careful."

Hawk nodded in agreement. "I know. Don't worry, I won't overdo it."

By physical reminder time, there was only one name that hadn't yet responded. "Well, that shouldn't take long. I'll get this one." Hawk rose from her seat.

"No, let me. You're supposed to be resting after all." Everest rose quickly and placed a hand on her shoulder from behind to stop her from fully standing.

Hawk smiled up at him. "Ok, hurry back though." She didn't want him to be gone when the announcement was made. It was important that she get to talk to him before that happened.

"What's the matter? Lonely?" he smirked. "Don't worry. It's just Mrs. Jenkins."

Hawk retorted, "That's the problem. She might be even lonelier than I am."

"I think I'll manage." And he was gone. Hawk was left alone.

She began thinking about which position she would give up. To stop teaching was out of the question. Hawk couldn't imagine *not* teaching. That left her to decide between her roles as a horticulturist or EPM.

She loved being around exercise equipment and having some time that was more private. Sure, she had Everest and, on occasion, a handful of other workers, but that was all. She had time to think and she was certain that would be harder to come by with her new duties.

Then she thought about her work in horticulture. Again, she had time to think there. Well, sometimes. When she wasn't working with Lark, she had time to herself. When Hawk *was* working with Lark, she had time with her friend. Giving up either position would be difficult.

Then her thoughts turned to an even more difficult task. Telling them. How could she tell either Lark or Everest that she wouldn't be working with them any longer? She knew both would try to be supportive and say they were happy for her. However, she also knew both would feel slighted. She wondered how Rowan decided what to give up. Maybe he would be the best person to talk to. She decided to ask if she saw him in the helm.

Everest returned quickly and took a seat next to Hawk. "Not as chatty tonight?" Hawk asked.

"Oh, I'm sure she would have liked to have been, but I got the feeling that I was needed here more." He turned and looked intensely at Hawk. "Is there something you would like to tell me?" His tail repositioned itself onto his opposite shoulder.

Hawk gasped. "How did you know?"

"You didn't say anything about the position all day. I figured you didn't want to think about it but when you told me to hurry back, I knew." Everest's face opened into a wide smile. "I'm sure going to miss you, kid, but I understand that you need to go."

"What?" Hawk wasn't sure that she understood what he meant.

"I know you got the position. There's no way you wouldn't get it. I'm guessing you didn't tell me because you have to give up EPM."

Hawk opened her mouth to talk but was interrupted. Everest held his hand up as if to cut her off. "It's ok, Hawk. I understand. You would be crazy to turn down an opportunity like this. I get it. Promise me you will stop by to chat every once in a while."

She couldn't stay silent any longer. "No. That's not it."

Everest looked instantly saddened. "Oh, I'm sorry. I can't believe they didn't give it to you. I know it's a hard job and all, but heck, you're the best! That council is full of useless, self-centered..."

"No! That's not it either. They offered me the position. I just don't know if I'm leaving my EPM position yet. I haven't decided."

Everest's smile returned. "Yahoo! I knew you'd get it." He

was on his feet now, pacing with excitement. Hawk stood too but remained in her original place. "Why didn't you tell me?"

"I thought it would be better to wait until the end. I wanted our night to be like normal. You know?"

"Yeah, I get it kid, but you were really going to keep me waiting for another two hours? Why did I have to hurry back then?"

Hawk sighed. "Not exactly. I didn't mean the end of the shift."

Everest looked puzzled for a moment and then startled as his wrist transmitter buzzed. Hawk did the same. They both looked down and read the message displayed: *The Council is proud to announce the selection of a new junior diplomat. Please congratulate Miss Hawk Larson!*

Hawk looked up towards Everest who was now looking at her with teary eyes. "Congratulations, Junior Diplomat Larson."

"Thanks," Hawk muttered as she looked past him into the EPR through the glass divider that partitioned the two rooms. There, on the wall, just as it would be on every living quarter's wall and public area in *Enlightenment*, was a short message with a giant picture of Hawk's smiling face beside it.

Her new life had just begun.

8

QUESTIONS AND GAMES

Hawk walked briskly through the hallways. She noticed lingering eyes every time she passed someone. If it was a group of people, Hawk heard whispers and imagined the people pointing in her direction behind her. She smiled politely and even gave a little wave at times. Nobody stopped to talk to her and she was grateful for that small piece of privacy.

Loris seemed very pleased when she opened the door. "Come in!" She ushered Hawk inside in an excited fashion. "What did you think of the announcement? I thought it should be short and congratulatory," she beamed.

"It was nice. Where did you get the picture?" Hawk had been wondering this since she had seen her face appear on the wall. She knew that they would show a picture but assumed it would be from the annual photo database that contained a posed head shot of all *Enlightenment* citizens. The photo that was shown was not that. Hawk had been smiling a genuine smile and it looked to her as if she had been laughing. She couldn't be sure, but she thought it had been from the day she found out that she had been selected for the internship.

"Did you like it? We took it from a security video. I wanted something that made you seem approachable."

Hawk couldn't argue that the photo used was much better than the force-posed pictures that she usually took. However, she again was not sure how to feel about this invasion of privacy. Hawk knew that there were security cameras in the common areas in *Enlightenment*, but she never imagined that the council took an interest in them unless there was a problem.

"It was a nice photo. I didn't realize that you had been watching me through the cameras." She tried to say this more like she was curious as opposed to angry. It was not easy to pull off.

"Oh of course dear! We check in on all candidates after they are selected for an internship," Loris stated as if it was an obvious course of action for the Council. "Does that surprise you?"

Hawk thought for a moment. Perhaps she was overreacting. "I guess not."

The two stood in silence for a moment. Loris spoke, "Please make yourself at home. Would you like some tea?"

Hawk accepted. The two sat together on the couch. "Hawk, I didn't invite you here to talk about work. We will be working together for a very long time. That's why I think it's important that we get to know one another. Things will become difficult on the Council if we don't get along." Her tone sounded very professional.

Hawk nodded as Loris continued. "I know that I can be intimidating, and I want you to get to know me for who I am, not from my public image. I'm sure you will find that who you are in private and who you are in the public eye will be different. You will see both sides of me. You've already seen the public side, now it's time that you see who I am outside of that." Hawk's head was buzzing. "Please, ask me anything."

Hawk sipped her tea while examining the woman in front of her. *Ask me anything.* What could she possibly ask? "If it's all the same to you, I'd like to just talk for a while. I'm not sure a person really gets to know someone by hearing them answer a bunch of questions."

Loris did not react at first. "That's why I wanted you. You see more than most people, Hawk." She nodded knowingly. "Tell me, what do you see in Rowan Sheridan?"

This question took Hawk by surprise. "He's all right." She thought again of his piercing blue eyes upon her and the blush on his cheeks and shifted uncomfortably in her seat.

"We've found that it's important for junior diplomats to have an ally. Someone who has been through the same experiences that they have, professionally speaking. It helps with the adjustment into the Council."

Hawk decided she should probably expand on her answer. "I like him well enough. He can be a bit..." she hesitated, searching for the right word, "tenacious."

"Tenacious?" Loris questioned. "What do you mean?"

Hawk sighed, questioning if she had picked the correct description. "He seems to be... I don't know... uncomfortable around me. He's always looking for something to say, something to get my attention. He won't let it go. Like he needs to be seen and be heard. It's not necessarily a bad thing, just part of who he is." She shrugged, trying to give the appearance that this quality didn't bother her as much as it really did.

"Oh, I see. I've never heard him described that way before." Her voice was subtly shifting to a more natural tone as the conversation continued. "Maybe you bring out that side of him." She looked as though she were trying to find a way to change the subject. Quickly. Her eyes darted around the room and finally landed on Hawk's ribs. "How are you feeling? I understand you had an accident during energy production."

"Oh, that." Hawk reached up instinctively to touch her ribs. "The shakes knocked me right off the treadmill."

"I heard that you were relieved of energy contribution for two weeks."

Hawk scowled at the reminder.

"You aren't happy with that then?" Loris' eyebrow arched towards the ceiling again with a quizzical expression on her face.

"Would you be?" She didn't wait for an answer. "It's how I clear my head."

"I'm guessing you will have a lot to think about over the next few weeks." Loris agreed. "I was restricted from use of arm equipment for six weeks once when I injured my shoulder. Being restricted from all equipment would be difficult."

"I'm only on day one of the restriction and I'm already feeling anxious!" Hawk could feel herself becoming jittery as the day went on. Her desire to work it off through exercise was intensifying.

"I guess you'll need to find something else to occupy your thoughts." The older woman looked legitimately concerned. Hawk was starting to feel more comfortable.

Loris rose and went to her dresser. Hawk watched as she pulled a wooden case from a drawer. Loris returned and set the box on the table in front of them. The top itself was a square composed of sixty-four smaller squares of alternating colors. Some squares were stained dark while others were lighter. It showed obvious wear; still, Loris set it in front of her gently.

"I inherited this from my paternal grandmother. It's been in the family since *Enlightenment* left Earth." She reached forward and opened a drawer on the side of the wooden box. Inside, there were sixteen dark brown pieces and sixteen light brown pieces sitting on a black satin liner. They looked similar to ones Hawk had seen in books. "This is a very old game called..."

"Chess." Hawk interrupted as she finished the sentence for Loris. She leaned forward to inspect the pieces. Hawk eyed the dark pieces first. She spotted two skyscraper buildings and two men on horseback. The other pieces appeared to be varying images of humans. The light pieces seemed to mimic the dark ones but were that of Onsellans. Instead of blocky skyscrapers, there were egg-shaped buildings. There were no horseback riders. Instead, there were two Onsellan riders on what appeared to be large dogs.

"You can pick them up if you'd like." Loris reached forward and grabbed an Onsellan rider. Hawk followed suit and reached for a human rider to investigate. It was carved from wood and stained to match the lighter colored squares on the top of the game board. "I had them re-stained a few years ago. Some of the pieces were beginning to splinter."

Hawk noticed that some pieces had fared better than others. She replaced the rider and reached for another piece, this one was a small man holding a shovel. The face of the figure looked as if it had long since chipped away.

"Do you know how to play?" Loris' question snapped Hawk out of her trance. She placed the small man back in the drawer.

"Not really. I've read about it. I'd heard rumors about some game boards in *Enlightenment*, but I didn't know if they were true." Hawk said dreamily.

"There aren't very many left. There weren't many brought on board to begin with from what I understand. Of the ones that were, most were poor quality. Few are left today. This one was made especially for the trip. My family has cared for it for many generations."

Hawk continued to pick up the pieces one by one to inspect them. She had just noticed that the small man holding the shovel was one of eight similar pieces when Loris' voice called her back to reality. "Do you want to play? I can teach you."

Hawk looked up, shocked. "With these? Is it safe? I mean, can't we damage the pieces?"

Loris chuckled. "We could, but we won't. Even if we do, what's the point in having something you can't use?" She reached forward and began removing pieces from the case and placing them on the board. "Here. I'll show you how to set it up."

Loris showed Hawk where all the pieces began on the board and explained how each one moved. Hawk didn't think she would remember it all, but they began to play anyway. Hawk asked many questions while they played. She lost count of how many games they played. The board had to be reset once as a result of the ship shaking the pieces off the board. Most games were short. A few were longer. Hawk was sure that Loris took it easy on her, even on the short games. The woman was patient with Hawk, and she turned out to be an excellent teacher.

Hawk found herself becoming anxious as the game continued. It was fun, but she couldn't help feeling uncertain about the upcoming visit to the helm. Loris appeared to have no intent to discuss it until they were there either. Finally, Hawk hit a button on her wrist transmitter to check the time. "Wow. Loris, it's almost 10:00!" She acted as if she hadn't been counting down the minutes.

"I guess we lost track of time. I haven't had anybody to play with for a long while." Loris began carefully placing the pieces back in their proper positions within the case. Hawk attempted to help but felt as if her fingers moved far slower and less delicately than the older woman's.

They walked together to the door. "Are you ready?"

The question was friendly enough, but Hawk couldn't help but feel as if it were ominous all the same. She nodded and gave what she hoped was a confident reply of, "I'm ready for anything." With that, the door closed behind them and Hawk followed half a step behind Loris.

Each step she took made her feel a little bit more comfortable about working with Loris Goring, but more uncertain about the work to be done in the helm.

Although Loris was standing next to Hawk, she did not look at her. They had said nothing the entire walk to the helm and now that they stood gazing out into the heavens, Hawk again found herself unable to speak.

"It's overwhelming, isn't it?" Loris was also staring out the helm window with eyes nearly as wide as Hawk's.

"Mm-hmm," was all Hawk could manage.

"The view is even better if you step up closer."

Hawk stepped forward and discovered what her mentor had meant. The glass wrapped around the sides of the helm allowing her to look outward in three directions. It was breathtaking.

"When you're ready, you can step up to the platform."

Loris continued on to the same platform where they had met earlier. Hawk was not in such a hurry to move. Even having seen it once before, she felt as if she would never be able to take in its entirety. The feeling only intensified as the view changed before her with each passing second as lights shot behind her out of view while still others appeared in the distance.

She heard the voices around her and knew that she must move, still, she struggled to pull herself away and move toward the voices.

Hawk entered the platform still dazed and feeling overwhelmed, but she did not have time to bask in the vastness of the universe. Today, all that mattered in the universe was taking place on a small platform with a handful of council members and their junior diplomats.

"We think we know where *Seeker* is located." Loris was saying. "We've adjusted course accordingly and we're hoping to establish a line of contact within the next two days or so. If we're right, we could make contact as early as tonight."

Hawk felt as if a heavy weight had been dropped on her chest. There was no air in her lungs to exhale but she tried anyway. The effect was her swaying on her feet feeling as if she might topple over. Before she could correct herself, she felt a strong hand upon her arm helping to keep her upright. Rowan had arrived. Despite his efforts, his presence had no positive effect upon Hawk's attempts to catch her breath.

Hawk's plight went otherwise unnoticed by the council members who were deep in conversation.

"Tonight? We are all staying here through the night?" Puma Stern clearly required more information. Hawk couldn't tell if the woman sounded excited or outraged.

"That's not exactly what I had in mind. The council needs to make arrangements for what happens once we arrive. We're needed elsewhere."

"Who then, if not us?" Diplomat Stern pushed on with her questioning.

"Junior Diplomats Sheridan and Larson, of course." Loris stated the names as if they were the obvious choice.

All heads in the room snapped toward attention as their eyes sought out the location of Rowan and Hawk. It was in that moment that Hawk's breath finally found her once more. She stood tall, acting as if she were already familiar with the plan. Her eyes sought out Loris questioningly but only saw pride in the woman's gaze as she met Hawk's stare.

Baffin Maxwell, the eldest of the group, spoke up. "You are entrusting something this serious to children?"

Hawk felt Rowan's muscles tense next to her and she was certain she had done the same. Loris, however, seemed unaffected by his doubt. "These two were the first to intercept the initial *Seeker* message. It was not easy to hear and still, they knew it was important and what steps needed to be taken. I see no reason why they should not be trusted again. They are best suited for the job. Better suited than any of us."

Her intense stare seemed to silence the group. Diplomat Maxwell nodded, indicating his willingness to comply with the plan.

"The rest will be discussed in the conference room." Loris said in a volume that bordered on yelling even though she could have spoken in a whisper and still been heard.

The group began to head for the exit leaving Hawk standing alone with Rowan. Before Hawk could think to speak, Rowan stepped in front of Loris. "How long will we be here?"

Loris arched an eyebrow disapprovingly at the question. "Until we send someone for you." She pushed past him and did not look back.

Hawk sat at the same table in the helm where they had first listened to the *Seeker* message. She gazed out the window in fascination as she watched the stars appear and disappear around her while Rowan sat at her side. The receiver let off a low hum of static.

Helm staff busied themselves by pulling levers and making adjustments on the screens in front of them. A young lady yelled across the room to Rowan. "Anything?"

"Not yet!" he hollered back. So far, they had heard nothing but static and the occasional metallic squeal.

Hawk glanced up at Rowan nervously. She had something on her mind but had not yet worked up the nerve to ask him. Finally, she spoke. "Why are they trusting me with this?" It came out in a rushed, direct sentence.

Rowan faced her, raising an eyebrow questioningly.

"I mean, there must be others who have proven themselves more than I have."

Rowan looked down at the table, his shoulders shaking with silent laughter. "Are you saying we shouldn't trust you?"

"No. It's nothing like that. It's just, maybe Diplomat Maxwell is right. This is big. *Really* big, and I just started," Hawk said, exasperated.

"Hawk, if Loris didn't think you were capable of handling something big, you wouldn't be in this position. Loris knew as soon as she heard the message that she needed someone extra special in this position. We all knew it. Whoever works under Loris holds a lot of power in *Enlightenment*. You know that. Don't you?"

Hawk didn't move.

Rowan continued. "We all know that when we get to *Seeker*, Loris will be the first one to jump in. But let's be real here, Hawk, she could put herself in serious danger. She needs someone that she can trust fully at her side if something goes wrong. Don't get me wrong, she trusts the Council, but Loris needs someone that she would trust to *take over* if something happens to her. She's been watching you for a long time, Hawk. She knows everything and everybody on this ship and she knew it needed to be you."

All the moisture in Hawk's mouth seemed to have disappeared. She managed to choke out, "Why?"

Rowan shrugged. "You would have to ask her. But trust me, if she says you're right for this, you are."

Hawk gazed out the window again unsure of what to say. Before she got the chance to respond, a faint whisper of a voice began sounding over the static. Hawk could make out the words "distress," "*Seeker*," and "help," but nothing more.

Rowan yelled toward the navigation area. "Hey! We've got something over here!"

The young woman hurried over to listen before sprinting back to a screen and keyboard, punching in information. The voice disappeared. "We're losing it!" Rowan barked in her direction without looking up.

"I'm on it." The woman continued to type feverishly. The ship shook aggressively as the voice became clearer.

"It's back!" Rowan bellowed. "And clearer!" He picked up the radio microphone. "*Seeker*, this is *Enlightenment*. Do you copy?"

Hawk held her breath, but there was no response. He tried again. "*Seeker*, this is *Enlightenment*. Do you copy?" His eyes darted from the radio to the window and back to the radio as if looking for a sign in the vast darkness outside the ship. The voice continued with no acknowledgement of the response. "They can't hear us." Rowan said loudly enough for the helm crew to hear.

"Wait a second!" the woman yelled back. A few seconds passed. Then, "Try now!"

Rowan took a deep breath. "*Seeker*, this is *Enlightenment*. Do you copy?"

They waited with bated breath. Nothing. Hawk sighed heavily, "Maybe we still aren't close enough to..."

"*Enlightenment*, this is *Seeker*. We're here. We hear you. We're here." The voice sounded shaky but strong.

Hawk made eye contact with Rowan before hitting the

button on her wrist transmitter that would send an emergency signal to Loris Goring. She needed to get there. Now.

The next few minutes seemed to stand still and rush by at the same time. Hawk stood at the edge of the table with a clenched hand held across her chest.

Several of the helm crew dashed to the platform. They stood in a circle around Hawk and Rowan. Nobody moved. Nobody spoke. If Hawk didn't know any better, she would have thought that nobody was even breathing. The only thing that could be heard was the sound of Rowan's voice and the voice emitting from the radio receiver.

"*Seeker*, this is *Enlightenment*. We hear you. Are you in need of assistance?" Rowan's voice trembled, but he spoke with authority. Hawk had no idea how he knew what to say or *if* he really knew what to say, but it sounded right to her.

The voice crackled back with obvious joy, "Thank God you found us. Yes, we need assistance." Hawk could hear what sounded like cheering in the background of the responding communication.

Rowan looked at Hawk as if she were the only person in the room. To Hawk too, the crowd around them seemed not to exist. He whispered, "What do I say?"

Hawk had no idea. "I don't know!" she mouthed. "Loris is on her way." They stared at one another with nothing but a low static hum and the gentle shake of the ship around them.

"*Enlightenment*? Do you copy? Are you still there?" The voice sounded worried.

They needed to respond. "Tell them we are waiting on approval for assistance and that our leader will be here shortly to confirm," Hawk said.

Rowan picked up the transmitter and after assuring the nervous man on the other end that they could still be heard, passed the message along. He then added something of his own. "Can you tell us your condition?"

Hawk heard a second voice coming from the radio. This also sounded to be a male, but he sounded much more confident. "*Enlightenment*, this is Councilor Pike Brighton. I am in command of *Seeker*. To whom am I speaking?"

"Junior Diplomat Rowan Sheridan. Our leader is on her way." Rowan breathed a sigh of relief. He no longer needed to pretend to be in charge.

Hawk imagined what it must be like in *Seeker*; the commotion of hearing another ship. Like *Enlightenment*, were they unprepared? Had someone paged their leader or had someone run to find him?

Loris Goring bustled into the room at full sprint pushing her way through the crowd of onlookers that had accumulated.

She looked to Hawk. "Fill me in." It was the first official command she had ever given Hawk and it was a very important one. Before Hawk could even speak, Loris grabbed the radio from Rowan without saying a word to him. He stepped aside with obvious relief and stood next to Hawk.

Hawk spoke very quickly and tried not to give too many details. She needed to be quick. "We've made contact with *Seeker*. They confirmed the need for assistance but have not told us why yet. Their leader has just taken control of the radio. Pike Brighton. Councilor. Councilor Pike Brighton. We told him that you were on your way."

Loris picked up the transmitter without a moment's hesitation. "Councilor Brighton, this is Diplomat Loris Goring."

The man answered back quickly. "Diplomat Goring, are you the leader of *Enlightenment*?"

"One of them, yes."

"Do you have authority to make decisions?"

Loris paused. "The Council makes decisions together,

Councilor. But I am a member of the Council and I can assure you that we will not hesitate to make a decision when it comes to this. Please, tell me, in what way are you in distress?"

The man paused again. "Diplomat Goring, I do not mean to offend you, but we've had some difficulties here. Can you confirm your identity? We need to be certain that you are who you say you are."

Loris looked up with obvious shock. When she spoke, it was not to *Seeker*. It was to the spectators. "I need all nonessential personnel to leave the helm." People looked at one another in blatant confusion. "Now!" she barked as people began heading quickly toward the exit.

She picked up the transmitter again. "I am clearing the room. Await confirmation."

Hawk looked at Rowan unsure if they should stay. He looked back with equal levels of apprehension. Loris finally turned to them. "You may stay. You must check with all personnel that has remained. Ensure that they are essential to the ship remaining functional."

There were only two people remaining. The pilot, who had not left the navigation area, and the small woman who had made the adjustments directly before contact. She remained at her station staring intently at her screen.

Hawk checked with the woman and Rowan checked with the pilot. When they returned, they did not speak. They just nodded for Loris to continue.

"*Seeker*, this is *Enlightenment* 15273. What kind of weather are you having there?"

Hawk felt useless. She had no idea what Loris was talking about. She could tell by the look on Rowan's face that he didn't know what was going on either. She found that to be somewhat comforting.

"A little foggy with a chance of rain. What kind of weather are you expecting?" The man responded.

"Sunny here with no chance of rain," Loris said.

The man on the other end of the radio sighed heavily into his microphone. "*Enlightenment*, I am so happy to hear you say that. We've had some trouble here. There's been an illness. There are few humans left living. Onsellans fared better. We had to reroute our power supply to keep electric and airflow. We've been standing still ever since."

For the first time, Loris looked scared. "How many survivors?" There was a long pause. "*Seeker*?"

"A little less than five hundred total." Hawk heard Rowan gasp in disbelief beside her. The man continued. "Four hundred Onsellans. One hundred humans. Give or take."

Loris placed both hands flat on the table, leaning forward so that her chin nearly touched her chest.

"I know that's not what you want to hear, but we are really in a tough spot. We've been sitting still for over four months and you are the only friendlies that have come along."

Loris' golden-brown eyes opened wide. "Friendlies? Have you had run-ins with others?" Hawk was thinking the same thing.

Another hesitation. "That's how we caught the illness to begin with. Another ship." He paused before adding ominously, "Trust no one but us. They could come back."

Loris sighed heavily. "Councilor Brighton, the Council will convene and decide on a course of action. Have someone standing by at your radio."

"Thank you, Diplomat Goring. We will be eagerly awaiting your reply." The tension in the man's voice was growing.

She picked up the transmitter once more but said only, "Signing off."

Loris turned to face the two junior diplomats who had been watching intently. Hawk spoke first. "What are we going to do?"

Loris stood straighter. "Isn't it obvious? We are going to help them."

Rowan rushed to speak. "Didn't you hear them? They're sick and have enemies. How can we justify the risk?"

Loris approached him slowly and with heavy steps. "Because they are our people. *Our* people. From Earth. They are in trouble and we are in a position to help them. Nobody said this was going to be risk-free. We are going into this knowing about the risk which is more than I can say for most things in life. We cannot and will not abandon them now."

Rowan nodded. A shiver ran down Hawk's spine as Loris pushed past them heading for the exit. "We will meet in the council room in ten minutes. Don't be late."

Hawk exited the helm, leaving behind the radio and Rowan. She knew he would be joining her soon in the council room, but for now, she couldn't stand to look at him.

How could he even suggest abandoning *Seeker*? People had died, others were at risk and he wanted to walk away? She agreed with her mentor. They needed to help the distressed ship and all of those left on board. She only hoped that the rest of the council would see it Loris' way.

Hawk entered the half-filled conference room unsure of where to sit. Loris sat at the head of the table. Hawk circled the room slowly before Loris noticed her arrival. "Hawk," she said affectionately, "your seat is next to mine."

Hawk eagerly took her seat next the woman she so admired. She felt the full enormity of the situation weighing on her. Hawk turned toward Loris and said simply, "I'm with you."

Nothing more was said between the two while the room continued to fill with both senior and junior diplomats.

It seemed to Hawk that there were assigned seats, even though she knew that there was nothing formally stated. The closer the diplomat was to the head of the table, the more power they held. Junior diplomats took their seats always to the right of the diplomat they served under. She was pleased to see Rowan's place toward the middle of the table was far away from hers.

The meeting began by Loris playing a recording of the conversation with *Seeker*. Hawk hadn't even known it was being recorded. When it was finished, the room sat in stunned silence. Hawk knew how they felt. She still hadn't fully processed it all yet.

Hawk was pleased when Loris spoke first. "We were able to acquire *Seeker*'s exact coordinates. Our course has been altered accordingly."

Cantil Gilchrist spoke next. He sat just to the left of Loris toward the head of the table, obviously important. "I think we need to discuss this further. Things have changed. This mission now comes with considerable risk."

Loris' voice was steady when she responded, but slightly louder than normal. "We knew there would be risks when we received the first transmission. Nothing has changed. We decided to conduct a rescue mission and that is precisely what we are going to do."

Cantil continued. "I think this should be up for further debate." He looked around the room in an attempt to find an ally. He was an older Onsellan man, but not the oldest on the Council.

Diplomat Maxwell, the eldest and longest-serving member, spoke next. "We are obligated to help these people. We know there will be risks going in."

Cantil looked wildly around the room once more. Puma

Stern responded to his pleading eyes. "I agree with Cantil. The risk is too great."

The room erupted at once. People began talking over one another in attempts to be heard. The junior diplomats remained silent.

The racket continued until Loris stood from her chair with her hand held out in front of her as if she could stop the assailing words with nothing more than her hand. "Enough!" she bellowed, and the whole room fell silent. Hawk sat straight-backed in her chair. She noticed several others do the same. "I cannot make anybody change their mind. We must take it to a vote."

Hawk could take it no longer. "This is why we're here!" she said forcibly.

All eyes turned toward her but she continued on.

"When the first Onsellans set out in search of fellow intelligent lifeforms, they knew that many of their people would not survive, that nobody aboard that first ship would likely live to see another planet. But they did it anyway. When they found Earth, they knew that they might be met with hostility and yet they still chose to reach out. Not for personal gain or even for gains of their home planet. They did it because they wanted to *learn*. To become something bigger than just themselves.

"Our ancestors did the same when they chose to leave Earth and start this venture. They left their homes knowing that there would be no turning back. For generations our families have lived in *Enlightenment* without ever having a planet to call home, all for the sake of bettering our races. And now, after all this time, we want to *abandon* those who are in need because 'it's too risky'? You ought to be ashamed of yourselves for even considering it. We owe it to our ancestors and to ourselves to push further once more and brave the risks!" Hawk couldn't recall leaving her seat, but she was now standing, taking heavy breaths and gazing around the room with wide eyes.

Hawk looked toward her mentor at the head of the table. She was openly staring at Hawk, as was the rest of the Council. However, Hawk thought she could see a hint of a smile pulling at the sides of Loris' lips. Her eyes darted towards Hawk's seat and she took that as the signal to sit down.

Hawk looked around the table once more to take it all in. Everybody looked shocked that she had spoken. She did not know if it was a rule or just an understanding that junior diplomats did not speak up in meetings. Either way, she had violated some sort of accepted agreement. The senior diplomats seemed somewhat upset at this, whereas the junior diplomats looked empowered. Hawk sat down holding her head up high.

If she had broken a rule, nobody verbalized it. Instead, Loris pushed onward. "Would anyone else like to add to this discussion?"

The room remained silent. "All right then. Let's vote." The ship shook ominously as she spoke the words.

9

THE PEER MENTOR

Junior diplomats were not permitted to vote, but it didn't matter. Nobody, not a single soul, voted to ignore the distress signal. They all agreed to dock with *Seeker* and to send in a handful of medical personnel.

After the initial vote, the Council discussed what to tell the rest of *Enlightenment*'s inhabitants. People would notice when the ship stopped. The artificial gravity relied on *Enlightenment* staying in constant motion. Although it could be adjusted to accommodate for a stall or decrease in forward motion, it would not go unnoticed.

They decided it would be explained away as maintenance. Given the recent increase in turbulence, they were confident it was a believable explanation. Hawk had hoped that the Council would agree to tell the truth, or at least a portion of it. However, this was an opinion that she kept to herself. Loris did not want to tell *Enlightenment* yet. She argued that it would create an unnecessary panic. There would be time to explain the situation to the community if need be.

Hawk did not have time to discuss it with Loris before the decision was made. If she had, she would have told her that, in her opinion, lying to *Enlightenment* would make more problems in the long run. What would happen if they needed to take on passengers? The Council would need to explain, and everybody would learn of their dishonesty. Things could become very uncertain for all of *Enlightenment* if that were to happen. However, despite her opinion, Hawk did not feel that breaching the understood agreement of silent junior diplomats twice on her first day would be wise.

Hawk walked with Loris to the helm to continue communication with *Seeker*. Both Loris' and Hawk's footsteps fell heavy in the hallway. Although there were others in the passages, Hawk was not truly aware of their presence. Her mind was full of uncertainty about her own actions. Had she overstepped when she had spoken up in the meeting? What if she had been perceived to be unstable or untrustworthy? Would she be dismissed from her position? Her mind raced faster than her heart, which was quite fast indeed.

When they entered the helm, they were the only two from the Council in the room. Others would be there soon, but for now, they could speak freely. The helm was nearly empty with only the two crew members they had left still remaining. Loris marched to the table in quick, confident steps. Hawk followed slightly behind her. When they sat, Loris positioned herself opposite of Hawk.

Loris took a deep breath before she spoke. "What you did in there," Hawk clenched her teeth, readying herself for the worst, "was the most remarkable thing I have seen any diplomat, junior or senior, ever do. Without your words, we might not be here now."

Hawk was speechless. She nodded appreciatively but said nothing more.

Council members began trickling in. The Council decided to have all members present for the continued communication.

Senior members crowded in around the table while the junior diplomats stood around the outside, all vying for the closest position. Loris ended up towards the center of the table. Hawk wished Loris was on an end. That would give her an excuse to stand closer. Instead, she stood in the middle of the pack with people she had never met. Rowan stood opposite her. She thought he was staring at her, but she couldn't be sure without looking. Still furious about his cowardice, she was unwilling to give him the satisfaction of looking back.

Nobody had said it, but it was clear that Loris would be the one speaking. Once everybody was settled, she picked up the radio's microphone and began communication. "*Seeker*, this is *Enlightenment*. Do you copy?"

"This is *Seeker*. We copy. Is this Diplomat Goring?" Hawk recognized the voice as that of Pike Brighton.

"This is Loris Goring. Please identify yourself."

He did so, confirming Hawk's suspicions that it was, in fact, Pike speaking.

"Mr. Brighton, the entire Council has decided to make themselves present for this discussion. Understand that certain responses may take more time than others if discussion is required."

"Understood ma'am. What decisions have you come to at this point?" His voice was thick with nervous tension. Hawk couldn't blame him. It didn't sound as though they had much hope outside of *Enlightenment*.

"We are committed to aiding you if possible. We are planning to dock within two days' time. Exact arrival time is still being calculated."

Pike breathed a sigh of relief into the radio. "Thank you to the Council. We will be eternally grateful."

"No thanks are necessary, Mr. Brighton. We take care of our own." She aimed a quick glance at Hawk. "We will allow a small number of medical personnel onto *Seeker* to assess the situation. From there, we will decide our next course of action."

"Of course. We understand. We are grateful for whatever assistance you are able to provide." Pike's voice was still shaky with emotion.

"We will be in touch Mr. Brighton. Our radio will be manned, please ensure that someone is available to speak on your end at all times. Is there anything else that we need to know at this time?"

"Ma'am, I think you are probably already aware, but it does need to be said. The illness I told you about, it was bad. Some people are still sick. We did the best we could with what we had, but our doctors, they died out early. At first, we didn't understand what was happening. We weren't prepared for it. It spread quickly. You would be wise to provide the proper equipment to ensure that the same doesn't happen to you."

Hawk noticed Cantil Gilchrist stiffen. There was no turning back now.

Loris continued on, ignoring the shuffling feet and fleeting glances that were being exchanged all around her. "We understand the risks sir, but we appreciate your concern. We will come prepared. Do you have medical supplies on board?"

"As I said, our medical staff didn't last long. We used what we knew but most of it has been left unused. I'm not sure what you will need but it's likely that we have it here already."

Cantil Gilchrist cleared his throat loudly. Although Loris didn't look up to acknowledge him, she must have understood his concern because she asked, "Can you elaborate on the illness? We can bring supplies from our ship if needed."

Pike sounded less sure of himself now. He spoke, but it was as if he wasn't sure that he should be saying anything at all. "Well, it's a little hard to describe. It started out small enough. Just some runny noses and watery eyes and such. Within a week their eyes were bright red as if they were filled with blood. People were cold. Very cold. They couldn't get warm. Then the vomiting started. There was blood. A lot of blood." His voice sounded distant, as if he was remembering.

Baffin Maxwell cleared his throat to get Loris' attention. When she looked up, he instructed, "Ask about the mortality rate."

Loris nodded acknowledging his comment. "Did anybody survive after getting ill?"

"Yes." Pike stated simply.

Loris waited for him to elaborate, but he didn't. "How many?" She asked after it was clear that he was not planning to offer the information without prompting.

His voice was slow when he spoke. "All of us. Everybody here had it. Anybody left in *Seeker* now is a survivor."

The room itself seemed to breathe as everybody simultaneously inhaled sharply. Cantil Gilchrist shook his head. "This is very bad. If they are telling us this much already, what are they not telling us? Nobody gives all their information to strangers. It must be even worse than they say."

"For God's sakes Cantil, they have nothing to lose. What else could they possibly be leaving out?" Diplomat Ambrose protested.

Loris held down the button to speak to *Seeker*. "Forgive us Mr. Brighton, but we are growing concerned. This is a lot of information to offer. From our experience, people tend to leave out the worst parts. Are you keeping anything from us that we need to know?" Hawk smiled at her mentor's direct yet kind approach.

"No ma'am. We are small in numbers, but we are a unified group. We agreed to tell you everything. You deserve to know. There will be no surprises here." He sounded earnest.

"Fair enough." Loris seemed to believe him. Gauging by the

looks from the rest of the council, Hawk wasn't sure if they were convinced. "You mentioned in our previous conversation something about another ship."

Hesitation again. "Yes." The word was stretched out to sound much longer than it was.

"Can you tell us what happened?"

"A ship contacted us. The initial message was in Onsellan, but they spoke English once we made contact. Don't ask me how they knew it. They told us that Onsella had become compromised and we were no longer welcome there, but that there was another planet. Their planet. They asked permission to board to discuss further arrangements. We agreed."

There was a buzz of concern among the group while wild eyes searched one another's faces for comfort. Hawk felt as if her heart had sunk into her stomach. Was Onsella really no longer their destination?

He continued. "When they entered, we could tell right away that they were untrustworthy. They looked at all of us like we were their next meal and our belongings were theirs. Anytime we asked how they spoke English, they wouldn't say. Finally, one of them referenced Earth, and we knew they were keeping secrets from us. They asked to view the navigation deck and we refused. We thought they might get angry but they didn't. They ate a meal with us and left. The symptoms started three days later."

"Were they Onsellan or human?" Loris asked.

"Neither. We had never seen a race like theirs before."

The murmuring around the room started again but died out quickly.

"Is there anything more that we need to know?" Loris sounded exhausted, as if this was more information than she had expected.

"No ma'am. Nothing more, but we will tell you anything

else that you feel you need to know. It is very important that you stay safe." He sounded sincere. The concern in his voice was almost fatherly.

Rowan spoke now. He was the first junior diplomat to do so. "Did they believe them? Is Onsella compromised?"

Loris stared at Rowan for a long time as if uncertain if she should ask. Finally, her finger hit the transmission button. "One last thing, Mr. Brighton. Do you believe that Onsella is still viable?"

"I want to Ms. Goring. I really do. Those people that did this to us, they weren't exactly trustworthy."

"Thank you, Councilor Brighton. We will be in touch."

Hawk was released shortly after the radio conversation. She was instructed to act normally and to tell no one of what was happening. She had a few hours before breakfast. Hawk went straight for her living quarters in hopes of falling asleep.

She slept very little, tossing and turning re-examining her actions from the night before. When she finally did get out of bed, it was nearly time for lunch. Hawk attempted to start her daily routine but quickly found one dramatic change: her wardrobe. Instead of the usual selection, she now had access to much finer materials. Hawk knew that she would be in the limelight today, so she opted for a mid-length black pencil skirt with a silky, blush-colored blouse. Hawk had never worn anything like it before.

She pulled at the skirt and smoothed her shirt as she left her quarters for the day. Fortunately for her, nobody seemed to notice her insecurity. There had been a short write-up distributed to everybody's wrist transmitter with information about Hawk. They even used short quotes from her interview for people to examine. People who had never acknowledged her before suddenly behaved as if they were close friends.

Strangers kept approaching her and shaking her hand in congratulations. Hawk continued to smile and graciously accepted all the positive words. She was already beginning to understand what Loris meant by a public life and a private life. She wasn't entirely sure how she felt about her public life so far. It didn't feel natural *at all*.

Really, she didn't want to eat with her friends today, but knew that she had to keep up appearances. Her stomach hurt whenever she thought about keeping such a big secret from the people she cared so much about, but she knew it was necessary. Hawk loaded her tray with a minimal portion of food and scanned the room for one of the few people on the ship she wanted to be with.

She could hear Caspian speaking when she approached the table behind him. He hadn't seen her yet. "Two sets of stitches and a broken arm all in one day. Not to mention the stomach bug that's been going around. I'm exhausted."

Lark was responding when Hawk sat down next to Caspian. "Two sets of stitches? How does that happen?"

"One was kitchen staff and the other was the butcher. Apparently working with knives is risky business in *Enlightenment* these days."

"I'm sure the shakes don't help that any." Hawk added trying to sound as if she had been there the entire time.

Lark turned her attention toward Hawk. "How was the first night on the job, superstar?" Hawk startled at the question. Until Lark had said the word "superstar," Hawk had been enjoying the few moments with her friends that felt like a time before everybody knew her name. Had the announcement really only been made the night before? To Hawk, it seemed to be years since she had sat at the cafeteria table last. *Oh, what a difference one night can make,* Hawk thought.

"Busy. You know how first days go." Hawk offered, but her friends wanted details.

"What was it like in the helm?" Caspian asked while he ate a piece of baked fish.

Hawk felt relief knowing that it was a question she could actually answer. "Beautiful," she said breathlessly. "It's like nothing I've ever seen before. I don't think words can capture it."

"Was it like the videos?" Lark looked as though it took a great effort to stay cheerful. She had never been to the helm or seen outside of *Enlightenment*. Even though she seemed content to stay in *Enlightenment* forever, Hawk knew how much Lark would like to see the outside.

Hawk tried to keep her description short so as not to hurt her friend's feelings. "Kind of. It's so... big. It's hard to explain how expansive the universe is when you're looking at it from the inside of a spaceship. It made me realize just how small we are in comparison." Hawk had always thought of *Enlightenment* as big, but compared to what she had seen, it wasn't even comparable.

"Why did you have to meet in the helm anyway?" Caspian questioned.

Hawk wished he wasn't so curious. "Oh, you know. Learning the ins and outs." She hoped that would be enough.

It seemed to be enough for Caspian, but Lark, being Lark, wanted to know more. "Do you like it? So far I mean."

Now that was the big question. Hawk wasn't sure how to respond. She had enjoyed the rush and the feeling of making a difference, but this had been a lot to take in in one day's time. Yesterday, her life had seemed so complicated to her: the prospect of a new job looming overhead, the injury to her ribs, being restricted from physical exercise, and constant emotional tip-toeing around her friendship with Caspian. Hawk would have given anything today to be able to relive that part of her life. However, she wasn't sure she would trade the night before even if she had the option of going back.

Before she had the chance to answer, the group was joined by an unexpected guest. Rowan sat himself down next to Lark, across from Hawk. Lark looked shocked, even a little displeased at first. Then she realized who had sat down next to her and a fabulous grin spread across her face. "Well, hello there. Friend of Hawk's?"

"Yes." Rowan replied while Hawk simultaneously responded, "No."

Neither Rowan nor Hawk seemed surprised by the other's response. Lark on the other hand, looked very interested. "I see. Well, are you going to introduce us, Hawk?"

"Caspian, Lark, I'm sure you recognize Rowan Sheridan. He's my *peer mentor*." She said the last words with great disdain.

Caspian reached his hand across the table, presenting it for a handshake. Rowan gripped it in response. "Nice to meet you, Rowan." Hawk was certain that Caspian's grip was harder than necessary. She couldn't be sure, but she thought Rowan's may have been, too.

"Hawk was just telling us all about her night," Lark squeaked out cheerfully, earning herself a glare from Hawk.

"Oh really?" Rowan raised a questioning eyebrow at Hawk. "What did she tell you about her first day?"

Lark remained as perky as ever, unfazed by the tension that had engulfed the table when Rowan arrived. "Just how beautiful the helm is. Of course, she told us how helpful her peer mentor is. You've made quite an impression on our Hawk here." Lark winked at Hawk as if to say, "you're welcome," but thanking her was not what Hawk had in mind. She wished that Lark was sitting across from her instead of Rowan. A kick seemed well-deserved.

"Oh, I doubt that." Rowan was facing Hawk now. "I think we may have had a misunderstanding. That's why I came to join you all. I thought some smoothing over might be in order."

"I see." By the embarrassed look on Lark's face, it seemed that she was finally catching on.

Caspian tried to hide a smirk but was doing a poor job of it. "Oh, don't take it personally, Rowan. I'm sure you two will get lots of opportunities to work it out. Or else more opportunities for miscommunications. Either way, I'm sure our Hawk won't hold a grudge." He nudged Hawk with his elbow. She grunted in response as she continued to graze on her meager salad.

"I'm sure." Responded Rowan as he eyed Caspian. He turned his attention towards Hawk again. "We are due back at the helm in half an hour. I thought we could walk together."

"Didn't you stay up late working last night? You're going back to work already?" Lark sounded disappointed.

Hawk swallowed her bite a little too quickly. It stung as the too-large bit of cucumber worked its way down her esophagus. She coughed slightly while saying, "Yes. We've got some things to take care of. Nothing to be concerned about."

She instantly regretted adding that last sentence. The look that Lark gave her indicated that she thought maybe there *was* something to worry about now that Hawk had mentioned it.

Oh dear. Hawk thought. *How am I going to keep this from her?* But it didn't matter what Lark suspected, Hawk would be able to tell her nothing.

Hawk agreed to walk with Rowan to the helm. It wouldn't have made much sense to refuse. They would be spending the next three hours together by the radio in case *Seeker* had any further transmissions. Avoiding him was pointless.

They didn't speak while they walked in the corridors. Instead, Hawk rushed ahead to lead the way. She did not want Rowan to feel as if he were in control of the situation. He had wanted to ignore pleas for help. She was angry with him, but furious with herself. She had started to trust him. How could she have misjudged him so completely?

Hawk begrudgingly waited by the helm entrance for Rowan. She wished that she had the clearance to open the door herself. She felt like a child with restricted privileges. She needed to remember to ask Loris when her clearance would be granted.

Once they were positioned around the radio, Rowan finally spoke. "I'm sorry. I was wrong."

Hawk looked up in acknowledgement but did not continue the conversation.

Rowan filled the silence once more. "I was afraid. I thought about my family, my brother, my sister, my parents. I couldn't imagine what would happen to them if they were to get sick and die like the people in *Seeker*. I was weak. I needed someone to remind me of what was important."

Hawk's body relaxed a little.

"You showed me what it really meant to be brave last night. You reminded me, and a room full of leaders, what we are really here for. I'm sorry."

Hawk hadn't expected this. She had assumed that he was going along with the Council's decision out of obligation, not because he agreed with her.

"Thank you for saying so." Hawk didn't want to tell him that it was ok or that she forgave him because neither was true.

She wasn't ready to give up the anger yet. He deserved to be hated for at least a little while longer.

As the night progressed, she found it increasingly difficult to stay angry with him. He told her about his younger brother and his parents. Hawk also learned he had another biological sister who had been raised by another family. Each couple in *Enlightenment* was only permitted to have two children in order to restrict overpopulation. *Enlightenment* would not be sustainable if the resources were spread too thin. Rather than allow for an upswing in population and then impose restrictions to fix the problem, *Enlightenment* opted for a family size cap. If populations started to decline, the restriction was lifted temporarily.

His sister had been the third child of the family. Per *Enlightenment*'s requirements, she was allowed to be adopted by another couple that was unable to have children of their own. In the case of his sister, she had been adopted by an inter-species couple. The adoptive mother was Onsellan and the father was human. Although Onsellan/human relationships were not unheard of, children were not possible by natural means for such couples.

With the family capacity restrictions and the difficulty for so many couples to have children of their own, adoption was fairly common in *Enlightenment*. Most families agreed to allow communication and even activities between the birth and adoptive families.

Rowan was eleven years older than his sister. He did not get to grow up with her, but felt very protective of her. She was the only child in her adoptive family. Five years ago, her adoptive father had died suddenly. Rowan did all that he could to be the best role model possible for her. He had a weekly visit with her that he used for playing games and helping her with schoolwork.

His brother was only a few years older than himself. He was a pilot. According to Rowan, he was very talented, but he had not taken as much of an interest in their younger sister. That caused the two brothers to drift apart. When Rowan decided to make his sister a priority in his life, his brother had difficulty understanding the decision. His parents, of course, had been thrilled. It was easier for a sibling to include themselves in an adopted child's life. Adoptive parents tended to be more protective in nature when it came to biological parents. Siblings were considered less threatening.

Hawk had always been envious of people with siblings. She often had pangs of jealousy when she watched Lark and Caspian together. Her parents had not wanted more than one child. They had each fought with their sibling incessantly and didn't want to subject their daughter to the same upbringing.

By the end of their shift, nothing had happened over the radio, but Hawk was no longer upset with Rowan. She understood fear. It wasn't always rational. At least he had been willing to admit he was wrong.

Hawk left the helm feeling much happier about her peer mentor. She was thinking about what the next day might bring and was almost to her room when her wrist transmitter vibrated. It was a message from Loris asking if she was still coming over for chess.

Hawk was exhausted from stress and lack of sleep, but she couldn't pass up the opportunity to talk with her mentor one-on-one again. Hawk turned around and began walking back towards Loris' room.

Loris had the chess board set up when she arrived. They swapped pieces so that Hawk was now the Onsellans and Loris the humans.

She expected more conversation about the events of the past few days, but Loris changed the subject whenever Hawk brought it up. Hawk was happy to give her mind a break. Although, break was not exactly the right word for the chess game. Hawk found herself in constant thought. She planned at least two moves ahead and was devastated when Loris foiled her plans. They played for a few hours and then decided it was time to call it quits. The pieces were shaken from the board twice while they played, but Hawk didn't mind this time. At least now she knew why.

Upon leaving, Loris gave Hawk a long hug and said in her ear, "After last night, I know with a hundred percent certainty that I made the right decision when I chose you. Well done." Hawk hadn't won a single game, but she felt victorious as she left the room.

10

DÉJÀ VU

That night, Hawk struggled to fall asleep. After tossing and turning for over two hours, she pulled a robe on over her pajamas and left her room. Hawk walked down the abandoned hallways in a familiar path. A path she only took when she was alone late at night. She moved past The Farm and through the door she had passed through many long nights before. Hawk stepped forward onto a long catwalk that wrapped around in an expansive half-circle. Thick glass separated her from the blue orb that was surrounded by the walkway. She had been told that the whole of the area was once filled by the power source, today it filled only a small fraction of the space. Despite its diminished size, it still let off a powerful, blue light.

Hawk leaned against the railing and looked past Blue Vigor. Looking directly at the substance was difficult due to its brightness. Instead, she watched the dancing reflections against the far wall while her eyes adjusted. Everything was tinted in blue. She felt her tension fade away as her eyelids started to feel heavy.

She startled when she felt a hand on her shoulder.

Suddenly wide awake once more, Hawk jumped and turned to face whomever had disturbed her peaceful state.

"It's just me!" Caspian stepped backwards. He had long ago been made all too aware of Hawk's tendency to swing out when surprised.

Hawk's chest rose and fell rapidly as she calmed herself. "Oh, it's you. I didn't expect to see anybody here."

"I didn't either. I thought you'd be sound asleep after your first day." His eyes fell to her side. "Did your ribs keep you up? Are you in pain?" Concern etched his face.

She tried to play it off as if trouble sleeping should be expected. "No. Nothing like that. I just had too much on my mind. First day and all." Caspian looked as if he wanted to ask questions but decided against it.

"I couldn't sleep either," he sighed heavily and ran a hand over the back of his neck. Hawk had the urge to press him for more details as to his own restlessness but decided better of it as she didn't want him asking questions in return.

Hawk moved to lean against the railing. Caspian joined her with another heavy sigh. "I guess I shouldn't be surprised to find you here. If I wanted solitude, I shouldn't have shown you my hiding place." It had been years since Caspian had first shown Hawk the viewing platform. It was open to the public, but few people used it.

Hawk felt instantly guilty. "I can leave if you want to be alone." She started to straighten up, readying herself to leave.

"No!" he nearly shouted and reached for her before pulling his hand back. "I'm glad you're here." He tried to lessen the alarm from his tone. "I mean, I could use the company."

Hawk returned to her slack stance, eyeing him suspiciously. "Ok." She wanted to say more, but didn't find the words.

Neither spoke while they watched the shadows bounce

around them. Caspian stated breathily, "There's so much beauty here."

"I'm surprised more people don't come to see it." Hawk said as her eyes continued to follow the blue lights cast against the walls.

"I didn't mean Blue Vigor." Caspian sounded surprised that she had misunderstood him. "I meant *here. Enlightenment*."

Hawk hadn't thought of *Enlightenment* as beautiful before. Sure, some parts of it were nicer than others, but most of the ship was tarnished and felt very old. "I suppose so," she said hesitantly.

"It's strange how I hadn't really thought about it before today." Caspian's hand bounced against the railing while he spoke.

Hawk looked towards Caspian with sad eyes. "How did things go with Mr. Davis?" She suspected the launching of his mentor into space played a role in his unhappiness.

Caspian looked surprised by the question and his hand stilled. "Fine. It was fine. He has a very nice family." He sounded distracted, as if his mind was far away from Mr. Davis' death.

Hawk opened her mouth to speak but closed it again without saying a word. Instead of speaking, they watched the reflections dance against the walls until neither felt they could stay awake any longer. They walked together towards their rooms. They came to Hawk's room first.

"I guess this is good night then," she said awkwardly.

"I guess so," he responded. He touched her arm tenderly as if to say goodbye. Hawk stared at his hand before gently pulling away. Caspian flinched as though he was caught doing something wrong. He took a step away saying softly, "Big day tomorrow," as he continued walking towards his room.

Hawk lay in bed afterwards feeling as if she should have

said more. She felt a deep ache in her chest that had nothing to do with her injured ribs when she thought of Caspian's distress. She had been too fearful of his return questions to even ask him why. Her failure at being a good friend stung. She vowed to find out more the next day. Her final thought before falling asleep was of his hand gently touching her arm, and questioning herself as to why she pulled away.

Hawk woke the next morning feeling as if she hadn't slept at all. The events of the day before weighed heavily on her mind and she kept replaying the radio conversations and meeting in her head. Hawk knew that Rowan and Loris had been proud of her for speaking up during the meeting, but she couldn't shake the feeling that she had made a few enemies already too. What troubled her even more was her conversation with Caspian. He had been cryptic, as if he wanted to say more but couldn't. She tried to push it out of her mind as she started the day.

She chose pancakes and bacon for breakfast the next morning and to her surprise, Hawk discovered that she was really quite hungry. After days of feeling too stressed to eat, her appetite had returned. She imagined that the extra adrenaline pumping through her veins had something to do with that.

Lark was waiting for her in the cafeteria as per their usual morning routine. She looked Hawk up and down with her lips pursed together tightly. Finally, in a caring voice she asked, "Are you feeling all right?"

Hawk translated that in her mind, *You look like crap, Hawk.*

"I'm fine," she responded in a clipped tone that came out far harsher than she had meant it to. She softened her voice to finish her thought. "I didn't sleep well, that's all."

"I'm sure I would have trouble sleeping too if I'd spent the evening with Rowan Sheridan." She peered at Hawk from the corner of her eyes. Then she asked, fishing, "What's the story with that guy anyway? Why didn't you mention him to me earlier?"

Hawk shrugged. "There wasn't much to tell. He's my peer mentor." Lark continued to glare at her. "I guess I was a little too preoccupied with my life-changing career switch to talk about boys." Hawk retorted defensively.

Lark dropped her eyes. "Did you work out that misunderstanding? He seemed to be genuinely sorry to me."

"Or else he looked genuinely *handsome* to you." Hawk quipped.

"That too." Lark continued to eat her breakfast.

Hawk shook her head in disbelief. Sometimes Lark overlooked the obvious and pushed her own agenda. "Yeah, we worked it out. He's not so bad."

"Good, because here he comes!" Lark waved at someone behind Hawk. She turned to see Rowan waving back as he walked across the large room. It looked to Hawk as though he had been looking for a place to sit and was waved over by Lark. He didn't seem to mind though. Quite the opposite. He seemed very pleased to have a place to go.

He sat down next to Hawk with a groan. Lark noticed right away. "Tired, Rowan?"

"Very. I hardly slept a wink last night." He rubbed his eyes.

"Really?" Lark stretched the word out and eyed Hawk suspiciously. "I guess it was a late night for a lot of people then."

Rowan looked confused. "More like a busy day, I guess. I had a lot on my mind."

Lark looked as though she didn't believe him. Her eyes darted between Rowan and Hawk. Hawk felt her cheeks burning pink and willed them to stop. Her friend had the wrong idea but she couldn't say anything in front of Rowan without making it even more awkward. "Big plans for today then?"

Hawk decided to tackle the question. Rowan seemed to be making things worse even if he didn't know it. "Not really. I've been excused from horticulture duties today for Council business. Until I decide which position to give up, they've limited my horticulturist and EPM shifts."

"You don't know which one you're going to give up, then?" Rowan asked curiously.

"Not yet." Hawk watched Lark closely to gauge her reaction. "I know for sure that I don't want to give up teaching. But really, I don't want to give up any of them. It's not an easy decision." Lark seemed unusually interested in her yogurt.

"I remember when I went through that. It wasn't so hard for me though. I gave up a kitchen gig. It wasn't exactly my favorite thing to do." He chuckled to himself. "Let me know if you need any help deciding."

"When do you need to give them an answer?" Lark was interested in their conversation again. Hawk couldn't tell if it was worry or just curiosity that tinted her friend's voice.

"Five more days."

Lark nodded and then turned her attention back towards her food. Hawk felt even more anxious about the decision now.

Caspian sat down next to his sister while eying Rowan. "Five days until what?"

"Until Hawk decides if she's giving up horticulturist or EPM." Lark said it cheerfully, but Hawk suspected she was hiding her true feelings.

"Oh man. That's a tough call. I'd quit being a horticulturist if I were you. There are all kinds of unseemly workers in that position. You don't want to be seen mingling with *those* types."

He pretended to hide his finger as he pointed playfully in his sister's direction. Lark retaliated by punching his arm. He rubbed the spot and mouthed, "see?" which earned him another hit in the same spot.

Caspian turned his attention toward Rowan. "I see you've come to join us again." It wasn't really welcoming or uninviting; just a statement of fact. However, his eyes did not show any signs of welcome whatsoever.

Judging by the way that Rowan tensed up, he had noticed this too. "I did. I'm trying to branch out. You know, spend some time with the new junior diplomat and all."

"Aren't we all?" Caspian responded. "It seems that she's in high demand these days."

Hawk could tell that Caspian did not like the sight of her sitting so close to Rowan. She decided it was time to excuse herself and get the rest of her day started. She had already eaten three pancakes as it was.

She had been instructed to meet Loris in the Council Room early. Only senior diplomats were required to attend, but Loris had told Hawk that she should attend as well. She had a lot to learn about the way the Council functioned, and she needed to learn it quickly. Rowan had opted to join her even though he wasn't required. He seemed to have a need to prove himself after what had happened the previous day. Much to Caspian's dismay and Lark's delight, they had left the cafeteria together.

Loris led the meeting again. There was little discussion this time. Mostly, the Council discussed plans for the future as it related to *Seeker*. Hawk learned that they were expected at *Seeker* by midmorning the following day. The Council planned to send out warnings to all citizens later that morning regarding the "scheduled maintenance" that would stall the ship the next day. Reminders would be issued again shortly before the stop.

Another meeting was scheduled for that evening to discuss exact roles while *Enlightenment* was docked with *Seeker*. Until then, they were to act as normal as possible so as not to raise suspicion. If any citizens questioned them about the "scheduled maintenance," they were to inform them that they were merely sending out scouts to inspect the exterior of the ship. This would explain the ships stopping and also account for any missing crew if they were noticed.

Hawk was given the task of radio communication again. Loris needed to speak with *Seeker* that morning to relay the plan, so she joined Hawk and Rowan, who had volunteered, to the helm. Loris spoke only with Hawk. She barely acknowledged Rowan's presence and when she did, it was with short, cold statements.

When Loris contacted the distressed ship, they did not hear the familiar voice of Pike Brighton. Instead, a woman responded. "This is *Seeker*. Councilor Kit Elderstein speaking." Hawk was fairly certain that she had heard the voice before, on the original recording. She had been the woman speaking Onsellan after the man's outburst.

Loris relayed the plan for the following day. They were hoping to dock around 10:00 in the morning with medical staff. Hawk had been expecting the discussion to go this way. What she didn't expect was what her mentor said next. "I will be leaving you now in the capable hands of my protégé, Hawk Larson and her colleague, Rowan Sheridan, with whom your crew spoke yesterday. If you need to contact *Enlightenment*, please address Junior Diplomat Larson."

Hawk was taken aback. It would make more sense to allow Rowan communication privileges. Apparently even with Hawk's forgiveness, Rowan had not managed to gain back the trust of Loris Goring. If he was surprised, he didn't show it.

Loris left. Rowan and Hawk were once again alone with the

helm staff. "She'll move past it soon enough." Hawk said in what she hoped was a comforting tone.

Rowan scoffed. "Yeah, we'll see about that."

Hawk had intended to ignore it and move past the whole situation, but something about the tone in his voice made Hawk hesitate. "You don't think she will?"

He was looking down at the table in front of him. "Oh, I'm sure she will. At least she'll act like she does. You can't always tell with her what's real, though." He looked up and saw the shocked, confused look on Hawk's face. "I mean... nothing. Forget I said anything."

Hawk wanted to ask more but was also afraid of the answers. She could tell by Rowan's body language that he did not want to elaborate. Hawk made a mental note to herself to pursue the topic again once they knew each other better and instead chose to preoccupy her mind with what was happening around the helm.

Although it was not fully staffed, there were more people working than had been the previous day. About half a dozen workers floated about, preoccupied with their tasks.

Rowan seemed eager to talk with Hawk more. She hated to admit it to herself, but she had been looking forward to spending time with him, too. He had been with her through some of the biggest moments of her life. Although she didn't look at him in the same way he looked at her, she enjoyed his company. Perhaps he was beginning to see their friendship in that way as well, because he seemed to blush less and was looking her in the eyes when he talked to her.

However, Hawk did enough blushing for the both of them when he asked her about Caspian. "He's a friend. Lark's brother, too."

"He seems awfully protective of you." Rowan acknowledged.

"We're a close group. We look out for one another." Hawk wished that her cheeks would stop glowing red.

"Is that all? It seemed like something else to me."

"That's all. I know he can come on a little strong, but he will warm up to you. Honest." Hawk knew why Caspian had been so protective. He didn't have a right to be really. They weren't together. That had been Hawk's choice, but it felt nice to know he cared. She felt a pang of regret thinking of what the next day would bring.

Hawk knew it was strange to be so willing to jump into danger and possibly risk death by debilitating illness while simultaneously being afraid to admit her feelings to someone that she knew reciprocated them. She thought about sharing the thought with Rowan but decided against it. She wasn't sure that their friendship was *that* strong yet. Still, it would be nice to talk to someone about it. Hawk had never actually said anything about her feelings towards Caspian aloud before.

Before she could say anything more, a strange screech emitted from the radio. "Dawn!" Rowan yelled towards the technologist who had helped make communication possible the day before.

Dawn responded swiftly and began punching buttons and screens. "We still have *Seeker*'s frequency. I'm not sure why you aren't picking it up correctly." She made more adjustments and a voice could now be heard faintly through a static sound.

The speaker was Onsellan. Hawk could translate the language and even speak it. She listened closely trying to decipher the words through the static. It was repeating itself. "Probably a recording." Rowan observed. He was also straining to make out the words. It was Onsellan, but the accent was different than either had heard before.

Unlike the last time, none of the helm crew came to listen.

They had learned their lesson after a stern discussion with Loris the night before. Rowan gasped and looked pale.

"What is it?" Hawk asked.

"You can't hear it?" his face showed astonishment.

Hawk listened harder until finally she understood. It was an invitation from Onsella itself.

11

CALLING ALL MEDICS

The message invited any ship within communication distance to join Onsella in their continued pursuit of knowledge. The message indicated that they were peaceful, but any violence would be met in kind by a superior military. The goal of Onsella was advancing the knowledge of the universe. Those who came to join them in their goal would be treated as revered guests.

Hawk and Rowan were both overjoyed by the news that Onsella was still what they had hoped. The last part of the message thrilled them even more. According to the voice, they were approximately five Onsellan days from the planet. This meant that they were a mere one Earth week away from their ultimate destination.

Hawk turned down the speaker volume. Nobody appeared to be listening, but they couldn't risk this information being leaked. If the news of *Seeker* would create a panic, the news of Onsella would cause chaos. The pair knew that they were in no position to act on this information alone. Hawk sent a page for Loris marked "urgent".

Rowan excused himself from the table and walked towards Dawn. She left her station and returned with two sets of headphones. Rowan graciously accepted them and began walking back towards Hawk. Dawn began to follow asking if she needed to adjust anything. Rowan insisted they could hear fine and that it was important she remain at her station. Hawk wished the message could be made clearer. She felt certain Dawn could help but understood Rowan did not want to draw any more attention than absolutely necessary.

They listened to the message quietly replay through the headphones four more times before Loris came rushing through the doors, surprising most of the helm workers. They had not been notified to expect a senior diplomat at all, let alone to expect the woman bursting through the doors and sprinting toward the conference table.

"You need to hear this." Hawk slipped off her headphones and handed them to the frazzled-looking leader. "You will need to listen through the static."

Loris put on the headphones. She bobbed her head up and down slightly with her eyes closed tightly, her eyebrows furrowed in concentration. Rowan turned up the volume. Loris put her hands up, cupping the earpieces.

Suddenly her eyes popped open, a look of complete astonishment on her face. She pulled the earphones from her head with a slight shriek. A mix of delight and concern spread across her face.

"Who else have you told about this?" Her tone was accusatory as she looked straight at Rowan.

"Nobody. We only contacted you," he replied hastily.

She turned her attention toward Hawk now as if to say, *Is that the truth?*

"Really. We've told no one." Hawk confirmed. "We turned down the transmission as soon as we realized what it was. Even helm staff doesn't know as far as we can tell." Her eyes darted around the room looking for any sign of eavesdroppers, but she found none.

"Good. Let's keep it that way. This information doesn't go anywhere outside of the three of us."

"You mean, until we tell the rest of the Council, right?" Hawk thought the rest of the Council would need to be told immediately. She expected Loris to send the notice for a meeting as soon as they were done discussing it together.

Loris looked lost in thought. "I'm not sure if that's the best idea."

Hawk was shocked. "What do you mean? Why wouldn't we tell them?"

"With our rescue of *Seeker* scheduled for tomorrow, we might need to keep this information private until after we hear what *Seeker* has to say." Loris looked to Rowan, expecting him to show signs of indignation, but he said nothing. His face remained emotionless.

Loris continued talking to no one in particular as if trying to convince herself. "Yes. Rescue of *Seeker* is priority number one for now. If this is a trap, they will know it."

"Do you think *Seeker* has access to this message? Why wouldn't they have mentioned it to us?" Rowan questioned.

"It's possible they haven't heard it." Loris said. "We altered our course significantly to approach *Seeker*. Onsella has a much greater range than any of the ships from Earth. If we just received this message now, it's possible that they never had access to it."

"So *Seeker* doesn't realize how close they are." Rowan nodded in agreement.

"Doesn't that mean we are actually moving away from Onsella?" Hawk asked, her mind was spinning.

"Probably so." Loris agreed. "It's hard to tell without knowing the exact coordinates from that message, and I don't think we can ask the crew to identify the source without playing our hand."

Hawk was conflicted. Helping *Seeker* was important, nobody agreed more than she did on that point, but Onsella was their ultimate goal. "Is it possible to return with additional help for *Seeker* after we reach Onsella? Surely they would want to help them as much as we do."

Rowan spoke before Loris could. "I wouldn't be too sure about that. We're assuming that Onsella is being honest about their motives, but we have no way of knowing that."

"We know that they sent ships out to find and bring back alternative life despite significant risk. Why would they want to harm us now?" Hawk replied, still trying to understand.

Loris apparently agreed with Rowan. "We know that over a thousand years ago their motives were pure when they sent out their original ships. We know nothing about them *now*. For all we know, the other ship was telling the truth about Onsella and the infection wasn't intentional. Or it was intentional and Onsella could be in cahoots with the ship that infected *Seeker*. We have no way of knowing. We need to see *Seeker* first."

The idea of Onsella was tempting. Hawk was still concerned. *Seeker* was important, but Onsella had always been her dream. "Why aren't we telling the Council this?"

"Hawk, I know how excited you are about Onsella. Now imagine a Council full of people just as excited as you are, if not more. Do you really think they would allow us to go to *Seeker* first even if it is the right call?" Rowan argued. Loris nodded in agreement.

"We will tell the Council," she added, "tomorrow. After we know for sure what happened in *Seeker*."

Hawk and Rowan remained on radio duty. They expected Loris to relieve one of them within the next four hours. Loris had concerns about allowing others access to the radio transmissions. If others intercepted the Onsellan message, she was certain that the rescue mission would be terminated. They planned to rotate between the three of them for the next twenty-four hours.

Four hours into the shift, the helm door opened, but Loris did not walk through it. Hawk scowled at Rowan as Diplomat Ambrose approached the conference table. She had just begun to trust Rowan again, now with his mentor walking closer towards them, she felt completely betrayed.

However, when she saw Rowan's face, she knew that it was not the case. He was just as surprised as she was by the unexpected guest. "He must be checking in. Don't mention anything." He urged her as he realized what she must be thinking.

"And how are things going in here?" he asked as he approached.

"Just fine." Rowan responded quickly. "No further communication with *Seeker*."

"May I?" the senior diplomat asked, as he reached for Rowan's headset.

Rowan cheerfully complied. Loris had insisted that Dawn recalibrate to make sure that the *Seeker* messages could come in stronger. They had not heard the Onsella message since, although it had been recorded. Loris had the recording with her to keep it safe.

"Not a peep then?" he asked his protégé.

Rowan cleared his throat nervously. "Nope. *Seeker*'s been pretty quiet after communication with Diplomat Goring this morning."

"I wasn't asking about communication with *Seeker*. I was asking about communication, period."

The man knew. To Hawk, her suspicions had been confirmed. Rowan must have told Diplomat Ambrose. There was no other explanation. "How could you?" she hissed. "I trusted you!"

"I didn't!" he responded defensively.

Hawk opened her mouth to tell him what a liar he was but was interrupted. "He's telling the truth," a voice called from behind Diplomat Ambrose. "Rowan did not tell Ural. I did."

Hawk had been so upset that she hadn't noticed Loris entering the helm. Hawk blinked in confusion. "You did?"

"Yes, she did. I was shocked to hear that you would keep something like this from me, Rowan. I'm very disappointed in you," Ural reprimanded. Rowan's eyes fell to the floor.

"Don't blame him, Ural. You know that he couldn't tell you anything without violating my trust." Loris came to his rescue, but Rowan didn't look as though he had been saved. His face looked pained.

"I'm sorry. I couldn't risk it," he said apologetically.

Ural did not acknowledge his apology. "Loris told me what happened. She asked me to come here to listen to the recording."

"We can trust Ural." Loris was talking to Hawk now. Rowan looked as if he wanted to sink through the floor of *Enlightenment* and fall into space.

Loris played the recording. She had one set of earphones and Ural had the other. His face was strained similar to how Loris' had been before. Loris listened thoughtfully but was no longer straining to hear. Loris looked as if she were trying to take in the moment and memorize it. Hawk knew the feeling; she had done the same.

While they listened, Hawk stood next to Rowan. "You couldn't have said anything. He knows that." No response. He stood staring forward as if in a trance. She reached out and grazed his arm with the back of her hand. He turned to look at her. "It's going to be ok."

He gave a weak smile back and nodded. "I know. I just wish she had given me the heads-up." Hawk had been thinking the same thing.

They both turned towards the table when they heard Ural set his headphones back on the table. "Are we sure it's from Onsella?" he whispered urgently.

"Without knowing the coordinates, there really is no way to be sure," Loris answered, "but we have no reason to think it isn't."

"What if it's from the ship that *Seeker* was talking about? Maybe they're trying to lure us to them."

"It's a possibility." Loris said skeptically. "But I don't think so. *Seeker* said that they were told about a different planet entirely. It wouldn't make sense for them to change their whole scheme now."

"None of this makes any sense," he looked annoyed.

"I know this is a lot to take in, Ural, but we need to find out more information. *Seeker* needs our help. The Council has already decided on that. Bringing this up now would only cause confusion and waste time. Time that *Seeker* may not have."

"I know Loris. You're right. I just have a bad feeling about this whole situation. Are we supposed to believe that all of a sudden we have contact with two different groups inside of one week when we haven't had communication with anybody outside of *Enlightenment* for over four hundred years? That seems like a pretty big coincidence for me. I'm not sure I buy it."

"That's why we need to meet with *Seeker* first." Loris insisted. "We can limit our exposure to the few who enter *Seeker*. Going to Onsella with so much unknown danger risks all of *Enlightenment*."

"I know. You're right." Ural agreed. "So, is it my watch on the radio then?"

"I was thinking you could take the next shift with Rowan. That would give me some time to talk with Hawk and get some rest before we take the next shift."

Rowan straightened himself and tried to look confident. Hawk knew he was dreading spending the next four hours with a man that felt betrayed by him, but he had survived a shift with her; she was certain that he could smooth things over with Ural Ambrose. After all, they had established a much stronger relationship than she'd had with him at the start of their shift.

Hawk left with Loris. Loris turned down the corridor heading for her room. Hawk followed apprehensively behind, unsure if she was supposed to be following her or not. "I know it's been a trying few days for you, Hawk," she said as they entered her quarters. "I didn't expect so much to happen so quickly, but I'm glad to have you by my side while it's happening."

"I'm still in a state of shock, I think. I knew I would have a lot of responsibilities as a junior diplomat, but I can honestly say that I didn't expect *any* of this." Hawk paused for a moment and then added, "It's quite a rush!"

Loris smiled. "This is by far the biggest thing I have faced in my entire career working with the Council. I doubt you will ever face more than what you are dealing with now. Then again, it looks like your career may be coming to a speedy end."

Hawk's heart sank. "Oh," she had known that questioning Loris' authority earlier was risky, but she had not expected to be dismissed.

Loris continued, "Once we reach Onsella, I'm not sure what will happen to the Council."

"Oh, yeah, me neither, I guess." Hawk was relieved to hear that she was not being fired, but until then she had not had the realization that her dream job would soon be nonexistent. "Do you think it's real? I mean, I want to believe it's real, but do you think it is?" Hawk had been eager to ask this question since she had first heard the transmission.

Loris frowned slightly. "I'm not sure. I will know more after tomorrow." She glanced at the time on her wrist transmitter. "It looks like it's time to meet with the Council about tomorrow's duties. You don't need to come to this one. Go home. Get some rest."

Hawk wanted to argue; to say that she was fine and continue to power through. However, she also had difficulty keeping her eyes open. She reluctantly agreed.

The hallways seemed never-ending as Hawk trudged her way towards her own living quarters. Many people smiled and waved at her enthusiastically when she passed. She did her best to look happy to see them. Nobody else knew what she was facing, and it was part of her job to maintain appearances.

When she finally arrived at her own room, she was sound asleep as soon as her head hit the pillow.

Hawk awoke when her wrist transmitter vibrated aggressively. She rubbed her eyes and then glanced at the screen. Loris had sent her a notification. She had a meeting in thirty minutes. Hawk was certain the meeting must have been scheduled earlier, but Loris had waited to send the notification knowing that Hawk was sleeping. She was very appreciative.

Rising from her bed seemed especially trying. Hawk cradled her ribs and remembered that she had not taken her second dose of recommended pain medication that day. She had been so busy, and her adrenaline had been so high that she hadn't noticed the pain until getting out of bed for the second time. Hawk groaned as she quickly rushed to get ready for the next meeting.

There was no way of knowing what the meeting was about, so Hawk felt a little nervous walking into the conference room. She took her seat next to Loris. Most of the seats were filled with the other diplomats. Some people spoke cheerfully to those sitting around them while others sat stiffly speaking to no one. Ural Ambrose and Rowan were two noticeable absences.

Hawk leaned in close to Loris. "What are we deciding on now?" She hoped to have at least somewhat of an idea before jumping into the meeting.

"No decisions this time. This is more of an informational meeting for the medical staff that will be entering *Seeker* tomorrow."

The last of the diplomats took their seats. Loris caught the attention of the room and asked for silence. "As you all know, the medical staff will be joining us tonight. We are here to show a united front and to come up with a plan that promotes safety for both the citizens of *Seeker* and *Enlightenment*."

"We are ready for the medical staff." She nodded to a junior diplomat towards the end of the table. He stood quickly and rushed to the door. Six nervous looking people walked through the door apprehensively. Hawk recognized the woman who was at the head of the line. She was one of Caspian's favorite doctors to train with.

It was then that Hawk was hit with instant dread. Surely there would be no medics who were still in training? The mission would require more experienced staff. She sat on the edge of her seat as she watched the doctors walk in. Her nerves intensified when she realized that the woman in the front was the only experienced doctor. All of the people walking behind her looked much younger.

Hawk's heart stopped when her eyes fell upon the last person in line. Caspian was walking into the conference room.

12

RECKLESS

Caspian didn't see her at first. He came into the room with a confident walk and his head held high. He was clearly in his element. He looked proud to be there.

Hawk continued to stare openly at Caspian, unable to move. Unable to even breathe. When Loris spoke, Caspian turned his attention to the head of the table. That was when he spotted Hawk. She shook her head slightly side to side with wild eyes. *Get out now Caspian,* she thought. *You don't know what you're getting into.* His eyes tightened questioningly, but he did not move.

"This is Doctor Paloma Lofton. She has been briefed minimally about our circumstances. As we discussed earlier, trainees are our best option for such conditions due to safety protocol. She has selected five medics-in-training to assist her with this mission." Caspian straightened himself even more, oozing with pride while Hawk inwardly kicked herself for sleeping through the last meeting. "The medics are not yet aware of the special circumstances surrounding their selection, only that they are needed for a special mission that has significant risk."

Or that they were selected instead of fully trained doctors because they are more disposable, Hawk thought bitterly.

Loris played the initial recording for the group followed by a recording of the conversation about the illness. The recordings had been edited to only include information that the medical personnel would need. Hawk could tell by the look on Doctor Lofton's face that she had not heard the recordings yet. Caspian looked just like she imagined she had when she first heard the messages. Stunned. Completely and utterly flabbergasted.

When the recordings started, he looked as though he might be sick and stared at the tabletop in front of him. His focus changed as the recordings continued. Instead, he looked straight at Hawk. A look of hurt and betrayal crossed his face followed by a look of mild confusion. Hawk couldn't tell if he was mad or just coming to grips with understanding.

The recordings finally ended. "Will you have sufficient medical staff and supplies for what this mission entails?" Loris asked the doctor.

For the first time, Doctor Lofton spoke. Her voice was quiet and calm. It was not what Hawk had been expecting. "It's difficult to say without being in *Seeker*, but I have confidence that we will get by just fine." She waved her arm to indicate the "we" to which she referred. "I've selected only the best to join me. This is the best medical team you could ask for. We will do everything we can to help those people." Hawk could tell that this was not just a job to her; she truly cared about the people she was going to help despite having never met them.

"Do you have enough hazmat suits and safety equipment?" Loris inquired. "Your safety is of utmost importance."

Doctor Lofton replied passionately. "I reviewed the hazardous materials supplies this morning. There are a dozen suits set aside for this type of event. We'll only be using six tomorrow."

"Seven." Loris corrected. "I'm coming with you." Hawk stared at her mentor in surprise. They had not discussed any of the Council members going.

"Eight." All eyes shifted towards Hawk. "You'll need eight suits because I'm coming too." Hawk knew it was risky, but she had to try. "You will need me." Hawk's eyes were wild and pleading as Loris turned to inspect her.

"Eight suits." Loris continued as if that were always the plan. "That'll leave four more suits in case reinforcements are needed."

Hawk did not like the word "reinforcements" being used. She thought it sounded like they were going to a warzone instead of a rescue mission. By the look on Caspian's face, he might as well have been entering a battle. His face was stern and tense as he scowled in Hawk's direction. He didn't seem at all pleased that she was joining him.

The medics were excused. Hawk heard Doctor Lofton say something to them about meeting first thing in the morning to prepare medical kits. The diplomats started walking towards the door. Hawk began to rise until Loris placed a gentle hand on her shoulder. "Stay. We have things to discuss."

Hawk sat back down and watched as the others exited the room. She found herself wishing that Rowan were there. He would mouth words of encouragement or give her a glance that meant everything would be all right. Instead, she was met with scrutinizing glances from diplomats as they headed for the door. They did not seem pleased with her stunt. She hoped Loris felt differently.

When the room was empty and the door was pulled tight, Loris stood and began pacing the full length of the room. Her hand was rubbing her forehead as if she had a headache. Hawk sat still as the woman walked back and forth twice before turning in her direction. "I really wish you hadn't done that."

"I know." Hawk said quietly.

"If something happens there, I'll have no one to take my place. With the new message from today, it really would be better if you stayed on the ship." She continued to pace, no longer looking at Hawk as she spoke.

"I know," Hawk managed to choke out again.

"Ural and Rowan will know, of course, but having you would provide more allies if the Council turned on them." Loris continued her rebuke.

"I know," her voice shook.

Loris turned ferociously, all her attention on Hawk. "So why did you do it then? If you know all of this, why did you say what you did? You said I needed you and I believed you but now I need to know *why*." She slammed an open hand on the table in front of her to punctuate the statement.

"I just," Hawk paused to take a deep breath, "I have to go with you. I insisted that this was our responsibility and that it was the right thing. I still believe that. I'm partially responsible for putting you and those medics at risk. I can't stay behind in safety when I know the dangers you're facing."

"You mean the dangers that *he's* facing. Right?" She arched an eyebrow at Hawk.

Hawk stared at Loris, not speaking for a long time. "It's all of you. I can't stay here and do nothing. I just can't."

Loris nodded. She started rubbing her forehead again as she did a full lap pacing around the room before turning back to Hawk. "You will stay with me at all times unless I tell you otherwise. Do you understand?"

Hawk nodded enthusiastically. "I understand. Anything you need, I'll be there."

"Good. Now we need to relieve Ural and Rowan. They're waiting for us." Hawk followed Loris as they exited the room.

Loris opened the door and looked out. "You can meet me there. I'll make sure Rowan stays by the helm to let you in."

Hawk didn't know what Loris was talking about. She planned on walking together to the helm. When she took a few hesitant steps forward, she discovered why Loris had altered the plan. Caspian stood in the hallway. Waiting.

"You two can use the conference room." Loris walked away without a backwards glance.

The two locked eyes as they stood in the hallway. Hawk finally stepped into the conference room and waited by the door for Caspian to step inside. She shut the door behind them. Neither made a move to sit.

"I knew you were stressed yesterday, but I had no idea." Caspian stepped toward her, his hand extended towards her face. Hawk stepped back. His eyes were intense, and she wasn't sure of his intentions. Noticing her reaction, he awkwardly lowered his hand by his side and took a small step away.

"That's why you were acting so strangely last night. You knew something was up, you just didn't know all of it." Hawk remembered his anxious mannerisms on the viewing deck.

"I know why you couldn't tell me. I'm just glad that I know now." His words held none of the animosity Hawk had expected.

Hawk felt instant relief. She couldn't hold herself back any longer. She rushed forward and wrapped her arms around his waist. He extended his arms and pulled her in closer to him. Her head pressed against his chest and she could hear only his heartbeat and her own breathing.

"I wish you didn't know. That would mean you were safe," she sobbed as tears streaked down her cheeks.

"Hey now, you know we'll be just fine. There are five hundred people over there with no medicine or hazmat suits and all of them are alive." Hawk felt his hand against the back of her head as he pulled her in even closer.

Hawk nuzzled closer into his shoulder. "And thousands who weren't so lucky. We still don't know what this thing is or how it's treated."

"That's for me to worry about. You just worry about getting all the information you can, and stay close to Diplomat Goring. She won't let anything happen to you." He sounded confident. Hawk wished that she felt the same.

She had become less certain of her choice to help *Seeker* after seeing Caspian standing with the other medics. She knew it was the right thing to do, but she hadn't imagined she would be putting someone so important to her in immediate danger. "Nothing is going to happen." He assured her. "I won't let anything happen to you."

Hawk thought that there was very little he would be able to do to protect her, but she didn't say it. "You know I can take care of myself. It's *you* I'm worried about," she sniffed.

"Oh yeah? Why's that?"

She smiled against his chest. "You're always rushing in to play the hero. I don't know if I'll be with you all the time in *Seeker* to tell you when you're doing something stupid. I can't exactly trust you to know it on your own."

Caspian smiled. "I think I'll manage. They wouldn't have asked me to go if I were *too* reckless."

"You mean at your job, right? They don't know if you're reckless elsewhere."

"Well apparently neither do you if you're classifying me as reckless." He laughed gently, causing his chest to vibrate beneath Hawk's cheek.

"Yeah, you're probably right about that. I can't remember the last risk you took, to be honest."

"Maybe it's time I change that then." He started to pull away.

"Hmm?" Hawk looked up, unsure what to make of this change, and was met with Caspian's lips on hers. Her mind told her to pull away, to tell him to stop, but she didn't. She closed her eyes and reached forward to pull his body closer.

They stayed in each other's embrace, unwilling to let go, knowing that when they stopped, the moment would be lost forever. Caspian pulled away slowly and placed his forehead against Hawk's. She tilted her head to face him fully, her eyes still gently closed.

"Now that, that was reckless." He pulled away quickly and left the room before Hawk could say anything more.

***

Hawk stood on shaky legs for a few minutes before she was able to leave the conference room. She rushed past the windows that lit the hallway with a confusing shade of reddish-orange as the "sun" began to set.

True to her promise, Loris had instructed Rowan to let her in the helm. A faint frown fixed on his face as she approached. "You ok? You look a little shaken up." He seemed genuinely concerned.

"I'm fine. It's just... Caspian will be one of the medics in *Seeker* tomorrow."

He seemed unfazed. "He's a big boy. He can take care of himself. Besides, he will be perfectly safe with his hazmat suit. You know how unlikely it is that anything will happen. It's a rescue mission. That's all," he assured her.

"I'm glad you feel that way, because I'm going, too," she said bluntly.

Rowan took a step backwards as if he had been slapped. "You're going? Since when?"

"Since the meeting. I'm not going to be left behind." She stood up straighter, daring him to argue.

"You don't have to do that, Hawk. They will be fine without you. There's nothing that you could possibly do in *Seeker* that someone else couldn't do."

"You sound worried, Rowan. You just said how safe it was. Why is it ok for them to go but not for me?"

Rowan scowled in response. He stood very still and said nothing. His jaw was clenched tight in frustration.

"Are you going to let me in, or not?" she pointed towards the doorway.

He turned towards the entry panel. His stiff movements showed that he was not ready to end the discussion, but he said nothing. When the second set of doors opened, he stormed down the hallway.

"Get some rest, Rowan! Busy day tomorrow!" Hawk called after him and was answered with the sound of his retreating footsteps.

Loris was sitting alone at the table with the radio in front of her. She handed Hawk a pair of headphones when she sat down next to her. Hawk sat looking out into space saying nothing but thinking of everything.

A helm worker whom Hawk recognized from the day before brought them each a chicken breast and salad at dinner time. Loris had brought a book and was reading quietly to herself. "Did you bring anything to keep yourself busy?" she asked.

"Not really. I didn't think about it." Hawk confessed.

Loris leaned across the table and handed Hawk a mystery novel. Hawk flipped through the pages and stared at the words in front of her. She reread the same page several times before deciding to turn the page, still unsure of the plot. Her mind kept drifting back to the conference room.

She imagined what the next day would be like. Not just the rescue mission but seeing Caspian again. He had left so quickly. Would he want to discuss it or just ignore it? For that matter, did she want to talk about it? It had felt right, but the future had become very uncertain. She stared at the pages harder, hoping they would suck her in and take her thoughts of Caspian away.

A voice came through her headset. *"Enlightenment,* this is *Seeker."* It was the voice of Pike Brighton.

Loris jumped. She hurriedly set her book down, *"Seeker,* this is *Enlightenment.* Please proceed." A slight tinge of panic presented itself in her voice.

"Ms. Goring, hello. We are confirming plans. Should we still expect you at 10:00?"

Loris sighed with relief. "That is correct Mr. Brighton. We will be sending in six trained medical personnel. Hawk and I will be joining them."

"We are pleased to hear that ma'am. Looking forward to meeting you in person."

The conversation was brief. "I wonder what that was about." Loris pondered aloud.

"I'm sure they're starting to get antsy. It must be difficult for them; just sitting and waiting." Hawk knew the agony of waiting.

"I suppose." Loris responded. "The whole thing makes me uneasy."

"Really?" Hawk was shocked. "You were so intent on going."

"So were you. Do you mean to tell me that you aren't nervous?"

Hawk laughed out loud. "Point taken. You just seem so ready for this." Hawk was extremely surprised that Loris was sharing her fears. The idea of such an impressive woman having doubts had not occurred to her.

"I don't think anybody can be ready for something like this. I know it's the right thing to do and I think I'm the best prepared that a person can be. I could tell you that it's nothing and that I'm not worried, but that would be a lie. This is the biggest thing that any of us have ever faced. Tomorrow, the door to *Enlightenment* opens for the first time since it left Earth."

Hawk nodded. "I'm scared too."

They sat very still. Hawk stared out the window and watched the stars appear and disappear behind them. Eventually, they continued with their previous activities. Loris reading and Hawk pretending to read but really thinking about the next day.

Rowan came to take the next shift around 10:00 p.m. Since Loris and Hawk were going into *Seeker* the next day, he and Ural felt that the two women needed more rest. He explained that he and Ural were splitting the remaining time between the two of them. They would work independently during the night so that each could get some sleep, then the two men would join up in the early morning to work together.

Hawk had the fleeting thought that she should stay behind and talk to him but decided against it. She liked Rowan, but she didn't owe him an explanation. Hawk had only known him for a few weeks, after all. Besides, she had enough difficult conversations for the day.

Loris did not mention chess and Hawk was relieved. Even with her nap earlier in the day, she was exhausted.

That night, Hawk dreamt that she was in *Seeker*, looking out the helm window. She was wearing a thick hazmat suit. She looked to her right and saw *Enlightenment* traveling next to them. Suddenly, alarms started blaring around her followed by the same message that she had heard earlier that day from Onsella. The lights flashed red. When she looked forward, Hawk realized that another ship was in front of them. It was heading straight at them. She started screaming and realized nobody else was there to hear her. She started hitting buttons and pulling levers, but nothing happened. The lights were no longer flashing and everything glowed red around her. Hawk looked up in a panic. The ship was directly in front of her now and she could see into the cockpit. Standing there, bathed in red light, stood Loris Goring. Laughing.

Hawk awoke gasping for breath just before the ships crashed into each other. Her pajamas were wet with sweat. "Time," she stated firmly. The wall shone 3:09 a.m. She took a shower and changed her clothes before crawling back into bed to get her last few hours of sleep.

The next morning's breakfast proved to be as awkward as Hawk had expected. Lark babbled away about an approaching social event. One of her jobs in *Enlightenment* was party planning. Her biggest task was planning the monthly Enlightenment Day Party. It was a way for people to mingle and, hopefully, not get cabin fever.

Lark had just finished explaining how she had talked Jasper's band into playing when Caspian came to join them. He sat next to Hawk. She turned to look at him and noticed he had dark circles under his eyes. Lark noticed too.

"What happened to you?" She obviously was not concerned with hurting her brother's feelings.

"Hmm? Oh, I didn't sleep well," he mumbled, "It's not a big deal."

Hawk thought of him standing on the viewing platform,

surrounded by blue light, alone. She suddenly wished that she hadn't gone back to sleep after her nightmare.

Lark looked annoyed. "All week people have been telling me they aren't sleeping or they are just busy and I shouldn't worry. It seems like people are keeping secrets here and I don't like it."

Hawk felt guilty but Caspian seemed used to his sister's tantrums. "Nothing is going on, Lark. You know that the ship's been tossing us all around. Some of us don't fall back to sleep as well as others."

Lark seemed appeased by his response and immediately changed the subject. "So, where's our new fourth member, anyway?"

Hawk looked at her blankly.

"Rowan. Where is he? I hoped we would be seeing more of him." She winked at Hawk. A gesture that did not go unnoticed by Caspian. His mouth became a thin line before he shoveled in another bite of bacon to mask it.

"I don't know." Hawk lied. "He's probably off working or spending some time with his friends or maybe even his family. How should I know?"

"You two seemed to be hitting it off, is all." Lark pouted. "I wish you'd tell me what's going on with him. I'd have to be an idiot to not notice."

"Nothing is going on with Rowan." Hawk felt her cheeks burning and wondered if Lark actually was, in fact, an idiot.

"Oh yeah? Then why are you blushing?" Lark smirked.

Caspian shifted uncomfortably next to Hawk.

Hawk squirmed as she asked, "Could we just drop it, alright?"

"Ok, ok. But sometime you need to tell me all about it." She winked again. Hawk focused on eating her breakfast.

Caspian stood suddenly. "I've got to get going. I have an early meeting."

Lark waited until her brother was out of earshot. "What's up with him?"

"How am I supposed to know? He's *your* brother." Hawk felt color creeping back up her cheeks once more. She hoped that Lark didn't notice.

She excused herself shortly thereafter. As much as Hawk enjoyed spending time with her best friend, she felt a little too stressed to be with her today. Hawk had given her a big, tight hug before leaving the cafeteria. Lark had been a little taken aback, but Hawk didn't care. She needed Lark to know how much she meant to her before getting in *Seeker*. Words failed her; the hug was the best Hawk could do.

Hawk had been excused from her teaching duty for the day. However, given that her students likely only had a few weeks' time left in *Enlightenment*, she imagined that they would forgive her.

The morning seemed to fly by. Hawk spent most of the morning alone in her room. She decided it was best not to visit her parents. She wasn't sure that she would be able to get through the visit without confessing all that was going on. Hawk realized then how much guilt went along with secrets. She hadn't known that being a junior diplomat would require so much dishonesty. Then again, the position had only recently called for so many secrets.

An hour before the expected docking time a message appeared on her bedroom wall and on her wrist transmitter, reminding residents about the scheduled maintenance. Hawk took that to be her cue to head towards the loading platform.

The first thing Hawk saw when she arrived was Caspian. He had most of his hazmat suit on. His helmet was sitting next to him on the bench. A medical kit sat in his lap. He didn't look up when she entered the room. His elbows were resting on his knees and he cradled his head in his hands.

Hawk looked towards Loris who was in the process of putting on her own suit. She hadn't spotted Hawk yet either. Hawk walked across the room and sat down next to Caspian. He didn't look up. She reached forward and put her hand gently on his arm. He jumped as if waking from a trance.

"We will get through it," she said gently.

"It's not the mission I'm worried about, Hawk." His eyes looked at her with such intensity that Hawk felt as if she couldn't breathe. "About yesterday..."

"It's ok. It was a pretty intense moment. Things just got away from us. That's all."

Caspian looked hurt. "Hawk, I don't regret what happened. I only regret that I didn't kiss you earlier. If you don't feel the same way, just say the word and I will go back to the way things were, but you need to know that these feelings I have for you, they're not going away. If I'm not what you want right now, that's fine. I get it. But I will be right here, waiting for the time when you are ready."

Hawk's mind raced with all the possibilities. She knew that she felt the same way and that her life would never be the same either way, but she still didn't know if she was ready to tell him the truth about her feelings.

"Hawk! Hawk! Over here!" Loris had spotted her and was waving her over.

"I've got to... I mean... Loris needs me." Hawk took a few hesitant steps before she turned around to face him again. "I'm sorry. I want to. I do, but I don't think I can make this decision right now." He looked disappointed. She added, "But I think we should talk about it when we get back from the mission. Ok? When we get back."

He smiled and nodded slowly. "When we get back."

Loris had Hawk's hazmat suit ready. She started with a thick, rubbery bodysuit that stretched over her entire body. Next came the bulky and heavy outer shell.

"Nervous?" Loris asked while she pulled on her suit.

"Terrified. You?"

"The same. But I'm ready." Her smile made Hawk think that she really meant it. She was ready.

"Me too." Hawk responded, and she really meant it. She was nervous, but more than anything, Hawk was excited. She was eager to help the people in *Seeker* and to find out if they knew anything about the Onsella transmission.

A green light flashed in the loading area followed by a voice over the intercom. "We are approaching *Seeker*. Ready yourselves for a change in the gravitational field."

Hawk noticed the others grabbing onto the benches where they sat. She positioned herself on the bench next to Loris and did the same. Within a minute, her stomach did a flip and Hawk felt as if she might be sick. As quickly as it had begun, it passed. Hawk looked at Loris and judging by the look the woman returned, she had the same experience. Suddenly Hawk felt as if she were very heavy. She gasped for breath but felt that her lungs were not working properly. Again, it passed within a few seconds. *Hold on to something. Yeah, that really helps.* She thought bitterly as the feeling of nausea returned.

Hawk glanced towards Caspian and her stomach sank but for an entirely different reason. Caspian looked as if he might get sick and she realized he was suffering from the same sensation. She wished that she could comfort him, but it was all that she could do to keep herself upright.

Her stomach started to settle. The voice returned over the intercom. "We are now docked with *Seeker*. You may open the exit port."

Hawk stood on shaky legs. Loris walked assertively toward

the exit, but Hawk could tell that she was slightly shaky as well. Hawk followed behind her trying to look equally confident.

She stood next to Loris, close to the exit door. Hawk could hear all the medics crowding behind her. She turned her head and saw Paloma Lofton. The others all stood behind her as if they were troops following their commander.

Loris turned to face the small group. "Before we embark, I want you all to know how proud I am of each of you. I know this is not an easy task. Any one of you could have chosen to walk away and left this whole mission behind you, but none of you did. You are all heroes to me."

She turned and looked Hawk in the eye through their helmets. "I mean it," she said matter-of-factly, before turning towards the keypad next to the door. She took a deep breath, looked towards Hawk, and then quickly typed in a series of numbers. She paused once more before hitting a red button beneath the keypad. The door creaked and Hawk had the fleeting fear that it wouldn't open at all, but then it slowly started to slide to the side.

13

FLOATING

A small room much like *Enlightenment*'s loading dock was revealed. Standing in the doorway was a small Onsellan man wearing a hazmat suit. He was smiling from ear to ear as he reached forward. He snatched up Loris' hand before her arm was fully extended and shook it vigorously.

"I'm so pleased to see you all. I know you said you would be here but I don't think I really believed it until just now." Hawk recognized the voice of Pike Brighton.

Loris tried to be polite, but she did not seem to enjoy the embrace. Dr. Lofton on the other hand greeted Mr. Brighton with a hug. Hawk could hear her saying, "I'm so sorry for all that you have gone through."

When he came to shake Hawk's hand, she extended her arm, but then seeing the look of joy and relief on his face decided to hug him instead. He seemed to have an almost magnetic pull to his personality. After he had greeted the entire group in his overly enthusiastic style, they clambered into the small room and sealed the entryway. Finally, he turned to open the entrance to *Seeker* itself.

Pike led them down a set of hallways that would take them

to the conference area. Hawk was shocked at how similar *Seeker* was to *Enlightenment*. She felt as if she could navigate the entirety of the ship without directions if she was given security clearance to do so.

Hawk did not see another person during the entire walk. It was eerie looking through the hazmat helmet, hearing her own breath echo in her ears and seeing nobody else. She felt like she was walking in a dream. She shook her head as if trying to wipe her mind clean and continued down the familiar, yet unknown, corridor.

She noticed one of the hallway imitation windows ahead of her and turned to see what scene would be displayed behind the glass. There was none. Instead, it looked like an empty, black screen. It was then that she noticed how dim the lighting was all around her. She had thought it was from looking through her protective screen in the helmet, now she suspected it was because much of the lighting had been disabled.

Pike took off his helmet as he walked. "I wore this blasted thing for your benefit, not mine. I've been exposed to all of this before. I'm not really sure how it spreads, but I know it spreads fast. I didn't want you opening up that door and finding an infected man on the other side. I wasn't about to breathe the same air as *Enlightenment*. Too risky for all of you. You all are taking a big enough risk coming here." He spoke quickly. Hawk could see the tip of his tail flicking every which way through the neck hole of his suit.

"We understand, Councilor. No need to explain yourself to us." Loris told him soothingly.

"Oh, but there is. You are risking your own safety just for the chance of helping us. We owe you everything." Hawk couldn't explain what it was about him, but he seemed to be trustworthy. He was an older man and, in many ways, he reminded Hawk of her grandfather.

He opened the door to the conference room. It was set up very similarly to the conference room in *Enlightenment*. Aside from the chairs being a slightly different design and the table being a shade lighter, the rooms were identical. Five other people sat around the table waiting for them. They had no masks or suits to protect themselves. Pike walked past them all and positioned himself in what would normally be, in *Enlightenment*, Loris' chair.

The others in the room looked just as eager as Pike. They stood when the *Enlightenment* crew walked in. Some looked as if they wanted to greet the crew while others merely shifted awkwardly from foot to foot. The *Enlightenment* crew stood in the back of the room uncertain of what to do next. This was a social situation nobody had encountered before, and it showed. Even Loris looked tentative.

"Please, have a seat. Anywhere is fine." Pike continued to beam at the group.

Hawk looked for Caspian and found him meandering towards the table. Hawk chose to stay close to Loris who had selected the seat at the end of the table, exactly opposite of where she would usually be sitting. Hawk decided to sit to her right, just like she would normally do in their own conference room. The hazmat suits made moving cumbersome, but what they lacked in mobility, they made up for in security.

Pike started introductions once they were all seated. The five waiting people turned out to be part of a makeshift council. Pike had been the only one from the original council to survive the outbreak. They had elected to change their titles from that of *diplomats* to *councilors* after the illness. They felt it was less formal. Onsellans made up the council with the exception of a sandy-haired woman with light brown eyes who sat next to Pike; Kit Elderstein, the only human on the council.

Pike explained again how the ship contacted them, claiming

to be from a safer planet than Onsella. They were welcomed onto *Seeker* initially. "When they left, their leader said, 'I'll being seeing some of you soon, if you're lucky.' I thought he meant if we survived going to Onsella, but after all this, I think he knew what was coming. They did this, and they're coming back for the survivors. The disease presented itself shortly after the encounter."

Loris and Hawk stared silently at one another while Councilor Brighton continued explaining their current situation. After the illness, there were too few people available for energy contribution. Without the extra energy from the EPR, they could not be mobile, have electricity, artificial gravity, heat, and life support. As a result, they rerouted the power provided by Blue Vigor to more essential features than movement. It was their only choice for survival. They had been sitting still ever since. That had been over four months ago.

Once Pike was finished explaining the situation, Doctor Lofton had the floor. She asked a number of medical questions. She was especially curious about the symptoms and the condition of the medical ward. A councilor took her and the other medics to the infirmary to examine the equipment. Only Loris and Hawk were left with most of the makeshift council.

Loris looked relieved once the medics had left. "Now that it is only council members present, we have a few things that we need to discuss. You told us that you will tell us everything. We appreciate that and hope that you will feel comfortable answering some questions."

They all nodded in agreement. "Very well. You should know that not all of *Enlightenment* knows about our situation. In fact, very few know that we have even heard from *Seeker* at all."

Hawk could tell that Pike was unsettled by this information, but he didn't argue.

"We need to know that the information discussed here will not leave this room. Not even the medics on board are privy to all of our secrets."

Pike nodded but it was Kit Elderstein who spoke up. "You hold a lot of secrets from your people, then?" Her voice was curt.

"We all have our share, I'm sure." Loris matched her tone. "We are in a position of assistance that we may not have been had we shared all of our secrets with the entirety of *Enlightenment*."

Kit Elderstein's lips were pressed into a thin, crooked line. Pike's eyes moved to Kit before speaking for himself. "We understand that you had to make some difficult decisions to be here. It is not our place to question what you have done."

Kit swallowed hard and attempted to make her facial expression more inviting. The effect was unflattering but less hostile. Her eyes never left Loris. Hawk squirmed uncomfortably but Loris acted as if she hadn't noticed.

"Thank you, Mr. Brighton. Now if you don't mind, we need to know everything you can tell us about that transmission from the unknown ship. What do you recall?"

"Ms. Goring, I can do better than that. We have a recording."

He brought a small radio into the conference room to play the recording. It was not the original hailing from the ship. They hadn't been recording during that time. Instead, it was the discussion afterwards. A woman who identified herself as Diplomat Maxine spoke to a masculine voice who called himself Zeb. Although Zeb had a thick and difficult to understand accent, he spoke in English.

"I'm not understanding you, Zeb. You don't want us to continue to Onsella?" The woman had a firm, almost harsh voice.

"It's not that I don't want you to go, ma'am. I just think you need all of the information before you go. The fact is, Onsella has turned hostile towards accommodating travelers. If you choose to proceed to Onsella, there's a good chance that they will blow you right out of the sky. We have another option. A safer option. Like you, our race was invited by Onsella. When we got there, we learned that their motives were not transparent. They attacked us. We fled. Fortunately for you, our planet is not far. Come with us and we will offer you a home. A *real* home." The man sounded pretty convincing.

"So, what are you proposing we do?" The woman sounded slightly panicked and there were many voices in the background murmuring.

"We would like permission to dock with your ship and meet with your leaders. We know this must be a difficult truth to face, but we have a safer alternative for you. If you choose to proceed onward to Onsella we won't stop you, but we cannot in good conscience let you go without warning you." He sounded earnest.

"Ok. We will allow a meeting," she sounded defeated.

Pike turned off the recording. "Of course, the rest is pretty obvious. They scheduled the meeting and here we are."

"Yes. Here we are." Loris muttered to herself. She turned to Hawk. "Did you recognize the voice?"

"No." Hawk responded quickly. She had been thinking the same thing.

"Me neither. I don't think it's the same as our recording."

"Your recording?" Pike questioned. "What are you talking about? Have you had contact with the same ship?" Now he sounded panicked.

Loris gave a meaningful glance to Hawk that did not go unnoticed by Pike or the others who were watching. "Ms. Goring, we have been completely up front with you. I don't think it's much to ask that you tell us what's going on. Our lives are entangled with yours. Are we at greater risk than we already were?" He had risen from his chair now. His voice quivered with anxiety and raw emotion.

Hawk turned to her mentor. "He's right. We need to tell them."

"I know." Loris turned her attention towards the *Seeker* Council. "We have received a message. It was a recording that looped repeatedly. We do not believe it to be from the same source as the ship that brought this illness, but we cannot be sure."

"Where else would it be from?" Kit questioned.

Loris took a deep breath and continued on. "If we can trust the legitimacy of the message, it is a welcome from Onsella."

The room buzzed with excitement. The councilors from *Seeker* began whispering enthusiastically. Pike sat silently taking it all in. He waited until the others were done talking.

"Do you think it's from Onsella?" he finally asked in an apparent daze.

Hawk felt that she could answer that question and did so. "That's what we're trying to figure out."

Loris added, "The voice from your recording does not seem to match the recording that we heard. It's very possible that it is from Onsella, but we can't be sure."

"There were many that boarded *Seeker* when the ship joined ours."

Loris straightened with excitement. "Would you recognize the voices?"

Pike sounded sad when he spoke. "I replay that day over and over in my mind every day. If I heard one of the voices again, I would know."

Loris reached into a pouch on the inside of one of her boots and pulled out a small tape recorder. "Then let's listen and see."

Pike rose from his seat and sat next to Loris on her left side. He was across from Hawk, but he didn't pay her any mind. It seemed that he wanted to be as close to the played message as possible. Hawk asked, "Did anybody else hear their voices?"

Everyone else shook their heads. Kit spoke, "I think we probably all saw or maybe even heard one of the people speak, but Pike would be the only one who met them all. We weren't councilors then."

Loris nodded and hit the play button. Pike leaned in closely and listened intently. The message cycled through several times. Finally, he started shaking his head. "No, definitely not. I've never heard that voice before."

Hawk felt a tinge of excitement. "Were there others left on their ship?" she asked hopefully.

Pike nodded. "There were a few, I heard the pilot over the radio. Other than that, I'm not sure. I didn't get the feeling that they were a very large group."

Hawk wanted to dance. There was no way to be sure that the message was from Onsella, but it was less likely that it was the same trap that *Seeker* had fallen victim to.

The room remained quiet, a fog of opportunity loomed over them all. Everyone was afraid to speak, as if they would break an unknown spell.

After a great deal of time, Pike said quietly. "So, what do we do now?"

Hawk waited for Loris to answer. It was a question that she desperately wanted an answer to as well. "I would be disappointed if we didn't seek out the origin of the message, but I can't make any decisions here. *Enlightenment*'s council will need to decide how to proceed."

Pike looked around the room at the faces of the others from *Seeker*. "We have talked a lot about our future here on this ship. Things have been uncertain for us for a long time. If *Seeker* gets a vote, I know that we are all willing to take the risk. We've already lost so much and all that we've ever wanted was to continue to Onsella. We know that it might not be what we thought it was, but we want to try. We have nothing to lose." The others around the table nodded in agreement. Nobody said anything to the contrary.

Loris nodded and assured them all that she would do everything within her power to ensure that they all made it to Onsella. Hawk could tell by the look in her eyes that there would not be much of a discussion when they made it back to *Enlightenment*. They would be searching for the origin of the message. Onsella was still their goal.

Kit stood. "I know that I speak for everybody here when I tell you that we appreciate that, Ms. Goring. Whether the message is from Onsella or not, I know that we will be better off if we find out where it is coming from."

Suddenly, Hawk felt a sinking feeling in her stomach. Of course the council from *Seeker* wanted to discover where the message was coming from. They had already nearly been killed off by a previously unknown alien race. If it turned out to be another trap, they at least had a chance of revenge. They truly had nothing to lose.

Enlightenment on the other hand was healthy and well-off. If they were to encounter the troublesome group of unknown origins, they would likely be infected. It was a big risk that *Seeker* was pushing for. However, even with the uneasy feeling in the pit of her stomach, she still agreed with Loris and Pike. Her hope outweighed her doubt.

Kit spoke again. "I've been selected to give you a tour of *Seeker*. I know I'm eager to see what your medical team is up to. Let's go see for ourselves."

Hawk and Loris rose and followed the woman out of the room. She did not seem overly friendly. Her words were always clipped with a bit of an edge. Kit walked briskly. Loris seemed to be in her element, but Hawk felt as if she were running. She noticed for the first time since she arrived at *Seeker* just how sore her ribs were, but she said nothing and continued to match the pace of the two women in front of her.

"It took us a while to realize how much danger we were in. We started wearing masks and restricting movement after we figured it out, but it wasn't enough. We all got it. The medical staff was hit hard, fast. We'd never seen anything like it. They had no way of knowing that they needed to be so careful. They were treating people like they would normally do." She paused and cleared her throat before continuing. "None of them survived long enough to even tell us what medicines they would recommend. I guess they never figured it out or they'd still be here." To Hawk, Kit sounded cold and uncaring. It was as if she hadn't cared for any of the people who had died.

Loris noticed it too. "You must have lost many of your friends and family. I imagine those were rough times."

Kit stopped and turned to face Loris. "*Those were*? No, *these are* tough times. Just because we haven't lost anyone in a while doesn't mean that we are out of the woods. Nearly our entire population died within two months. A person can't help but change after watching that kind of suffering."

"I meant no disrespect. I'm trying to understand everything that went on here."

"Everybody died. That's what happened here." She turned on her heels and began her brisk walk again. Hawk found herself wishing that the hazmat suits were lighter, but she kept going. She didn't want to make Loris look weak. "Our medical wing is this way." She turned to the right.

"I know." Hawk muttered under her breath. The whole mission had been surreal to her. Everything was the same, and yet nothing was the same at all. She still hadn't seen another living soul outside of the people in the conference room.

"Where are all of your people? I thought there would be around five hundred people here?" She called ahead, curiosity getting the better of her.

Kit yelled over her shoulder instead of turning to answer the question. "We all stay in our separate living quarters as much as possible. Too many people in one area is too risky. No point in spreading the illness if we can avoid it."

"I thought everybody had already been infected?" Hawk asked.

"We have been; we think. There were a lot of symptoms. We can't be sure that there isn't more than one virus involved." She never slowed as she marched onward. "Like I said, the medical staff died off early. We aren't really sure what we're facing here."

Hawk expected to see patients lying in bed screaming in agony when she entered the medical ward, but it was nothing like the dramatic scene playing in her head. There were no more than fifteen people laying in beds. The hazmat-wearing medical crew poked and prodded the people in front of them; most were Onsellan. Hawk saw Caspian towards the middle of the room taking blood from a middle-aged human man. The man was grimacing and facing away from the needle. Another medic was starting an I.V. on a woman who was looking very thin and extremely pale.

Kit stopped before moving any further into the room. She pulled out a mask from her pocket and grabbed a set of blue medical gloves from a jar on the desk. She motioned towards Doctor Lofton. The doctor quickly approached the group looking eager. "I need you to come with me, Doctor."

She nodded and joined the group. Kit led them down the center aisle, weaving between the patients and doctors. Hawk followed but was no longer sure where they were going. She was being led to an area in which she had never been in *Enlightenment*. The group walked through three doors that all required Kit to be scanned before entering. Finally, they walked into a small, metallic room.

Hawk could see Kit's breath rise in front of her. Hawk did not feel cold inside of her hazmat suit, but she could see that the walls were frosty. Ten metallic, square doors lined the back wall reminding Hawk of the freezer doors in the kitchen. Kit walked up to one and opened it. She slid out a shelf with a thick, black plastic draped over it. Loris, Hawk and Doctor Lofton all moved closer to stand next to the shelf.

Kit pulled back the plastic to reveal a body. Hawk turned her head and let out a sigh of disgust. She had never seen a dead body before and hadn't expected it now. When Hawk worked up the courage, she turned her head back to the scene in front of her. It was the body of a woman. Hawk tried to focus on her face but found that to be difficult. The woman's eyelids were red with dark streaks all around them that made it look as if she had scratched at them ferociously. Hawk noticed blood spots around the woman's ears. Finally, Hawk decided it was best to focus on the living people who were with her.

Doctor Lofton was leaning in close, examining the body. Loris, like Hawk, looked very uncomfortable. She was looking towards the wall.

"She was one of the first. We were preparing her for a funeral, but for obvious reasons, that never happened." To Hawk's surprise, she paused as if gathering her emotions. "We kept the first ten bodies. That's all we had room for. We discussed launching them with all of the others, but we decided it was best to keep them to study. Could they help you, Doctor?"

The doctor nodded. "They might. I would like to take some

samples and run them through a diagnostic test. We might be able to figure out why these people died and why you survived."

"We'll leave you to it then." Kit turned abruptly and headed for the exit.

They left the doctor in the icy room, alone. Hawk looked back and saw that she was already taking supplies from her equipment.

They continued to follow Kit. She led them back to the medical ward where the medics were busily working. She stopped next to a man in a bed at the end.

"This is Altai. He was one of the last people to show any symptoms and has been having a hard time of it lately. We've been monitoring him closely and he seems to be getting better. How are you doing today, Altai?" Her voice sounded compassionate for the first time. She leaned forward and held his hand. It was a stark difference from what Hawk had observed from her earlier.

"Feel better already, Kittie. It sure is nice to see these folks." He let out a light cough when he finished speaking. Hawk felt the urge to run even though she was fully protected. Kit however, didn't move at all.

"I feel the same way, Altai. We're very lucky they answered our pleas for help." She smiled affectionately at the man before walking away. Loris and Hawk continued to follow.

"I think you should see the helm," Kit stated as they walked towards the exit.

"Is there something wrong with the navigation?" Loris questioned her.

"No, nothing like that. There are just some things you should see to really understand what we've been through."

Loris shot Hawk a puzzled look. They continued down the corridors following the same path that they would have followed in *Enlightenment*.

Kit opened what looked to be the same two doors before entering the helm. When Hawk walked in, she noticed right away that something was very different from *Enlightenment*'s helm. The windows which had always shown the beautiful expanse of open space were all covered with what looked to be bed sheets. There was only one person in the helm working. However, working was a loose term for what he was doing. He was an Onsellan man who sat at the meeting table. His feet were propped up and his chin drooped against his chest. His head rose slightly with each breath. Apparently when a ship was sitting still, it didn't require many staff.

Kit turned towards the table. Hawk thought she was going to wake the man up, but she didn't. Instead, she walked past the table until she stood next to a window. Loris stepped forward hesitantly. Hawk did the same.

"About half of the ship's population was still alive when we had to redirect the power. We couldn't move forward any longer. We were sitting ducks. Now that would have been bad enough, but people were still dying." She reached towards the sheet and gave an assertive yank downward. The window became visible, but the view was not the beautiful, starlit sky that Hawk had come to love. Instead, she saw bodies. Too many bodies to count.

14

SHOWERS

Hawk felt sick to her stomach, but she couldn't look away from the grisly scene. Kit continued. "You know, I always thought that when we launched them into space that they were *launched*, but that's not how it works." She turned to look out the window. "No, they aren't launched so much as *released*. When the ship is moving, we just leave them behind. That's not the case when you're sitting still. They just float around the ship. They have nowhere to go."

Hawk remembered reading about graveyards in her books about Earth. She thought how similar those cemeteries must have been to this sight, only instead of bodies, there would be markers to show where the bodies were located. She thought a headstone would be much nicer than what was floating around them.

"We covered it up, of course. Nobody wanted to be in here with *that* right outside. Now they're still there, but at least we can pretend they aren't. It makes us all feel a little better somehow."

Hawk stepped forward as a body floated close to the glass. Pike had said that there was a lot of blood, she could see now that he was telling the truth. The eyes, ears, mouth and nose all were visibly stained red. Hawk guessed that the survivors didn't have time to clean the bodies, or else didn't want to risk becoming infected. Hawk stared out the window in disbelief. She looked towards Loris and saw that she was doing the same thing. The horror of the scene was almost mesmerizing.

"We are truly sorry for all that you have been through." Loris finally choked out. "But why are you showing us this? We came here to help you. We already know what you've suffered through."

Kit arched an eyebrow. "Do you really? You hear a story like ours and you think you understand, but you don't." She pointed towards the window. "These people are not just a story to us. They are our friends, our family. You see a dead body; I see the man who used to bake cookies. I get that you want to help us, but now you should understand that this mission can't just be a want. You *need* to help us. We need to escape all of this."

"Ok. We've both seen it, now please, cover it back up." Loris pulled her eyes from the sight in front of her and walked toward the sleeping man. Hawk turned to watch but did not follow. When Loris reached the table, she pushed the man's feet off the side of the table. He let out a snort and opened his eyes in confusion. When he saw Loris standing in front of him in her hazmat suit, he let out a little yelp of surprise.

"I'm sorry. So sorry. I've been up all night. I—I must have dozed off," he stuttered when he saw Kit.

"I'm not here to criticize you. That's not my job." Loris sounded aggravated. "What I want now is for you to do yours. Is this the radio you've been using to contact *Enlightenment*?"

"Yes ma'am."

"I would like to use it." She was already reaching for the radio.

"Yes ma'am." The man stood quickly and rushed to stand

next to Kit. His eyes shifted to the window before he began staring at the floor.

Loris sat down where he had been. "*Enlightenment*, can you hear me?"

Rowan's voice shook as he responded. "Loris? Is that you? What's going on over there? Have you looked outside?"

Loris sighed into the radio. "I have. That's why I radioed. How is everyone doing over there?"

"To be honest Loris, we're all a little freaked out. The rest of the Council came up here to be close to the radio. When we were preparing to dock, a body hit our windshield. A human body, Loris. The closer we got to *Seeker*, the worse it got."

"I know, Rowan. They had to get the bodies off *Seeker* somehow."

"I know that, but couldn't they have gotten them off a little further? This is crazy!" Hawk had never heard him sound so upset.

"We aren't concerned with the dead, only the living. We are here with the survivors now. That's our mission; helping the survivors. I know it's not pretty, but this is what they've been facing every day since this illness hit. That's why we're here."

Hawk knew that Loris did not contact *Enlightenment* to give Rowan or Ural a pep talk. She was speaking to all the other diplomats. It was them that she sought to reassure. She imagined how difficult it must be for all of those in the helm of *Enlightenment*. They were seeing the same thing that she was and she doubted that they had covered the windows yet. Hawk was grateful that her family and Lark couldn't see it.

After viewing the carnage from the helm, Kit brought them back to the conference room. Pike was still there waiting for them, but he was the only one. "Have you seen everything you need to before making any decisions?" he sounded hopeful.

"I don't think that's something we can decide on until after the doctors are able to tell us about their results."

"Do you think that you will be able to take us with you? To Onsella I mean. Now that we know it's so close and all."

"We don't *know* it's close." Loris corrected. "We all *hope* it's close, but we don't know for sure."

"Of course. I guess I'm just being optimistic." He sat back down. Hawk was struck by the thought that optimism seemed to be a normal state for the man. "So, what exactly are you thinking of doing with us? You didn't come here just for the tour, I'm sure."

"I hoped that you would all be cleared medically to join us, but now that I've seen everything here, I can't imagine that will be the case," Pike's smile melted into a frown, "but I think we can treat those who are still sick, maybe even find out exactly what caused it. After that I think we would be better off going for help. If the message really is coming from Onsella, I'm sure they could send a transport ship that would be better prepared for this type of situation."

"So, you'll just leave us here?" Kit sounded alarmed.

"I'm not sure what else we could do. If anyone in your group is still contagious, we can't bring you on board. We agreed to help, but I will not risk the health of our entire civilization."

Kit looked annoyed, but she didn't argue. "How long will you be staying here?" Pike asked.

"I need to talk to my medical staff to find out an exact timetable, but I would like to return to the ship before the end of the day. Hopefully we can be on our way to Onsella by tomorrow. We've told the others that we stopped for required maintenance. We can't stay still for too long or that excuse won't hold up."

"Why didn't you tell your people the truth?" Kit sounded just as confrontational as she had seemed earlier.

Loris stared at her for a short time as if she was trying to decide if she should answer. Finally, she did. "You are a small group and you have been through something very traumatic. It seems to have brought you all together. I applaud you for the community you've created here despite everything else that has happened to you. *Enlightenment* has never seen such a tragedy. The worst we've had was a food shortage, and that was short-lived. We came here out of duty, but if we had told everybody, there's a big possibility that we may not have been able to agree to come at all. This kind of thing creates fear. I don't want *Enlightenment* to be ruled by fear."

"What will your people say when they realize you've lied to them?" Pike asked. He sounded much less harsh than Kit, more curious than angry. Hawk wondered if that's why he asked the question, so that Kit wouldn't.

"I'm not sure, but it doesn't matter. I'm not in my position to make everybody happy. I'm in the position I am in because I have always chosen to do what was right for the better good. Hopefully the people will understand that these decisions aren't always easy and they only get more difficult if more voices are involved. I had to make a hard choice and I did so by limiting the voices telling me what to do. That's why we have a council in the first place. To make the hard choices that large numbers of people aren't able to make."

Kit scoffed. "You're not giving your people enough credit. You didn't even give them a chance."

Loris glared through her face shield at Kit. Hawk held back a smile. What she really wanted to do was shake Kit's hand.

"It wasn't their decision to make. It was mine." Loris' tone told them all that the conversation was finished. "I would like to check in with my medical team now."

Pike stood and walked towards Loris with his hands outstretched to show friendliness. "Of course, Ms. Goring, you are welcome to come and go as you please. What's ours is yours. All council members have been instructed to allow you full access to any and all areas of the ship."

"Thank you. I need to meet with Doctor Lofton to assess our next move."

Pike offered to walk her to the medical ward. Hawk walked behind the two, listening to Pike attempt to ease the tension. He joked and laughed. Loris acted as if all was well, but Hawk got the feeling that she would be holding a grudge against Kit for quite some time. As much as Hawk liked her mentor, she was still afraid to question her so blatantly as Kit had done.

Instead of walking ahead and leading them, as Kit had, Pike walked next to Loris. They were about to make the last turn before entering the medical ward when Doctor Lofton met them halfway down the hall. She was moving briskly. "Diplomat Goring, we need to meet with *Seeker*'s council right away. We found something."

Pike quickly assembled the Council. They met in the same conference room that they had earlier. They all looked nervous, but none as nervous as Paloma Lofton.

The room was still and silent. All eyes were on the doctor standing at the front of the room. She fidgeted inside of her hazmat suit. The tip of her tail whipped frantically around her face. Finally, she spoke. "I can tell you have all been through a lot, but I don't think it's over." She paused. Hawk expected someone to speak, but nobody did. They all remained silent and transfixed on the woman in front of them.

"You were very wise to limit contact amongst your citizens. It may have saved your lives. We ran several labs on both the living and the bodies you've preserved for us. From what I can tell so far, you were most definitely infected, but not by *one* pathogen. Your ship has been subjected to a cocktail of ailments. Some of them look pretty easy to treat with antibiotics and the like; others are unlike anything I have ever seen before." The room remained very still but a few heads seemed to bob up and down as if their suspicions had been confirmed.

"I think we may have identified the pathogen that is causing the deaths. All of the deceased that you have preserved have it, but it is nearly entirely absent in the living."

Pike looked concerned. "Nearly?"

Doctor Lofton nodded. "Yes. Nearly." She swallowed hard, an action that was visible even behind the protective shield in front of her. "I found only one living person so far that has the virus. I'm doubtful that there is anything that we will be able to do for him other than keep him comfortable until he passes."

Kit was on the edge of her seat. "Who?" she asked, but Hawk felt that she already knew the answer.

"Altai Kinley."

Kit's body slouched into a defeated posture. Still, her voice was strong when she asked, "Nobody else? The rest are safe?"

Doctor Lofton looked concerned again and shuffled back and forth on her feet as if nervous to continue. "I don't know if I would say it quite like that. We've only tested the people who were brought down to the medical ward. There is no way of knowing about the others. Additionally, the people in the unit have now been in close quarters with Altai. If this thing spreads as fast and easily as you say it does, those people are all at serious risk. We've quarantined Altai to his living quarters and sent all of the others back to their rooms with strict instructions to stay put, but that doesn't mean they are safe."

"Nobody's safe." Hawk heard one of the council members mutter under his breath.

The doctor continued. "I feel that it is important for all of your citizens to be tested. Now that we are pretty sure what we are looking for and that it is still active here, we need to see each citizen, one by one. There is no reason to put people together when we still aren't sure how this is spread."

"So, what do you propose?" Pike asked.

"We need to test everybody on this ship in their own living quarters. We can use the emergency wash shower to disinfect our suits after each visit. We can step in the shower with our whole suits on. We can take blood samples from each person and see who's infected with the deadly virus."

"How long will that take?" Loris questioned.

Doctor Lofton looked even more nervous. "We would need to stay for at least a week. That would allow us to observe the course of the disease and be sure that everyone else isn't infected. Then we could find a way to make space in *Enlightenment* and bring the uninfected people with us. I know it's a grim idea to leave the dying behind, but I don't see any other way to help here. We don't have any way to treat this."

Pike looked toward Loris accusingly. "I'm sure there's another way. Right, Ms. Goring?"

Loris pursed her lips tightly before speaking. "Continue your tests, Doctor. I need to discuss this matter with the Council." She rose from her chair quickly and turned toward the head of the table. "I need someone to contact *Enlightenment* and let them know that Hawk and I will be joining them shortly. They need to meet us in the conference room."

Pike didn't have a chance to answer before Loris started walking away. "And I need one of you to open the exit so that we can return to *Enlightenment*."

Hawk and Loris were alone when they entered the loading area. Before taking off their suits, they walked straight to a decontamination area and sprayed their suits heavily with the disinfectant available. They were careful to remove their suits without touching anything else around them.

As soon as her suit was off and located in a sealed locker, Hawk backed away from it as if it were a bomb. She turned to Loris with a fearful look and said, "Come with me." She didn't wait to hear if her mentor replied or even if she was upset at Hawk giving her an order. Hawk turned and sprinted towards the medical wing. She rushed past people in the hallways while being careful not to touch them or anything but the floor beneath her feet. She rushed into the medical ward with her hands held up as if she were under arrest. Hawk was relieved to find Loris directly behind her doing the same thing. "I need a decontamination shower. Now!"

The medical team didn't argue. They opened doors and rushed the women to the shower area. Hawk knew where it was already from her experiences with *Seeker*, but she didn't tell them. She rushed into the shower with her clothing still on and allowed the burning hot liquid to wash over her entire body. Hawk wasn't sure if it would be enough. She wished there had been a shower in the loading area, but of course, *Enlightenment* wasn't equipped for a rescue mission like this. For the first time, Hawk thought back to the speech that she had made before the vote and questioned if she had made the right decision when she insisted on going to *Seeker* herself.

Hawk stripped off all of her clothes and left them in a sopping wet pile on the shower room floor. She scrubbed her skin until it was red. Hawk ran her fingers through her hair so much that she wondered if it would fall out. Finally, she yelled to the medical staff that she needed clothes. They brought her a paper-thin gown and Hawk was all too happy to step into it.

Loris met her in a similar gown outside of the shower rooms. She asked the medics to notify Diplomat Ambrose of their location and to instruct him to bring additional clothing. They obliged. Loris turned to Hawk. "We don't want to create a panic. Better not let everybody see us walking around the ship in medical gowns." Hawk agreed. She wished she had her wrist transmitter to call for the clothing on her own but it was in a locker in the loading dock. She hadn't taken it with her to *Seeker*.

The medics stayed outside the room. They paced awkwardly as if they were unsure of what to do next. Hawk was certain they had many questions, but neither she nor Loris offered any information. The only thing that either woman said to the group was when Loris instructed them to wear gloves and a mask when grabbing their discarded clothing and that it would need to be destroyed. This only added to the looks of confusion from the medics, but nothing more was said.

Ural arrived, panting for air as if he had been running. He had two sets of clothing, neither of which looked particularly appealing to Hawk, but both were better than the gown she was currently wearing. He handed them to the women quickly and then stepped outside of the door once more with crimson cheeks.

He waited while they changed but came in shortly after. He was wearing a medical mask and stood towards the end of the room. "Are you ok? What happened over there?"

"We're fine, Ural. We're just taking precautions." Loris said dismissively.

He did not look pleased. "Where are your hazmat suits?" His voice sounded accusatory.

"We disinfected them with the spray the medics gave us this morning and left them in the loading bay. You didn't expect us to wear those all over *Enlightenment*, did you?"

"So, they worked then? You didn't come into contact with anything?"

"We wore the suits the whole time. We just got a little concerned taking them off is all. We were around some pretty sick people, Ural." Loris tried to sound reassuring, but Hawk could tell that her mind was working overtime. She was not thinking about the hazmat suits anymore. "Ural, we have to tell the rest of the Council about the Onsella message. Nobody in *Seeker* recognized the voice or the accent. I don't think it's a trap. It could really be them."

He took off his mask to reveal a wide grin and walked forward to give Loris a hug. She smiled back but her arms remained pinned to her side while he hugged her as if this was the last thing she wanted to be doing.

"Ural, my transmitter is in the loading area. I need you to send a message to the Council. We need to meet right away."

"They're already there." He looked surprised that she didn't already know. "When *Seeker* messaged to say you were on your way, we thought the conference room would be the best meeting spot."

Loris nodded. "I need Rowan there too. Another junior diplomat can mind the radio. Onsella won't be able to reach us this far out anyway. *Seeker* has heard nothing from them at all."

Ural nodded and looked down at his wrist transmitter. Hawk saw his fingers move rapidly over the screen before it beeped indicating that he had sent a message. He looked up excitedly. "Let's go, then."

15

BACKGROUND PEOPLE

The entire Council watched as they walked in. Rowan was already seated in his usual spot. He started to stand when they walked in as if he wanted to rush towards them in relief. He sat back down without anybody else noticing. Hawk felt the pink return to her cheeks. Whether she wanted to or not, she liked that he noticed. She liked that he couldn't hide his emotions. Most of all, she liked that he was excited to see her. Even if she wasn't interested, she was flattered that he was.

She walked behind Loris and took her seat towards the head of the table. She was eager to start the meeting. From the looks of it, the whole Council was.

Loris began abruptly and without introduction. "Our medics are still in *Seeker* doing their work. It appears the symptoms are not isolated to one illness. Several sicknesses were released in *Seeker*. Some of them are relatively harmless. From what they can tell, there is only one that is deadly."

Diplomat Maxwell cleared his throat. "How much longer will they need?"

"I was getting to that." Loris continued, obviously annoyed by the interruption. "Doctor Lofton and her crew will need at least one more week to observe and collect all of the samples." The other diplomats began to mutter to their neighbors. Loris held up her hand, "I'm not done, folks. They will need at least another week, but it is dangerous. The virus that is killing their people is mostly gone at this point. They have done an excellent job at preventing it from spreading. However, there is at least one man who is still infected."

Cantil Gilchrist spoke up through the whispers of his colleagues. "We are going to stay attached to a ship with a very deadly, very contagious illness for more than a week?" He sounded stunned.

Loris stood as if preparing herself for a fight. "No. I think we need to separate from them while our medics work."

Cantil continued to argue. "So we just float around them for a week? With the bodies? I don't know about the rest of you, but I don't want to add to that graveyard floating around outside our windows. We need to revise our plan."

"I couldn't agree more." Loris conceded. Diplomat Gilchrist opened his mouth as if to speak, but no words came out. The whole room was shocked into silence. "I think we need to seriously consider another plan." She turned to Rowan. "Did you bring the recording?" He nodded. "I think it's time that we share it with the group."

Rowan pulled out a small recorder similar to the one that Loris had brought with her to *Seeker*. He placed it in front of himself on the table. "Are you sure?" He looked towards Loris.

"Play it." She gave a single, assertive nod.

The recording began. Just as Hawk had done, the group listened intently as if they were trying to make out the words. The recording was repeated over and over. Hawk watched as realization hit members of the group at different times. Some held their hands over their mouths in shock, others gasped, and some looked as if they were going to fall from their chairs. One by one, they all came to understand the significance of the recording.

Loris signaled towards Rowan and he turned off the player. "This message was received yesterday—"

"Yesterday?" Cantil interjected. "And we're just hearing about this NOW!" His face began to redden and his fists were balled up in front of him.

Loris continued as if no such outburst had occurred. "We received the message yesterday after the decision to continue with the rescue mission to *Seeker*. I decided that it was best to find out all that I could before bringing it to the attention of the Council."

Diplomat Maxwell spoke up in his soft, yet authoritative, voice. "And what did you find out, Loris?" He didn't sound angry, but he clearly wanted all of the information before he acted.

"While at *Seeker*, we listened to the recordings of the initial communication with the mystery ship. That communication was in English but we were told that the message they initially broadcast was in Onsellan, just like this one. We asked the *Seeker* crew if they recognized the voice. According to their leader, if this is the voice of someone from the mystery ship, they never entered *Seeker*.

"If this is a ruse, they completely changed their game plan. The first message was trying to scare people away from Onsella, but this one is inviting people to go there. It doesn't make sense for it to be the same people. I think this is Onsella."

Nobody spoke. Hawk had expected excited murmuring, maybe even a celebration, but nobody moved. Loris sat back down in her seat as if she thought the worst was over. She began speaking again. "I think if the medics need more time, we need to give it to them, but we also need to find the source of that message. If it is Onsella, I'm sure they would help retrieve

Seeker. They would probably be more equipped to handle the outbreak than we are."

"And if it's not Onsella?" Diplomat Maxwell asked.

Loris took a heavy breath. "I think it's them. We all want to believe it's Onsella, but there is no way to be sure. If it isn't, then it's for the best if our medics remain in *Seeker*."

A small woman Hawk knew to be Diplomat Raven Montgomery spoke up in a small voice. "Can we play the recording again?" Hawk thought there were tears in her eyes.

Rowan pushed play once more and the message began cycling through again. Hawk watched the room. The same people who had been listening so closely before seemed to be doing the same now but in a very different way. Hawk watched Diplomat Montgomery closely. She thought her lips were starting to move with the message towards the end and her face seemed to be tight with emotion. Finally, she spoke and Rowan turned off the message. "It sounds sincere. I think we should go."

"Any further discussion?" Loris asked.

Diplomat Maxwell stood. "Our goal has always been Onsella. If we have a chance now, we have to take it."

Nobody argued. When Loris called it to a vote, Diplomat Maxwell and Montgomery stood rather than raise their hands in support. The gesture was soon supported by the other members. The sole hold-out was Cantil Gilchrist. He watched as one by one, each council member stood in support. After seeing that he was the last one remaining in his seat, he reluctantly stood to join his peers, his face in a grimace as he did so.

Hawk knew that she should feel overjoyed at the prospect of Onsella, but she didn't. She felt a growing pit in her stomach when she thought of the medics being left behind. Caspian was still in *Seeker*. Not only was he in *Seeker*, but he would soon be *left* in *Seeker*. He would be working very closely with people who were very sick, some of whom were dying. And this time there would be no way for her to stay with him. He would be on his own.

Hawk turned towards the woman she so admired sitting next to her and asked earnestly, "What do we tell everyone?" She was thinking of Lark and of her family. They would notice Caspian's absence.

Loris' face broke into a large smile. "We tell them the truth. That we received a transmission from Onsella, and we are close."

"And what do we tell them about *Seeker*?"

Loris waited a bit to respond and did so thoughtfully. "It's time we tell them the truth about that as well. They don't need all the details. They just need to know that we were contacted by *Seeker* and we provided aid. We can tell them that we left a small medical team in *Seeker*, and we will be sending ships from Onsella to retrieve them as soon as we arrive. It's time they get the truth."

Hawk hesitated a moment before asking, "We aren't going to tell them about the illness there?" She agreed that it was time to tell the citizens of *Enlightenment* the truth, but she thought they needed *all* of the truth.

"There's no reason for them to know about that right now. Everybody here is safe." Loris gave Hawk a look that said this time she needed to stay quiet.

Hawk thought of the brazen look on Kit's face and decided that she needed to push further. "They're safe for *now*. What about the ship that infected *Seeker*? We don't know if they will come back. Shouldn't we at least tell them that much?"

Loris looked annoyed now. "We aren't going to let another ship dock with us so we are perfectly safe. Telling them about that will only create unnecessary fear when we should all be celebrating. We are heading to Onsella. *That* is the most important thing."

Hawk couldn't help but think Loris was wrong. *Caspian was the most important thing.* She opened her mouth to argue but stopped herself. She could tell by the look that Loris was giving her and the way that the others were looking at her that this was not a battle that she was going to win. Hawk nodded to show her agreement, but she gave Loris a look that showed she did not support the plan.

Loris moved on as if the interruption had never happened. "I will go to *Seeker* tonight to tell them the plan and send the medics back for the night. We should give them a night here to be with their families and gather anything that they will need for their time at *Seeker*. It will give *Seeker*'s council some time to create a safe area for our people too. I'll work with Doctor Lofton tonight and make sure they can set up procedures to keep our medics safe. We can't leave until we are sure they will be safe."

That made Hawk feel a little better, but she wasn't sure that she would ever be ok with leaving Caspian behind on a ship with a deadly outbreak of an unknown illness.

She listened to the discussion as it continued, but nobody disagreed with Loris. They decided to make a formal announcement in the dining room that night. A message would be sent excusing everybody who was nonessential for ship functionality from work after dinner. Hawk sat in a near trance-like state. She felt excited yet terrified.

When she left the room, she didn't even look at Loris. She knew it would cause problems for her later, but didn't care. Hawk headed for the loading dock to fetch her wrist transmitter. She was nearly there before she heard footsteps rushing up from behind her. She turned around abruptly, expecting to find Loris hurrying after her, but it wasn't her mentor. Rowan was by her side. "What?" she asked harshly before she could stop herself.

"You'll need someone with clearance to get in."

Hawk felt her defenses melt as he walked next to her saying nothing while she retrieved her transmitter from the locker. She reminded herself that it wasn't Rowan's fault Caspian was being left behind. Hawk looked at the hazmat suit hanging in its container and wished that she could put it back on and rush to Caspian.

Rowan stayed by her side while she walked toward her room. Hawk was certain he had been as scared for her while she was in *Seeker* as she was for Caspian now. It was comforting to know that he had just endured the same experience, however unpleasant the experience was.

Hawk turned the corner and nearly walked into the bundle of excitement that was her best friend. "Oh, there you are, Hawk! I've been looking everywhere for you. I ran into Mrs. Gonzales at lunch and she said that you had been given the morning off from teaching for council business. I was starting to get worried after you missed lunch. Is everything ok? Someone said that you and Diplomat Goring went to the infirmary."

Hawk was taken off guard. She had not expected to see Lark. Hawk fought back her annoyance at now having to manage her friend's emotions and answer questions. It wasn't Lark's fault. Lark was just being her normal self and had no way of knowing all that Hawk had gone through that day. Still, Hawk couldn't find it in herself to match her friend's enthusiasm. "I'm fine," she mumbled.

Lark stared as if expecting an explanation. "And?"

"I'm fine. I really can't talk about it right now."

"Oh." Lark looked to Hawk and then let her eyes scan over Rowan. "Then let's talk about it tonight."

Hawk thought that would be better. Perhaps after the

announcement Lark would understand a little bit of what she had been going through. "Sorry. Yes. Tonight then." She walked away from her friend at a brisk pace. Rowan continued to walk next to her without saying a word. Somehow, she found that incredibly comforting.

When she reached her room, he spoke for the first time since arriving at her side. "I'm glad you're all right." He gave her a crooked, awkward smile and turned to leave without hearing her response. Somehow, she found that comforting, too.

Hawk felt exhausted when she was finally in her room. Her ribs still ached. She considered walking to get her pain medication but decided against it. She didn't want to leave her room until absolutely necessary. Instead, Hawk took another shower and changed clothes once again. They had taken all the best precautions, but she couldn't get the image of the floating bodies out of her head. She tried to take a nap but found it difficult. As soon as she closed her eyes, the face of the woman with the clawed-at, bloody eyelids popped into her mind.

Hawk folded her bed back into the wall and sat on her small couch. She looked towards her dresser and saw the smiling faces of her ancestors in front of the waterfall. Smiling back at them, she slid off her couch and, without even bothering to wear gloves, retrieved the lockbox from her wall and began looking through all the photos that she already had memorized. Her eyes examined all the faces. Some she knew to be family; others were people who just happened to be in the way of the camera when it snapped a photo of some iconic place. She hadn't paid much attention to those faces before, but today it was all Hawk could think about.

Her family had always been important whenever they

appeared in the images, but today her focus was on the background people. She stared at the faces and wondered what happened to them. Hawk felt a tinge of guilt for having never cared for those people before. The people whose images had been stored in her room for most of her life, yet she never bothered to think of them.

Hawk stayed in her room looking at the photos until it was nearly time for dinner. She had received the message about the "special announcement" on her transmitter, same as everybody else. She walked from her room with a slow, exhausted gait, but didn't head straight for the dining area. She had no desire to eat dinner that night. Instead, she walked towards Loris' room.

Hawk took a deep breath before knocking on the door. She wasn't sure how Loris would react to her presence or if Loris would even be in her room at all. Hawk was both delighted and unsettled when the door slid open to reveal Loris standing behind it. She looked neither angry nor pleased to see Hawk. Instead, she looked very tired. Loris said nothing but stood to the side to allow Hawk entrance.

The bed was still down. Loris folded it back into the wall and Hawk sat down in her usual spot. Loris did the same. "I get it." Loris said finally. "Why you're so worried. I get it."

"You do?" Hawk wasn't convinced that she did. If Loris knew why she felt so strongly about sharing all the information, she would have agreed to do so already.

"I know that you're close with Caspian. I can't imagine how difficult it must be for you to leave him behind."

Hawk was astonished that this was all that the brilliant woman was taking from the situation. "If you think that's all of it then you really don't get it."

Now Loris looked surprised. "It's not about him then?"

"No! It's about the people's right to know what danger we could all be in. They will know virtually nothing about what's happening in *Seeker*, and I can admit *that part* has a lot to do with Caspian. But what about the part with the renegade starship that's going around infecting people with a deadly illness? Or that we aren't even a hundred percent sure that the message is *really* from Onsella. I'm not saying that people should be allowed to make the decisions, I'm just saying that they should understand the magnitude of the decisions that were made for them."

To Hawk's surprise, Loris smiled. "That's why you're my protégé, Hawk. You aren't afraid to speak up for what you think is right."

"So, you'll tell them?" Hawk felt optimistic.

"No."

"But you just said..."

"I said that you aren't afraid to speak up for what *you* think is right. That's a quality we share. Unfortunately, this time we disagree on what the right thing is."

Hawk wasn't sure how to respond. She felt she should say something, maybe even argue, but no words came out.

"I don't know what the next few weeks will bring for us, Hawk. This is the first time in the history of *Enlightenment* that we've had a shot at something bigger than ourselves. All of this came at once, and I don't think any of us really know the exact right thing to do. There's no road map for something like this. All I can do is my best, and that's what I'm going to do. I think giving these people hope is what's needed right now."

"Even if it's false hope?" Hawk felt a little angry at her mentor's words.

"Better false hope than false fear. If we're going to instill some sense of emotion in our people, I would rather it be a positive one."

Hawk's anger immediately dissipated. As much as she wanted the truth to be revealed, she didn't want to be responsible for the whole ship succumbing to fear. She knew the way she had been feeling over the past few days had kept her on edge. Did she really want to do that to all of *Enlightenment*?

"I know that you don't agree with me, Hawk, but I need to know that you will support me anyway. You are my protégé after all. I'm hoping you can put our differences aside and know that there will be more bad than good if you can't stand beside me on this. And it's only been a few days, but I think you make *me* a stronger person when you're with me. Don't throw that away. Can you stand with me on this?"

Hawk nodded hesitantly. "Yes, I understand."

Loris smiled. "Good. I want you next to me when I make the announcement tonight. There will be a lot of excited people!"

Hawk imagined watching her parents and seeing the expressions on their faces as they looked up towards her and heard the good news. She couldn't help but smile.

16

OUT OF THE BLUE

Hawk walked next to Loris as they entered the dining area. Neither one had eaten lunch nor dinner. Both were too nervous to think about food. When they ascended the stairs that led to the stage, Hawk felt her knees start to tremble. She looked out towards the crowd hoping to see her parents. As best she could tell, all of *Enlightenment* had come for the announcement. Because all non-essential work duties had been excused, everybody knew that whatever was going to be announced must be very important.

When she saw her parents, her heart swelled with joy. Not just because Hawk knew they would be getting good news, but also because of who was sitting with them. Next to her mother sat Lark and Caspian's parents, the Malcolms. Lark sat across from them. Next to her was someone that Hawk hadn't expected to see at the announcement ceremony. Caspian.

Hawk knew that they would be boarding *Enlightenment* in the evening but hadn't considered exactly when that would be. Seeing his face made her feel even more nervous. He was one of the few who was not smiling. Hawk realized that he didn't know yet that he would be left behind. He had no knowledge of the Onsella message.

She sidled up close to Loris. "Caspian doesn't know yet, does he?"

Loris turned her body so that the audience would not be able to see her lips move. "There wasn't time to brief the medical team before the announcement. We will meet with them after. You should come."

Hawk nodded. She wanted to be there when he found out. Hearing the announcement about Onsella would no doubt give him hope. She hated the idea of his happiness being changed so suddenly to dread.

Loris stepped up to the microphone and the crowd immediately fell silent with anticipation. "Hello everyone. Today is a very important day in *Enlightenment*'s history."

Hawk stood next to Loris, facing the audience. She could see the large, projected image of both Loris and herself displayed on the back wall. In fact, their images were shown on all of the walls. Hawk pushed a lock of her long, dark hair behind her ear nervously. She had never had so many eyes watching her before.

Loris continued with her speech. "I must confess, I have been less than honest with you all, but for significant reasons. Today's stop was not due to maintenance like you were previously told." The audience looked confused by the unexpected direction the meeting was going. "We have recently made contact with *Seeker*, a ship that was launched from Earth prior to *Enlightenment*. They were stalled and in need of medical assistance for some of their passengers. Without knowing the entirety of the situation, we chose to remain silent about *Seeker* until everything was known."

There was a rumble in the crowd, but Loris did not stop.

"We agreed to dock with them to provide medical aid. That is the real reason why we stopped today. We will continue to provide care for a short time. However, there are more important things to discuss."

The murmuring stopped almost immediately. "We received a transmission yesterday from Onsella. They are inviting any ship within distance to join them."

The energy in the room changed instantly from tense unrest to excitement. "According to the message, we are about a week away from Onsella. As of today, we are officially making preparations for arrival."

Hawk saw many people with their mouths hanging open in shock. Some people wiped away happy tears, but Hawk's eyes were set on her family. Her father had his arms wrapped around her mother and they looked as if they were too shocked to move. Tears shone in her mother's eyes and her father pulled her closer to him in a loving gesture. His face still showed signs of shock while he stared at the stage.

Hawk's eyes drifted towards Lark and Caspian. Lark also looked surprised. For as long as Hawk had known her, Lark claimed that she didn't care if they ever reached Onsella; *Enlightenment* was her home. However, after seeing her reaction, Hawk knew now that she had only been putting on an act. Her mouth was set in a tremendous smile. Her hands were clasped in front of her as if she were ready to throw them into the air in celebration.

Caspian, however, had an expression that was difficult for her to read. His mouth hung open and his eyebrows were pulled inward. He looked excited and confused. Hawk knew that he must be contemplating what this meant for him in *Seeker*.

Loris continued with a lilt in her voice that showed her own enthusiasm. "Tonight and tomorrow, all non-essential work shifts will be cut. Supervisors, it is up to you to decide how to cut these hours. Please do so fairly. I am certain that everybody has preparations they would like to make. We will be keeping you all informed as we know more. For now, I think a celebration is in order!"

The crowd erupted into cheers and clapped their hands together loudly. Someone from tech services ran towards the media closet and soon music was blaring through all of the speakers. People began hugging one another and dancing to the music. Hawk wished that she could stay, but instead, she followed Loris toward the exit. It was time to meet with the medics.

———

Hawk assumed that they would meet in the conference room, but that was not where Loris headed after the announcement. Much to Hawk's surprise, she turned towards the helm. Hawk immediately saw the bodies floating outside when they entered. Having seen it before, she was not as surprised as previously, but was just as disturbed by the scene. She sat with her back to the windows.

The medics filtered in shortly after, following Ural Ambrose. They all looked nervous. From the looks on their faces, Hawk thought they must have had an idea of what was going to happen. Caspian met her gaze and held it. She wanted to look away but didn't.

Loris began explaining the plan. Nobody looked surprised or even scared. They looked determined. "We know that the people in *Seeker* will likely die if they do not have trained medical staff there to help them. Additionally, your assessment of the patients will greatly aid the Onsellan rescue ship when they arrive. That being said, your safety is very important to the

Council. We will stay docked with *Seeker* until proper arrangements can be made for your safety. I've already had a discussion with Councilor Brighton. He has assured us that there is a wing that was unused at the time of the outbreak. It has remained isolated. It will be yours to do with as you feel necessary to keep yourselves protected."

Paloma Lofton looked eager. "We will need our own oxygen supply for those rooms which will remain completely separate from the people in *Seeker*. We can continue to use the rebreathers in the suits while we see patients, but we will need our own air supply for that wing. That's the safest way until we know how this is spread."

"We can do that." Loris agreed.

"We will also need our own food supply. I don't think their food sources are tainted, but we need to be safe," the doctor continued.

"Not a problem. That can be done." Loris agreed.

"We will also need a shower transformed into a decontamination area. We need to ensure that our suits are not contaminated with the pathogens each time we change. That is very important."

Loris nodded. "I will talk to Mr. Brighton right away. I'm sure we can make that work."

Doctor Lofton stood straighter. "Other than that, we're ready to stay."

"It should only be a few weeks." Loris assured them. "How long do you expect we will need to stay docked with them?"

"As long as they can make the decontamination area for us, we will be ready tomorrow."

Caspian broke eye contact with Hawk when he heard the timeline. "Tomorrow? *Enlightenment* will leave tomorrow?"

Loris looked his direction in recognition. "I doubt we will be leaving tomorrow, Caspian. We would stay an extra night for you to make preparations and say your goodbyes." Her eyes shifted towards Hawk when she said the last part.

Caspian nodded but did not respond. He met Hawk's eyes again. She felt as if he wanted to say more, but not with everybody else there. The medics filed out after they had been briefed. Loris used the radio to make arrangements with *Seeker* to set up the decontamination area. Pike insisted that they would start working on it right away.

Afterwards, Hawk was alone with Loris in the meeting area. Loris started to leave, but Hawk stopped her. "Loris?"

She turned to face Hawk. "Yes?"

"Why did we need to meet in the helm? The conference area would have been just as good." Her eyes shifted to the grisly scene behind the glass.

Loris sat across from Hawk. "We met here so that the medical staff could see what they will be working for. It's not easy being left behind, but we are doing it for a good reason. They need to remember that."

Hawk continued looking out the window and thought how she, too, had been struck by the importance of the medical team when she saw the bodies floating outside. Even though she hated the thought of leaving Caspian behind, she knew that it was the right thing to do for the victims in *Seeker*.

"You should go now. Celebrate! I know it's not everything you thought it would be when the time came, but that doesn't mean you can't enjoy it." Loris tried to sound enthusiastic, but Hawk knew her well enough to tell that it wasn't genuine.

Hawk rose from her spot and started walking towards the exit. About halfway there she hesitated. "Aren't you coming?"

Loris looked up. "I think I will stay here for a while. Somebody needs to monitor the radio."

"Yeah, but anybody can do that now. The secret's out. All the Council knows. It doesn't have to be you."

"I need a few minutes to myself first." Hawk decided it was best not to argue. When she walked out the door, she turned to look back at Loris. She sat stone-still, watching the bodies float past the window. A chill went down Hawk's spine as the door closed in front of her.

Hawk had expected to see Caspian waiting for her outside the control room, but he wasn't there. She could hear the celebration from the dining area drifting down the corridors. It sounded as if a full-fledged party had broken out. Hawk headed towards the sound of music and merriment hoping she could find Lark and her parents in the commotion.

The music's volume continued to increase as she got closer. Hawk could hear cheers from groups of people as she walked into what had once been a dining hall. People were dancing and singing along to the music. Many people still had happy tears trailing down their faces. She scanned the room and although Hawk recognized most people, she didn't see anybody that she had been searching for. She inched her way through the crowd, scanning faces as she went. When she reached a group of women scarcely older than herself, one woman broke away from the crowd and enveloped her in a gigantic hug. Hawk patted the woman awkwardly on the back as the women she had been standing with moved closer and produced cheers of happiness.

Hawk broke away from the excited group and waved a feeble goodbye as she continued looking for her friends and family. She found her parents sitting close to their usual spots. They leaped to their feet when they saw her approaching. Her mother quickly embraced her in a hug.

"I see why you've been too busy to talk these last few days."

Onyx nudged her in the ribs with his elbow which caused her to wince. "Oh, yeah. Sorry about that kiddo."

"It's been an exciting first week for you, I see." Poppy was all smiles. "I can't wait to see it for myself!"

"Yeah, me neither." Hawk tried to sound enthusiastic. Truthfully, she was really eager to reach Onsella too. However, her joy was tainted with the concern she felt whenever she thought about leaving *Seeker* and what they might be heading towards. Or worse, what might be heading towards them.

Hawk excused herself as quickly as she could and again started pushing her way through the crowd. She wanted to find Lark. Of all the people she knew, Lark was the one who would enjoy this type of atmosphere the most.

It didn't take long to find Lark. She had apparently convinced Jasper to dance with her. Lark held him close and rocked back and forth, completely lost in the moment. Jasper did not look as enthused. He scanned the room over the top of her head as if looking for an escape. Hawk approached the two but did not make it there before she was pulled unexpectedly to the side by Caspian's firm grasp against her arm.

Hawk turned to face him; although she could see his lips moving, she couldn't hear any words. "What?" She tried to yell over the music but was certain that her words didn't make it to his ears. He frowned. His hand slid down her arm and grasped her hand as he began pulling her towards the exit. The crowd seemed to part before them as if sensing the tension that Caspian was emitting.

When they reached the hallway, he turned to face her abruptly. "I..." he stumbled over his words as if unsure what he was going to say. Hawk didn't blame him. She had thought about it all day and still didn't know what she was going to say to him either.

Before she could overthink it, she leaned in and stood on her tiptoes. She gently placed her lips against his before quickly returning back to her flat feet. Caspian looked surprised.

"I don't know what tomorrow brings," she told him, "But I know that I can't keep pretending that these feelings aren't there. We've both been trying to hide from our feelings for a long time now, but I'm done hiding."

Caspian pulled her in close but did not kiss her. Hawk laid her head against his chest and they stood together just as they had in the conference room the previous day. He caressed the back of her hair as he held her close.

He didn't say a word as he released her and grabbed for her hand. He pulled her beside him as he moved further away from the music behind him. At first, Hawk wasn't sure where he was taking her. She didn't want to question him or break the silence in any way. The tingling she felt in her chest and head felt fragile and she didn't want to risk breaking the spell.

Soon, she realized where he was heading. They moved through the hallways, past the windows that were now showing scenery blanketed in darkness, walked past The Farm and stopped only once they were bathed in the cobalt light emitted by Blue Vigor.

Caspian turned to face her and once again pulled her close. "Hawk, I know that I need to go back to *Seeker* and I'm not going to back out of it, but I can't imagine how difficult it will be being away from you."

She laughed as she pulled away from him. "That will be the hard part? Not the dying people or the risk of your own death? Or the fact that everybody you've ever known will be heading towards everything you've always dreamed of and you can't be with them?"

He smiled. "It's more like everything I've always dreamed of will be flying further away from me." He gave her a meaningful look and she blushed.

"I can't believe it took us so long to come to our senses," he admitted sheepishly.

"I guess when you're faced with death and a brand-new life all in the same day it makes you reevaluate your priorities."

"It's all going to be ok. You know that, right?" Suddenly, he looked very serious.

Hawk thought about the mystery ship that had infected *Seeker*. "No, Caspian. I don't know that, and neither do you. What if that ship comes back while we're away? We still don't know what their end game is."

"You'll only be gone for a few weeks, Hawk. They've been gone for nearly five months. Why would they come back now?" He sounded as if he were trying to convince himself.

"I know, but why would they stay away? It doesn't make sense to infect a group and then just *leave*. You need to be careful. I just got you. I can't imagine losing you." Hawk gave a shy smile. It didn't feel right to think of him as being hers, but she didn't know how else to say it either.

"Nothing's going to happen to me. You know the precautions we've been taking."

Hawk nodded, but she didn't feel any better about it. Caspian moved to sit on the platform. His legs dangled over the edge. Hawk sat down next to him and put her head against his shoulder. Wispy blue tendrils of light seemed to reach out towards the pair as they pulled one another closer. She wanted to say so many things but couldn't find the words for any of them. Instead, Hawk held Caspian's hand and traced small circles over the back of it with her thumb. She felt all of her tension melt away as they sat in a comfortable silence.

Hawk couldn't be sure how long they sat there. She only knew that her eyes were beginning to fall shut and she could feel Caspian's breathing starting to slow. "You've got a busy day ahead of you tomorrow what with the saving lives *and* moving and all of that." Hawk chuckled awkwardly, unsure of what to say next.

"I guess we both do. You've got to get things ready for Onsella. I'm sure being on the council means you will be pretty busy right now, huh?" Caspian looked concerned.

"I'm not sure," she said truthfully. She had no idea what the next day would bring. "But you're probably right."

"We should get some sleep then, I guess," he said apprehensively. Hawk nodded while yawning. She didn't want to leave his side but didn't know if she would be able to stay awake either.

"Ok. Yeah. See you at breakfast?"

"For sure, and tomorrow, once I'm back from *Seeker*, right?"

"I wouldn't miss it!" Hawk gave him a peck of a kiss on his cheek before she stood and began a slow walk towards her living quarters. She imagined him watching her walk away and found herself wishing he would follow, but she knew that he wouldn't.

The next morning, Hawk took extra care in getting ready. She knew that her day would be packed full of things that Loris had planned for her, but that wasn't the real reason for putting in the extra effort. She wanted Caspian to see her at her best, at least in the morning. She was early heading to breakfast. She got her favorite, French toast, again, and sat down in their usual meeting spot. Lark joined her with a cheerful, "Good morning!" and launched into discussion about the night before.

"Where were you? You disappeared after the announcement. The party was amazing!" she gushed.

Hawk laughed to herself. Of course Lark would be focused on the party instead of *why* the party was taking place in the first place.

"I was there for a little bit. I guess we just didn't catch up with one another." She blushed thinking about who she wound up with instead. Lark didn't seem to notice.

"I spent the whole night dancing with Jasper. He is *so* great!"

Hawk remembered his vacant expression as he scoured the room for somebody to rescue him. "I'm not so sure about that guy. I get a bad feeling from him."

Lark looked disappointed. "Really? You've never mentioned it before."

"Trust me, he's bad news."

Lark dropped the subject of Jasper immediately. Hawk knew Lark wasn't going to take her advice, but she'd had to try anyway.

"So, where's Rowan this morning?" She glanced at Hawk sideways.

"Lark, really, there's nothing going on with him. Can you just drop it?" Hawk wondered how Lark would take the news when she found out that her best friend was dating her brother.

"Why not?" Lark pouted.

"Look, Lark, he's just not my type. Besides, I've kind of been interested in someone else lately." She didn't want to tell her who until Caspian was there to help break the news.

Lark looked like she might explode from excitement. "What? Who? When were you going to tell me? I *knew* there was something going on with you. Spill!"

"It's a really new thing." Hawk tried to calm her down before telling her the rest. "I've been so busy I haven't had a chance to tell you anything."

"Tell me now, then!"

Hawk looked around the room hoping Caspian would be close. He wasn't. "I..." Hawk wasn't sure how to keep her friend from pushing her further.

"Hawk, you can't say something like that and then not tell me!" Lark squealed.

Hawk played out the choices in her head. Option one: she

could continue to evade the topic and put it off until Caspian arrived. However, that would be difficult and might make Lark angry once she was actually told the truth. Option two: she could flat out lie. That seemed like a very bad choice given the nature of the conversation. Option three: she could just tell her the truth and hope that Caspian understood. That option seemed the best, but she hadn't discussed with Caspian what they would be telling people. Especially his sister.

"I don't want you to freak out or anything," she tried to ease in gently.

"Who's freaking out? Why would I freak out?" She started to get a wild look in her eyes. "Hawk? Why would I freak out?"

Then, the only person who could make the conversation even more awkward arrived. Rowan sat down directly next to Hawk, a little too close for her comfort.

"What's happening?" He looked at Lark in confusion. "What are we freaking out about? Onsella?"

"No. Hawk's..."

Hawk cut her off. "Yes, thank you! If there was ever something to freak out about it would be the fact that we are within a week of Onsella. That, that right there is what we *should* be freaking out about!"

Rowan looked bemused. "Oh, changing the subject, are we? This must be good." He settled in as if expecting a good show.

Hawk not so subtly tried to continue to steer the conversation far away from the topic of her love life. "A week, people! I can't wait to see it! It's got to be better than those old recordings and pictures that we've got. I bet it's beautiful." She saw Caspian walk through the entrance and join the line to get his meal. She hoped she could keep Lark at bay until he made it over to their table. It wouldn't be easy now that Rowan and Lark had joined forces.

"Stop changing the subject!" Lark squealed.

"What exactly is the subject anyway?" Rowan turned his attention back to Lark.

Lark actually looked a little embarrassed, as if she didn't want Rowan to know but also didn't want to *not* know herself. Hawk thought that perhaps Lark wasn't quite ready to give up her dream of Hawk and Rowan being together.

Caspian was picking up his tray and selecting his breakfast. *Hurry, Caspian. Please!*

"This must be good if *you* don't even want to tell me." Rowan looked like he was enjoying watching both women blush.

Caspian was walking in their direction now. *Thank you!* Aside from being happy to see him in general, his timing was excellent.

"Well, Hawk was just telling me about..." Lark hesitated and looked to Hawk for approval. She seemed unsure if Hawk would be ok with Rowan knowing.

Caspian sat down on her other side, glaring at Rowan's close proximity to Hawk.

It was time to come clean. She leaned over and bumped Caspian lightly with her shoulder as if to say he needed to ready himself. "Lark just caught wind of the fact that I've been, sort of, seeing someone."

"Oh, did she now?" Caspian questioned.

Rowan looked surprised. "Oh. I guess I didn't realize." He stumbled over his words as he spoke.

"But I didn't tell her who." Hawk looked up at Caspian's face and saw his mischievous smile appearing.

"Knowing my sister, the anticipation must be killing her." Lark nodded feverishly. "You should probably put her out of her misery and tell her." When he finished speaking, he very obviously reached for Hawk's hand and held it brazenly on the surface of the table.

Hawk's cheeks reddened as Lark's eyes widened. Rowan's face reddened also, and his mouth became a very thin line.

"You mean... I didn't... You two?" Lark pointed towards their intertwined hands while her eyes flickered back and forth between the two of them.

Hawk held her breath waiting for the surprise to wear off. She felt Rowan slide away from her as if she were infected with the illness in *Seeker*.

Lark suddenly broke into a wide smile of genuine joy. "Why didn't you tell me? How long has this been going on?"

Hawk breathed a sigh of relief. "It really just became official yesterday, but it's been a long time coming." Caspian responded. Hawk was grateful that she didn't have to try to speak yet. Her face was still burning from embarrassment.

"You mean that you've known this was coming for a while and neither one of you said anything about it?" Even though she tried, Lark couldn't make herself sound angry. Delight overpowered any mock anger she tried to project.

"I don't think either one of us thought anything would actually happen, but after the announcement last night, we couldn't keep our feelings quiet any longer." Caspian spoke as if he were thoroughly pleased with himself. Like he had somehow planned it. Hawk looked up to check his expression and found him gazing down at her, smiling affectionately.

Lark was now standing on her seat and reaching across the table. Hawk knew that she could easily escape, but chose to let her friend enjoy the moment. Lark had both Hawk and Caspian in single-armed hug. One arm wrapped around each of them while she pulled them in as close as possible leaning across the table.

"This is the best news I've gotten all week!"

Hawk laughed. "Really? Do you remember yesterday's announcement?"

"Of course I do, and I still stand by my statement. This is the best. The BEST!" Lark reached across the table once more and put them both in the semi-headlock hug again. When she released them, Hawk leaned in close to Caspian, feeling as if she had just had a big win. She looked to her right expecting to see Rowan, but instead found only an empty seat.

17

THE FAMILY

Hawk wasn't sure what the plan for the day was but felt certain that Loris would be in the conference room or the helm. Since she didn't yet have the clearance to enter the helm by herself, she decided to try the conference area.

She didn't hear any voices upon approaching the room. Hawk hesitantly continued onward assuming she had selected the wrong meeting place. She opened the conference door expecting to see an empty room. To her surprise, Rowan sat in the room, alone. He sat in what would normally be Loris' seat.

Startled, he stood when Hawk walked in. He shuffled away from the chair. "They're meeting in the helm." He didn't make eye contact when he spoke.

"Ok." Hawk turned to leave but couldn't find it in herself to walk out the door. She turned back to face him. "Then why aren't you there?"

He took a few more steps away from the head of the table. "I just needed a few minutes to myself."

"And you decided to take your private moment here?" She pointed towards the head of the table. Hawk couldn't help but worry about him sitting by himself in the dark room.

He glared at her for a few seconds but answered anyway. "I always thought of my future as being here. In *Enlightenment*. Maybe even someday, here." He motioned towards the chair he had just vacated.

Hawk nodded. "I guess we've all had to change our plans pretty suddenly, huh?"

Rowan moved back towards the table and sat down in his desired seat. "Yeah, I guess we all did."

"I'd probably better get to the helm." She turned to face the door, but before stepping into the hallway she looked over her shoulder. "I'm sorry I didn't tell you about Caspian. I should have."

She walked towards the helm. Soon she heard Rowan's footsteps approaching from behind. "Hawk, wait. Did you get clearance yet?"

Hawk shrugged. "Not yet. Apparently they've been too busy with other things."

"I'll let you in."

He pushed past her and led the way. His pace was brisk as if he were running from something.

When they got to the helm, Hawk expected to see the entire council. However, it was only Loris and Ural. They sat closely together at the table. Loris had the radio in hand and barely looked up when Rowan and Hawk approached. The two sat down next to their mentors and listened.

Pike's voice could be heard emitting from the radio. It sounded as if he was giving an update about the decontamination room. His breathing was audible through the receiver as if he were out of breath. "We have almost completed the alterations. We have been careful to keep them sterile. It should be ready by the end of the day."

"And how are our medics progressing?" Loris asked.

Pike cleared his throat before continuing. "They arrived

within the last hour. According to your lead physician, they are making progress with collecting blood samples from each of our citizens. Doctor Lofton still thinks that there is only one deadly virus. So far they've been able to identify fifteen separate pathogens in the blood work."

Hawk met Rowan's eye. He was watching her, gauging her reaction. She tried not to show it, but she was afraid for Caspian.

"How is Altai?" Loris sounded concerned.

"He's been quarantined to his room. Kit went to visit him last night. Sounds like he's been getting worse but remains in good spirits."

"How much time does he have?" Loris' voice shifted to a gentle tone.

"Your medics aren't sure exactly. If it progresses like what we've seen before, we think it will only be a few days now."

"How's Kit holding up?" Hawk was surprised to hear Loris express any concern for Kit.

There was a pause before a voice answered, but it wasn't Pike. "I'm fine. Why wouldn't I be?"

Loris seemed surprised by the change in people, but she hid her shock when she replied. "Kit. Hello. I know you're close with Altai."

"I've been dealing with all of this for a long time now. I know how to handle myself here." Kit's voice had the clipped, defensive tone that Hawk was starting to become familiar with.

"Understood. I know that you are very capable. I won't ask again." Although her tone managed to stay polite, Hawk could tell by the look on her face that Loris was irritated.

Pike returned to the radio. "We are getting by. Your medical staff are making everybody here feel a lot more comfortable."

"I spoke with Doctor Lofton this morning. She sounded optimistic about the outcome."

"We are too, Ms. Goring."

Loris smiled even though he couldn't see her. "I think we are past the formalities. Please, call me Loris."

When the conversation was over, Ural stayed behind to monitor the radio. He seemed very eager to do so. Loris walked with Hawk explaining the plan for the day. Rowan stayed behind with his mentor.

"We need to stay in the public's eye until we arrive at Onsella. So far everybody is excited for the arrival, and nobody has shown too much concern about *Seeker* as of yet."

"That could be because they don't know everything that's involved with *Seeker*." Hawk quipped back.

"That's true. The family of the medical team will be briefed today on the extended stay of their loved ones."

"How much will they know?" Hawk's mind turned to Lark. She had been so happy that morning when she learned about Hawk's involvement with Caspian. How would she feel once she realized that Caspian would not be making the rest of the trip to Onsella with them?

"They will know that their family member has been selected to be a part of the medical team being assigned to *Seeker* and that they will be retrieved by an Onsellan team once we arrive. They will also know that we are following proper protocol for quarantine procedures."

"What will they know about the illness?" Hawk was worried for Caspian, but as Loris had pointed out, this was supposed to be a happy time for the rest of the community. She didn't want them to worry.

"They only need to know that their loved ones will be safe. That's enough. No sense worrying them any more than we have to."

Hawk nodded in agreement this time. Her view about how much of the truth to tell was starting to sway.

"We'll be meeting with the families this morning." Loris continued on.

"Whoa, wait. *We* are going to be the ones telling the families?" Hawk stopped walking and remained in place in the middle of the hallway.

Loris turned back to face her. "It's not like the medics will have time to tell their families themselves. When they arrive back from *Seeker* tonight, they are going to be getting things ready for their extended stay and saying goodbyes. If an explanation is included, they might not have enough time to finish everything. Besides, it's hard to tell what they would say to their families if the explanation was left to them as individuals. We're better off giving the news." Loris looked thoughtful. "Would you rather I tell Caspian's family alone?"

"No!" Hawk said in a rush. "I want to be there. It might be better if it comes from me anyway."

Loris' eyes traced Hawk's posture and facial expression. Hawk tried to look sure. She must have succeeded. "Ok then. After we tell the families, we will be heading over to *Seeker* to monitor the progress."

Hawk nodded. She hoped that seeing all the progress at *Seeker* would help her feel calmer about leaving Caspian behind. She knew that telling Caspian's family personally was the right thing for her to do, but it didn't make her feel any better about it.

They went to see Paloma Lofton's loved ones first. Hawk was surprised to see that she had a family of her own, a husband and a young daughter. The little girl had her hair in pigtails and wore an adorable pink flowered dress. Hawk guessed that she was probably around six years old. She hid behind her dad's leg as he opened the door but still smiled up at Loris and Hawk as they walked in. He introduced himself as Hoel and the daughter as Yara.

Hoel looked nervous and fidgeted with his hands when he sat down. "To what do we owe the pleasure?" he asked curiously.

"Hoel, thank you for meeting with us on such short notice."

"No problem at all. Is there news about Onsella?" He didn't sound as worried now but he still looked uneasy.

"Not exactly. Last night we mentioned encountering *Seeker*. They are in need of a medical team."

He responded hesitantly. "Yes. I remember." Hawk thought he was starting to understand where the conversation was heading.

"The Council sent a team to *Seeker* yesterday. Your wife was part of that crew."

Hoel blinked the confusion out of his eyes. "Is she ok? I saw her this morning and she looked fine."

"Everything is fine, Mr. Lofton. Your wife is fine." He looked relieved. Loris continued. "The work she is doing in *Seeker* is invaluable. For the time being, we have decided that it is in everybody's best interest for the medical team to stay in *Seeker* while we proceed to Onsella."

Hoel blinked rapidly and shook his head. "You mean you're leaving her behind?" He sounded panicked.

"Only temporarily, sir. Once we reach Onsella, we should be able to send a spacecraft that will allow both our medical team and the citizens of *Seeker* safe transport."

"Safe transport? Is she in danger there?" His voice rose several octaves as he asked the question.

"It is only a precaution for the people in *Seeker*. Your wife is fine." Loris reassured him. "We have been doing everything within our power to ensure that the medical team is safe. You have nothing to worry about as far as your wife's welfare is concerned. All that we are requiring is time. I know that it's an exciting time right now with our impending arrival at Onsella. I am very sorry that your wife will not be here to celebrate with you. She will join you at Onsella after we arrive."

He sat very still. The little girl crawled into his lap and buried her head into his chest, but she said nothing. "And you've talked to Paloma about all of this? She's ok with this?"

"Yes. Your wife knows the entirety of the situation and she has decided to remain in *Seeker* to help those in need."

He nodded. "When will I see her?"

"She's in *Seeker* now but will be coming back tonight. Tomorrow morning, we will depart for Onsella."

"Ok." The word was stretched out. He sat still and watched Loris and Hawk for a few moments. "Anything else?"

"That's everything." Loris rose from her seat. "Let me know if there's anything that I can do to make this time easier for you."

He nodded again as he moved his daughter out of his lap, set her in the seat next to him, and stood. He walked towards the door and showed them out without saying goodbye. He did not seem angry, just unsure of how he should feel or what he should say. Before the door closed behind them, Hawk saw him looking at his daughter with a pained expression. She instantly felt guilty.

The rest of the visits went about the same. Families asked questions. Some could be answered, others couldn't. Loris did most of the talking. Hawk's part in the conversations was primarily introductions and goodbyes.

The last family would be the hardest family for her. The Malcolm family. Hawk knew Lark would be with her parents, eagerly awaiting Loris' arrival. She wondered if they expected Loris to be alone or if they knew Hawk would be coming.

She walked the familiar path to the Malcolm family

quarters. Lark didn't live there any longer. Neither did Caspian. However, Hawk and the two Malcolm children visited often. Hawk felt her heart grow heavy as she approached the door. She wondered if Caspian had told his parents about their new relationship. Hawk supposed it didn't much matter for the sake of this conversation. It would be hard either way.

Loris turned to Hawk outside of the Malcolms' living quarters. "Are you sure you want to be here for this?"

"I need to be." Hawk replied. And then added, "I think that I should do most of the talking this time. They know me."

Loris nodded knowingly and stepped aside for Hawk to ring the buzzer.

The door slid open to reveal Lark's smiling face on the other side. "I was hoping you would be coming!" Her enthusiasm was unmistakable. Even Jade and Aden seemed excited to see Hawk and Loris. They were clearly expecting good news.

Hawk sat down in the chair opposite the family. She tried not to look too stressed sitting in front of them, but their expressions quickly turned to apprehension and she realized that she had done a poor job of hiding her emotions. "I need to talk to you about Caspian." She cleared her throat before continuing on. "As you know, he is an excellent medic."

Hawk tried to make her voice more professional to keep herself from crying. She focused on the facts. His parents sat straighter with pride. "Because he is so good at what he does, he has been selected for a very important mission."

Lark looked as if she had a sudden realization. "*Seeker*. They mentioned medics last night at the announcement."

"Yes. *Seeker*. He has been helping in *Seeker*." Hawk was grateful that Lark had said it first.

"Helping with what, exactly?" Jade asked hesitantly.

Hawk looked towards Loris for guidance, but Loris said

nothing to help. "Some people in *Seeker* required medical care. He's providing the care they need."

Jade seemed to accept the answer, vague as it was. Perhaps she understood that Hawk wouldn't keep things from them unless she had to.

"Because of the nature of the work, the council has decided that the medical team will stay with *Seeker* while we proceed to Onsella. After we arrive, we will send a crew to retrieve Caspian and the rest of the medical team as well as the residents of *Seeker*."

"Why can't the people in *Seeker* join us for the last week? We have enough food I'm sure." Lark asked, searching for alternatives. Her eyes darted back and forth between Hawk and Loris.

Loris joined the conversation, "We would not be able to accommodate the citizens of *Seeker* and we are not equipped to make their ship mobile. This is the only way."

Jade put her hand on Lark's knee to help steady her daughter's bouncing leg. "The Council wouldn't do this if it wasn't necessary, honey. You know your brother. He *wants* to help people. I'm sure he wouldn't be there if he didn't want to be." She looked to Hawk for confirmation. Hawk nodded her head in agreement.

"He is safe. He wouldn't be there if he wasn't. I know it will be hard without him," Hawk's eyes started tearing up, "but it's what we have to do."

Lark nodded. "I just can't believe we're leaving him behind. Now, of all times. We're so close!"

Hawk moved to sit next to Lark and lovingly wrapped an arm around her. "I know. I wish there was another way."

Loris sat awkwardly in her seat, unmoving. She turned her attention towards the parents rather than acknowledge Hawk's exchange with Lark. "Your son is very brave and very capable. I cannot tell you how much we appreciate what he is doing for us."

They didn't respond. Loris remained sitting while Hawk comforted her friend, although Hawk wasn't sure who was really doing the comforting, herself or Lark. When Lark and Hawk separated, Loris caught Hawk's eye. "We need to be going now. We have another commitment."

Hawk left with a slow walk as she looked back at the Malcolms. She knew that Lark understood. Still, she hated seeing her friend so distraught.

They headed for the loading dock. Apparently, arrangements had been made with Pike already to open *Seeker*'s hatch. Hawk put on her hazmat suit quickly. She handled it as if it was a bomb that could explode at any moment. She wore gloves to touch it and held her breath while she faced it. Hawk knew it had been disinfected, but she still didn't like touching the outside of it.

Pike greeted them in the same joyful fashion as he had the previous days. He wore his protective suit just as they did and was careful not to remove it until he was through the second set of doors.

When he turned to face her, Hawk could see that he looked very tired. He had dark circles under his eyes and looked almost ashen.

"Are you feeling ok, Pike?" Hawk immediately thought of the worst possible reason for his appearance.

"Oh, I'm fine. We were up most of the night getting things ready for your medics." Pike blinked his eyes several times while he spoke.

"I didn't realize you would be so involved with the project?" Loris said it as if it were a question.

"There aren't a lot of us here. We need to take care of each other. I wasn't about to ask anyone to get out of bed to do it, so the Council did the majority of the work last night."

Hawk was impressed. She liked Pike a little bit more, which was saying a lot because she liked him a great deal already. Loris didn't say anything, but Hawk thought she must have been thinking the same thing. Once again, Loris walked next to Pike and Hawk walked a few steps behind. She wanted to hear their conversation if they started talking.

"Are we going to see the progress regarding the medics' living area?" Loris asked.

"I can take you there now, but I'll need to put my helmet back on. We've been very careful to ensure that all pathogens stay out of that area."

Hawk was pleased to hear that they were taking the risk seriously. She didn't want to leave anybody in a position that would allow them to be infected with a deadly disease, especially Caspian.

"The far wing was not in use at the time of the contamination due to a population decrease. Once the outbreak started, we decided to keep it as a safe zone. By the time we realized how much danger we were all in, we were all showing varying degrees of symptoms. Rather than contaminate it with our own illnesses, we decided to reserve it as an uncontaminated area in case a rescue team arrived. Honestly, we had almost given up hope."

Loris chuckled. "I gathered that. The first transmission we received wasn't exactly hopeful."

Pike blushed bright enough that it could be seen through his hazmat helmet. "That wasn't exactly my best moment."

"Oh, we rather enjoyed it. It helped us to understand the gravity of the situation. Don't you think Hawk?"

"We were all pretty surprised." Hawk responded. She didn't

want to sound harsh, but it had been a surprising message to receive, to say the least.

"I'm sure it was a tough time for all of you." Loris said thoughtfully.

Pike sounded distant. "You have no idea. We all thought we were going to die. We had been calling for help every single day since we cut supply to the engines. We had nothing else to do but sit and watch more and more people die. It seemed to be under control, but we were still restricted to such limited interactions. It was awful." He turned to face Loris and then looked back at Hawk. "We are all so grateful to have you here."

Loris snorted and then quickly looked as if she regretted it. Hawk was surprised. She had always thought of Loris as under control, but she didn't seem to be able to control her feelings this time.

"I know some people come off a little harsh. But really, we are *all* grateful. We had no chance without you."

"We're happy to help." Loris sounded a little embarrassed for her display of feelings. Hawk thought that she must really hate Kit for feelings about her to show even a little bit. She was glad that Pike didn't take it badly.

They headed towards the far wing. She was amazed to see that they had partitioned the area leading into the wing with a thick, plastic barrier. When they passed the barrier, there was a short room made from the plastic sheeting. Cans of disinfectant were ready for use. They sprayed themselves liberally before exiting the makeshift room and finding themselves in another plastic-coated room.

Upon exiting the second plastic partition, they entered a wing that looked familiar. Hawk could hear banging and whirring sounds. She noticed that the door to the first room was fixed open. It seemed that Pike was leading them there.

When they entered, she could see that the entire room was

being remade into a decontamination shower. People worked inside of cumbersome protective suits. Although progress was being made, it was obvious that the suits slowed them down. He led them across the hall next to another room. It looked to be a storage room for the hazmat suits. Next, he led them further down the hallway. When they hit an area where the hallways crossed, it was also made into an area with protective plastic walls. Pike said that he would not go any further. Nobody from *Seeker* had actually stepped past the partition. He explained that they would have the choice of moving in two directions once inside of the plastic, forward or to the left. Either direction was safe to travel in. Loris decided to move forward.

On the other side of the plastic, the hallways looked just like the living areas of *Enlightenment*. They walked the hallways but did not enter any of the rooms. They left quickly. Hawk didn't want to be in the area for too long. She felt like a ghost walking the empty hallways.

Next, they went to the conference room to meet with *Seeker*'s Council. Everybody looked just as tired as Pike. Hawk knew that she should feel bad for them all, but instead, she just felt impressed. She had seen the Council of *Enlightenment* in action long before she had become a part of it and they had never come together like the Council in *Seeker*. Even more impressive to her was the fact that these were not people who had been chosen prior to the outbreak. They were merely the most capable during a bad situation. Some seemed feeble and as if they were much better suited as followers than leaders, but they all pulled their weight when needed.

They discussed the plan for the next day. They were all in agreement that *Enlightenment*'s continuation to Onsella was important. Although they couldn't be certain of the origin of the message, they needed to try. They would be leaving mid-morning the next day. The medics would eat breakfast in

Enlightenment and would then go to *Seeker*. Loris would board one more time to say goodbye and then *Enlightenment* would depart. They would stay in contact for as long as possible. Paloma Lofton would check in every day until contact was lost. The *Seeker* council seemed happy with the plan.

Pike was the one to walk them to the exit after the meeting. "I think this is the best way. It has to be Onsella." Pike paused momentarily to muffle a weak cough. "It wouldn't make any sense for it to be the group that boarded us."

"Whether or not it is Onsella, we will be returning to *Seeker*. You can count on that." Loris said flatly.

"If there's one thing I've learned from all of this, it is how much we can count on *Enlightenment*. You all have been..." He coughed harder. He leaned against the wall for support. Loris moved forward to stand in front of him.

"Are you ok?" She sounded alarmed. Hawk moved closer.

"Yeah, I just need to..." What he needed to do, they never found out. He started to sway back and forth. Hawk moved forward just as his knees buckled and his body slammed into her.

18

SECRETS

Hawk stumbled backwards as Pike's weight hit her. She hastily wrapped her arms around him and lowered him to the ground as gently as possible. Hawk looked towards Loris whose eyes were wide with panic.

Loris was shuffling backwards in quick, stunted steps. "I'll get help!" Loris stammered out when she seemed to get control of herself. She turned and began running down the corridor in the direction they had come from.

Hawk sat alone with Pike, feeling helpless. She stared down at his face which was now resting in her lap. "Pike! Can you hear me, Pike?" He let out a groan. "Open your eyes!"

His eyes fluttered as if he were trying to open them but his eyelids were too heavy to do so. Hawk looked frantically down the hallway hoping to see someone coming, but there was no one. She thought he may be trying to speak but she could not make out any words through his moans and the protective helmet muffling his voice. She pulled off his helmet and placed a gloved hand on his cheek. "Pike?"

He groaned softly and finally she could hear attempts at words. "Mmm... I... eh..."

"Pike?" Hawk felt her heart surge with joy that he was responding at all. Now if he could only make sense.

His eyes open jerkily; he seemed to look through her rather than at her. "Ha... Hawk? What happened?" He looked around in confusion. "Why am I on the floor?"

He sounded meek but it still made Hawk smile with relief. "You fell. How are you feeling?"

He rubbed his eyes and sat up with Hawk's help. "I'm fine," he hesitated and then added, "tired though."

Hawk arched her eyebrow. "Really? Tired? That's why you started coughing and ended up on the floor? Because you didn't sleep much last night?"

Pike smiled up at her. "Or something like that."

Hawk heard footsteps rushing towards her. She turned to see Kit leading the way with two people in hazmat suits following closely behind. Kit stopped when she was a few steps away and allowed the suited people to pass her and kneel next to Pike and Hawk.

Kit's eyes were wide with fear. "Pike? Are you sick?"

Pike sounded irritated by the question. "We're all sick, Kit."

She matched his tone and replied, "You know what I mean," but did not step any closer.

Pike looked up at her sternly. "If I thought I was dying, I wouldn't have been spending my days around people, Kit. I don't know what happened, but I would never put all of you at risk."

Kit nodded and started to step forward. Pike held up a hand in front of his face. "I wouldn't. I don't think I'm dying but that doesn't mean I want you to risk it either." Kit nodded in response and took a few steps back.

Hawk turned her attention to the people who were assisting Pike. To her surprise, it was Caspian and Loris. She had expected Paloma Lofton to be one of the medics assisting him. "Where are the others?" Hawk asked.

"It's just me." Caspian responded. "The others are all busy with other patients." Hawk knew there weren't many medics, but she had assumed at least a few would be available for the leader of *Seeker* collapsing.

"So, what do we do?" Hawk knew that without other medics to help, the burden would fall on herself and Loris to assist.

"We need to get him to the infirmary right away. Can you help me get him up?" Caspian responded.

Hawk stood on one side of Pike with Caspian on the other side. Loris stood in front of him and helped to ensure his feet didn't slide out from under him. Pike was able to assist quite a bit with standing but was wobbly when he tried to walk. Caspian and Hawk continued to walk with their arms wrapped around his waist. Loris shifted her position to walk behind them with her hands up as if she were prepared to catch Pike should he start to fall backwards.

"I don't know what all of the fuss is about." Pike was not pleased with all of the attention. "I've been working hard and you know everybody has been sick, including me. I'm just exhausted. Get me to a bed and let me sleep for a while and I'll be fine."

Caspian ignored his protests and turned to Kit, who had been leading the way ahead of them. She was quite a distance away, so he had to shout. "Did others collapse before?"

Kit kept walking but shouted over her shoulder. "Not really. Most people stayed in their beds."

Caspian turned towards Pike now. His face shield was inches away from Pike's face while he helped to support the man's weight. "When did you start feeling worse?"

"Just today. I told you, I'm tired. It's been a busy few days here." Despite Pike's insistence that he was fine, he didn't push them away or refuse their help. Hawk could tell that he was weak.

They made their way to the infirmary. Kit put on a mask and gloves as she entered and did not get too close to them. They were the only ones in the room. All the other medics had been working with people inside of their living quarters.

"I need to take a blood sample." Caspian said as he looked through a nearby cabinet for supplies.

"You haven't taken his yet?" Loris sounded surprised and upset.

"He insisted on being one of the last." Caspian responded without looking up from his task.

Kit glared at Pike. "That sounds like him."

"I am telling you people, I'm fine!" Pike tried to yell but it only came out as a forceful whisper.

Kit spoke from her position against the wall. "Listen to the doctor, Pike. He knows what he's doing and you're too important to die. If he says they need a blood sample, they need one."

"You are making a big fuss about nothing." Even while he argued, he rolled up his sleeve to expose his arm, a gesture that showed he would submit to the tests but with protest.

After the blood sample was taken and Caspian had finished all of his tests, Loris and Hawk helped Pike to his room. Caspian had instructed that he needed to rest during the day. To be sure that he did so, Caspian quarantined Pike to his room. "If you won't rest for yourself, do it for all of the other people you work so hard to protect. Until we know what's going on with you, you need to stay put. It's not just for *your* safety."

Loris suggested that she and Hawk stay until the results of the test were known. She wanted to be in *Seeker* until they were certain of Pike's condition. The tests didn't take long to come back. The lab in *Seeker* was just as equipped as the one in *Enlightenment*.

Loris and Hawk waited with Kit in the conference room. Caspian had assured them that he would join them as soon as he knew the results. Kit still wore her mask and gloves. She did not sit at the table with the two women. Instead, she paced back and forth along the far wall distancing herself from the table.

Hawk sat in silence. She felt as if there was no way to comfort Kit. Loris tried, but it didn't seem to help. "He's a tough man. I wouldn't rule him out just yet." Loris tried to assure her.

"He's a very tough man." Kit agreed. "That's why this is so concerning. I've never seen anything, *anything,* bring that man down like that. Whatever is going on, it's bad." She nervously picked at her nail beds while she continued to pace along the back wall.

Nobody spoke again until Caspian entered the room. Kit stopped pacing but did not move closer to the group. Caspian sat down. He looked frazzled. "I don't know how to say this."

"He's dying." Kit stated in a monotone voice.

Caspian didn't speak right away. He looked at the table with sad eyes and Hawk knew that Kit must be right. Finally, he continued. "If we are right about which virus is the deadly one, then yes. He's dying."

"So, what are you going to do about it?" Kit demanded.

"For now, I'm going to try the same medications that we have Altai taking. It doesn't seem to have cured the illness, but it has slowed the progression. It might buy him some time."

"Some time before he dies you mean." Kit clarified. "You aren't trying to keep him from dying, just trying to make him die slower. Am I understanding you correctly?"

Caspian looked somber as he addressed her. "I will do everything that I can. For now, that's the best I can do."

Kit nodded as tears shone in her eyes. Suddenly, the tears

turned into sobbing as she sunk to the floor. Hawk stood to move closer, but Loris stepped in front of her, extending her gloved hands outward. "We've touched him. We need to stay back."

Hawk felt helpless as she watched the strong woman struggle and fail to gain control of herself. Caspian moved next to Hawk and pulled her close. Hawk stared at the wall next to her and tried not to look at Kit. It wasn't much privacy, but it was the best that she could do.

When she was able to, Kit wiped the tears from her eyes and rose stoically. "Have you told him yet?" Her face was set to a stern expression.

"Not yet." Caspian confirmed.

"I will be the one to tell him." It was not a question. Kit was giving an order.

"Then let's get you a hazmat suit." Caspian started to walk towards the door. "Come with me."

They walked with Kit to Pike's room. His smile fell when he saw that it was Kit standing in front of him in the suit. Hawk heard him say, "All right then," before the door slid closed behind Kit. The *Enlightenment* crew did not enter.

Hawk moved closer to Caspian. "What do you think she's saying?"

Caspian shrugged. "What can she say? They've seen it happen before."

When Kit left the room, she had tear streaks down her cheeks. She stood in front of his door and addressed the group. "We need to convene the Council. You are welcome to attend."

Hawk and Loris made their way towards the conference room. Caspian did not join them. Instead, he returned to his work. The Council responded quickly. Most looked as if they had been sleeping before the call for the meeting. They staggered in, yawning and rubbing at their eyes.

Kit, who had taken off her hazmat suit, sat at the head of the table. Loris and Hawk had disinfected their suits before the meeting and were able to sit with the Council.

Kit began, "As you can see, Pike is not able to attend today." Hawk saw several of the councilors exchange meaningful glances. They clearly had experienced similar meetings before. "Our worst fears have come to fruition," she continued, "Pike is very ill and will likely die."

She stopped and let her words sink in. A few councilors wiped away tears; however, most sat still without moving or showing any emotion at all.

"He has asked me to take his place. I will meet with him daily. I am only his mouthpiece for the time being. Pike is still in charge, and he will be for as long as he is able." Kit showed none of the emotion that she had exhibited earlier.

The room fell silent. Hawk had expected somebody to say something, but nobody did. Although people looked sad, they seemed hardened to the harsh realities they faced. They were desensitized to death.

Kit rose from her chair again. "So until then, we need to continue on with our work. The decontamination area is nearly complete. It will be done before the end of the day. Treatment is being fine-tuned for the illnesses. Anything that the medics need, we supply. That is our mission now. Keep up the hard work."

Hawk and Loris looked at each other with expressions of confusion. They had both expected a longer, more emotional meeting rather than a quick fact-providing blurb of a meeting.

Kit turned to them next. "I know Pike was walking you out before this all happened. I can take you now."

They followed her again. Once again, she preferred to lead

the way rather than walk next to them. Whenever she had something to say she would toss the words carelessly over her shoulder. Hawk couldn't help but compare her to the far more personable Pike Brighton.

Their arrival back to *Enlightenment* was much less dramatic than the previous day. They had arranged for makeshift showers to be brought to the loading area and had better means to disinfect the suits. Hawk still felt a bit uneasy and nervous as she took the suit off, but nothing like the day before.

Despite being safely in *Enlightenment*, her mind continued to drift back to *Seeker*. Hawk imagined Caspian moving from room to room, finding more people who were sick or even dying and having to be the one to tell them the news. She thought of Kit managing the place with her harsh, emotionless demeanor and wondered what life would look like for the medical team during the upcoming weeks.

Loris hadn't scheduled anything else for Hawk to do. Instead, she was instructed to "stay visible" and "be diplomatic." Hawk couldn't help but think how much she hated both of those things given the current circumstances. Hawk moved around *Enlightenment* concentrating her efforts in known communal areas. She changed locations often. There was an increase of people gathering around common areas due to the fact that most of the people had been excused from work.

The atmosphere of *Enlightenment* buzzed with delight and anticipation. Although for Hawk it was a time of worry, for the rest of *Enlightenment* it was a time of celebration. She seldom saw anybody without a smile on their face. Laughter wafted down the corridors from every direction. Hawk did her best to fall into character, but it was difficult when she thought of the turmoil taking place in the ship next door. The ship that few others had even uttered the name of since the announcement had been made.

She stopped by her parents' living quarters and asked them to meet her in Commons Area C. Hawk wanted the familiar, calming location but also felt it was important to talk with her parents. They didn't know everything, and they wouldn't be allowed to know. Still, Hawk felt it could be therapeutic to explain to her loved ones what little she was able. Per Loris' instructions, she needed to do that in a public space to "stay visible" for the others.

Onyx and Poppy were cheerier than she had ever seen them. They were a laughing, smiling, ideal poster-couple of *Enlightenment*. "This must be so exciting for you, Hawk! You must feel very lucky to have been selected as junior diplomat *now*. This is the most exhilarating time in all of *Enlightenment*'s history!" Poppy was unable to contain her enthusiasm.

You have no idea, Hawk thought. But said instead, "It's pretty exciting that's for sure. I'm really looking forward to seeing Onsella." At least that was a truthful statement. She hoped she sounded more enthused than she really felt.

"Do you know what your duties will be when you get there?" Onyx sounded excited but didn't talk nearly as quickly and enthusiastically as his wife.

"Not yet." Hawk responded. "Right now, we are focusing on getting there and our work with *Seeker*." She was hoping that *Seeker* would come up in conversation. Hawk couldn't tell them everything, but they could at least know the basics.

"That's right." Onyx nodded as if he were being reminded of a faraway thought. "Diplomat Goring mentioned that last night. How are things going over there?" He seemed curious.

"It seems to be working out ok. We are preparing to depart tomorrow morning. Caspian has been selected as one of the medical personnel that will be staying behind." She tried to sound nonchalant when in fact this was where she had wanted to steer the conversation all along.

"Oh really!" Poppy sounded thrilled. "That must be quite an honor!" There was no worry in her tone nor any showing on her face. Hawk envied her mother in that moment.

"It is. He's very good at his job." She paused and wondered if she should tell her parents more. "I don't think I mentioned that Caspian and I have been seeing each other."

This caught Onyx's attention right away. "Oh, are you now?" His smile did not reach his eyes and he sounded more confused than curious.

Poppy stared at her husband as if waiting for him to continue. He didn't. "Well, that's great, honey!" Poppy added in her overly-supportive mom way.

"Mmhmm. It's only been a few days but I'm a little concerned about leaving him behind." Hawk understated it knowing that if she said what she really felt her parents would know that there was more to the story.

Poppy chimed in. "I know Caspian will be fine. It will only be for a few weeks anyway, right? They'll send a team back for them after we reach Onsella?"

"That's the plan." Hawk tried to sound positive, but she was still worried that Onsella wouldn't be able to send a return vessel. Whether it was a rational fear or not, she was still worried. After all, they hadn't had any contact with Onsella to make a plan with them. They were operating on hope alone.

"It must be a treat to see another starship." Poppy had a dreamy, envious expression on her face.

Hawk shrugged. "It looks exactly like *Enlightenment*."

Poppy blinked twice before responding. "You've seen it? You've been holding out on us young lady." Her chastisement wasn't sincere.

Hawk hadn't realized that her trips to *Seeker* weren't common knowledge. "I went with Loris. It's not a big deal," she shrugged.

Poppy made eye contact with her daughter and held it. She seemed lost for words. Poppy opened her mouth as if she were going to say something and then quickly shut it, pursing her lips tightly.

Onyx's eyes darted between the two. "What will he be doing in *Seeker* anyway?"

Hawk shrugged. "You know, doctor stuff. Supervising and checking in with people." She tried to keep it vague.

"I guess that'll be a bit of a vacation for him after spending all of his life here." Poppy added in a tone that suggested she was still not pleased with being kept out of the loop.

"Something like that." Hawk didn't think the word *vacation* was the right word, but to her parents the trips to *Seeker* probably sounded relaxing. She wished that she could tell them more but knew that she couldn't.

The rest of the conversation was lighthearted although Poppy clearly felt jilted. Onyx moved the conversation forward at an uncomfortable pace. He was clearly more content with his wife leading their conversations.

The visit with her parents had helped some, but overall, Hawk felt frustrated that she couldn't tell them her real concerns. The rest of the day consisted of her plastering a fake smile on her face and talking to people she didn't really know about all the possibilities and how perfect Onsella would be. Her cheeks hurt from constant strain, but she continued to smile along.

Hawk said the words and went through the motions, but she was having more doubts about what Onsella would be like. So far, they were only *approaching* Onsella, and they had already faced disease, death, and mysterious people from an unknown origin who may have tried to kill an entire civilization. If life on Onsella was like life approaching it, Hawk wasn't sure they would be better off on the planet. To Hawk, *Enlightenment* seemed a safe haven compared to the rest of the universe that she had experienced so far.

19

HAVEN

As dinner approached, Hawk became increasingly nervous about her evening. She was looking forward to seeing Caspian, but wasn't sure what to expect from her last night with him before he was left behind in *Seeker*. Rowan joined her for the last few hours before dinner. It helped to keep her mind off what was going to happen that evening. It felt nice to be around someone who understood the magnitude of the situation.

Rowan changed the subject whenever Caspian came up. Hawk was grateful for his avoidance in a way. As much as she wanted to talk about Caspian and *Seeker*, Hawk also liked pretending that everything was normal.

Lark joined them shortly before dinner. Hawk enjoyed that part of her day the most. She was able to laugh and smile without feeling like it was forced. It gave her hope for the upcoming weeks. Hawk was still nervous for Caspian, but, despite his impending absence, she felt as if she might be able to enjoy some of the time during which she was separated from him.

Dinner was by far the largest feast she had ever seen.

Anything that could be made, was. The dessert area overflowed with sweets. Apparently, the cooks had taken the order to celebrate very seriously. Hawk watched as Lark piled desserts onto her plate. She turned to Hawk. "It's not like we need to worry about a food shortage or anything at this point and who knows what food will be like on Onsella. Better enjoy it while I can," she said to justify her indulgence.

Hawk took a heavy helping of pork roast and tried a few types of cookies but did not eat near as much as Lark had put on her plate. Caspian had told her that he would meet her for dinner and she was eager to see him. The food was a nice distraction, but not distracting enough to keep her mind from wandering back into Caspian's embrace.

Hawk sat down opposite of Rowan and Lark. She wanted to leave room for Caspian to sit next to her. Although Lark didn't say it, she was sure that Lark had caught on and asked Rowan to sit by her instead of next to Hawk. Caspian came in shortly after. He seemed tired but pleased to see her. Hawk nearly jumped to her feet in excitement when he came up behind her.

"Hey there," he said as he put his tray down with one hand and ran his other hand along the curve of her shoulder. Chills went through her body and she found it difficult to concentrate on the conversation taking place in front of her. Hawk was certain that she had been talking with Lark and Rowan, but she could no longer remember what the conversation had been about.

He took his seat next to her in close proximity. She had trouble eating with him so close to her. Every time Hawk lifted her arm, she grazed his forearm with her elbow, but she didn't mind. It was worth it to feel the warmth coming from his body.

Lark beamed with happiness as she watched Caspian sit down next to Hawk. Rowan on the other hand seemed extremely focused on his food.

Lark jumped in with conversation. "I guess we won't be seeing you for a while after tonight." Her tone shifted as the realization of his impending absence hit her.

Caspian looked up at his sister for the first time since sitting down. "I was wondering when they would tell you about that." His face showed that he felt guilty. "I couldn't say anything. We were instructed that the Council would handle it."

"Yeah, Hawk came by with Loris and told us. Of course 'told us' is a loose phrase." Lark sent a mock glare in Hawk's direction. "She didn't tell us much. Just that you would be in *Seeker* helping for a while and another ship from Onsella would come to get you after."

"That's all of it then." Caspian smirked at his sister. He looked calm, but Hawk felt his muscles tense when he heard that she had been the one to share the news.

"Yeah, I didn't figure you would tell me anything more." Lark stabbed at the food on her plate but did not eat any of it.

Rowan joined the conversation. "It'll be fine, Lark, and as an added bonus, we get a break from Caspian here." He pointed his fork at Caspian while he spoke and tried to play it off as if he were joking, but Hawk wasn't sure that he was.

Caspian sent a sarcastic smile his way. "I'm sure all of *Enlightenment* will throw a party to celebrate my absence."

"Maybe not because of your absence, but I think you might be right about the party part." Hawk said as she looked around the dining hall. Decorations peppered the walls. The noise level in the mess hall was much louder than normal. People laughed and yelled across the room to friends whom they had spotted. Everybody looked happy and cheerful.

Caspian joined Hawk in surveying the room. "I guess they have a lot to celebrate these days." A frown appeared on his face. Hawk thought again about how miserable his next few weeks were going to be and her heart fell.

Lark seemed to notice the expression as well. "I know you're going to miss out on the trip, but you'll be helping people! You'll get to see *Seeker* and whatever ship they send to fetch you. I'm sure *Seeker* will be celebrating too. It might take them a bit longer to get there, but they are also Onsella-bound!"

Caspian gave a heavy sigh. Lark seemed to take his change in emotions as mere disappointment at not seeing Onsella with the rest of *Enlightenment*, but Hawk knew better. Rowan seemed to understand as well, but neither could say anything about it with Lark sitting with them. There would be no celebrations in *Seeker*. Instead, he would be watching death creep in on people he was just beginning to know.

"It'll only be for a few weeks. You know that the Council wouldn't leave you behind permanently." Rowan offered.

That didn't seem to make Caspian feel any better, but he opted to continue on with the conversation anyway. "Things should be pretty exciting this week that's for sure."

Lark, being Lark, was ready to focus on the party activities of the week. "So, do you all want to go to Haven tonight? I'm sure it will be crazy!"

"Sure. It might be nice to get out." Rowan chimed in.

Caspian glanced at Hawk. "We have plans tonight. Maybe we can meet up with you later in the evening."

Hawk nodded enthusiastically. She was happy to hear Caspian was thinking the same thing that she was thinking. Hawk wanted to spend time with Lark, but she also wanted some time with Caspian without the watchful eyes of Lark and Rowan.

"Oh. Ok." Lark sounded disappointed but recovered quickly. "Then Rowan and I will go and maybe we will see you there later?"

Rowan also looked disappointed. He looked at Hawk with sad eyes but didn't dispute her decision.

The rest of dinner was uneventful. The room continued to exude excitement. Everybody ate until they could eat no more. As they waddled out of the dining room together feeling as if they couldn't eat another bite, Caspian started talking about the spread of food. "Where did they get all of this food from all of a sudden?"

Food was usually heavily restricted. People were able to eat enough without rations per se, but the kitchen only made a set amount each day and only added to the meal marginally as people required more. Food was rarely wasted. People were encouraged to limit their food consumption. On the contrary, the meal from the feast that they had just attended would likely have excessive waste and people were encouraged to eat as much as possible.

"We had a surplus in supply that the Council approved dipping into. They aren't as worried about saving for a rainy day when there's only a few weeks' time in *Enlightenment* left." Hawk answered.

"So, should I expect to see feasts like this in *Seeker*?" He asked in passing but Hawk was sure he was genuinely concerned.

"We've transferred a lot of food into your living quarters. Most of it requires very little preparation though. You won't have a lot of access to kitchen appliances." Hawk started to fidget uncomfortably while she walked. She rubbed a hand over her bicep awkwardly.

Caspian stopped and gently grabbed her hand. "I'm sorry. We shouldn't be talking about that now. I want to spend as much time as possible with you, *not* talking about work."

Hawk smiled as they strode hand in hand down the hallway. "So, what's the plan then?" She had not made any plans for the evening and wasn't sure if he had either.

"I thought we could start at the commons area and then see where we wanted to go."

They headed for her favorite commons area and sat beneath the artificial trees. The conversation felt natural and easy for Hawk. The difficult part was avoiding talk about the upcoming events. Instead, they joked about Lark's reaction to their relationship and discussed past shenanigans. The conversation even turned to what they thought Onsella would be like, but they were careful not to mention that they would be arriving at Onsella at different times.

"I'm sure they will have doctors there. At the very least, they will need you to teach the Onsellan medics about human diseases and anatomy." Hawk told him.

"I don't know about that. Onsellan anatomy and human anatomy is surprisingly similar. Although a lot of diseases seem to affect the two races differently. It's really fascinating actually."

"See, you'll have a job there. You'll be miles ahead of them when it comes to human health." She paused before adding in a whisper, "I'm still not sure what I'll be doing there."

"Oh come on. As a junior diplomat, I'm sure they will have you doing all sorts of things."

"Me too, I just don't know what they'll be. Human relations?" Hawk laughed realizing how the term took on new meaning when it was applied to another planet.

"I'm sure Loris will keep you busy." Caspian replied.

"You're probably right about that. I'm actually looking forward to seeing what she's like when we aren't in crisis. When I took this job, I thought I would learn a lot from her, but so far we've just moved from one tragic situation to another."

Caspian looked around the room. A handful of people sat in the area. "Maybe we should change the subject. I don't want people overhearing."

Hawk nodded knowingly. She searched her mind for something else to talk about, but found herself quite distracted by *Seeker* and Onsella. Suddenly her mind shifted to the look of disappointment on Lark's face during dinner. "Maybe we should head to Haven for a bit? We can catch up with Lark." Hawk purposely left out any mention of Rowan even though they both knew he would be there.

When they entered Haven, the music was loud. Recordings played instead of a live band. Hawk was glad for that. People moved in all directions with exuberant energy. She moved in close to Caspian and said loudly in his ear, "She's usually over there!" She pointed towards the dance floor. They made their way through the crowd. Caspian led the way with Hawk staying close behind so as not to be separated.

As they approached the dance floor, Hawk's eyes were pulled to a table towards the side of the area where Rowan stood on a chair and was waving his arms wildly in their direction, beckoning them over. Hawk lightly poked Caspian in the back. He turned and she pointed out Rowan's location. He nodded and once again began weaving through the crowd, this time heading for the table.

When they arrived, Hawk was pleased to notice that the music level was much more tolerable by the tables. Although they still needed to shout to be heard, they didn't require being directly next to one another. She sat at the table opposite Rowan. Caspian sat next to her.

"Where's Lark?" Caspian questioned loudly once he was sitting.

Rather than shout a response, Rowan rolled his eyes in an exaggerated fashion and pointed towards the dance floor nearest them. There, they saw Lark, but she wasn't alone. A young, tall man whom Hawk only knew by sight had his hands wrapped firmly around her petite waist. He had lifted her into the air and was spinning in quick circles. Lark's arms were thrown up in the air and her head was tossed back in a fit of laughter.

"Who's that?" Hawk questioned as she scrutinized the man with her friend.

Rowan laughed. "I have no idea. She said she wanted to dance. I said I wasn't really the dancing type so she went off by herself. The next thing I knew..." He pointed with his thumb back to the dance floor.

"At least Lark's having a good time." Caspian scowled at his sister spinning above the dancers while he spoke, as if he weren't as supportive as his words suggested.

The song finished and the man set Lark back on the floor, looking very proud of himself. A beaming Lark turned towards the table. Her eyes widened when she spotted Hawk and Caspian. Hawk watched in awe of her friend as Lark dismissed the man she was with. She did so with such grace as she patted him affectionately on the chest and then walked towards her friends as if nothing were out of the ordinary.

"Hawk! Caspian!" Lark squealed in delight as she approached the table. "I didn't think you would actually come!" She embraced Hawk in an affectionate hug before doing the same to her brother.

Caspian laughed. "Oh, you know us; we can't stay away from the party."

Lark scoffed. "So, you're going to dance, then?"

Hawk usually enjoyed dancing, but not like Lark did. Hawk was more of the dance-when-no-one's-looking type. However, as she looked around at the jumble of moving bodies in front of her, Hawk realized nobody seemed to be watching anyway.

She looked up towards Caspian who was also watching the crowd and then turned her attention towards Lark. "Sure! Why not?"

The new song began to play. It had a heavy bass beat that

repeated in a quick rhythm. Lark grinned and reached out for Hawk's hand. Lark pulled Hawk along to the same area where she had been dancing with the tall man. She began to jump and move in a way that reminded Hawk of the ribbons that fluttered from the air system above. Hawk unsuccessfully attempted to imitate her friend's movements while not jarring her still tender ribs. When she felt Caspian slide in next to her, Hawk felt her tension melt away. Her movements felt much more natural. She turned from Caspian to watch Lark again and was surprised to see Rowan dancing next to Lark. Although his movements appeared tense and robotic, his smile suggested that he really was having a good time.

They danced for a few songs before sitting back at the table. Hawk fanned herself with her hand as she attempted to cool herself off. Lark sat for less than a minute before excusing herself to find Jasper. "He told me he'd be here." She insisted as she disappeared into the crowd.

"Maybe that tall guy can lift you up again. It was a good vantage point!" Hawk called after her with a chuckle.

Once Lark had left, an uncomfortable silence fell over the table. Hawk was very relieved when Rowan suddenly spotted someone over her head and began waving enthusiastically. Ural Ambrose slid into the vacant seat next to him.

"What a zoo!" he yelled over the music. "I've never seen it so busy here."

Hawk laughed silently to herself at the thought of Ural Ambrose frequenting Haven.

Rowan joked with his mentor and soon the table was filled with conversation that neither Hawk nor Caspian knew anything about. Caspian cleared his throat. "Hawk and I weren't planning on staying too long. Maybe now would be a good time for us to take off."

Rowan grunted an acknowledgement in their direction and

Diplomat Ambrose picked up his hand in a rushed wave without pausing his conversation.

"Tell Lark we'll see her tomorrow." Hawk said while she left the table. She wasn't sure if Rowan had heard or not, but wasn't going to wait to find out.

They walked towards Caspian's living quarters, which was closer than Hawk's. When there, they sat on the couch. Hawk leaned against him, and he wrapped an arm around her.

"If someone had told me last week that this is where I would be today, I wouldn't have believed it." Hawk said as she leaned against him.

Caspian laughed. "Me neither. I've thought about having you in my arms so many times, but I never thought it would actually happen."

"I guess we just needed something life-changingly big to bring us together." Hawk smiled.

"I wanted this for a long time." Caspian sounded very serious now. "I just didn't think you wanted me, too."

"I did." Hawk responded. "I just didn't want to risk all that we had."

"So why risk it now?" Caspian asked.

Hawk tilted her head upwards to see his face and saw that he was gazing down at her. "I realized that nothing was worth hiding from this any longer. Everything about our lives is changing now. If it's going to change, I want my life to change *with* you. The fear of our lives going in separate directions was enough for me to realize I wanted to go forward with you regardless of the risk." She repositioned her body to face him now. "What about you? I mean, you kissed me first. What made you do it?"

Caspian sighed heavily. "I had wanted to for so long, I guess I couldn't stop myself any longer." He leaned forward and put his lips on Hawk's. She pushed herself deeper into the kiss and felt his body against hers. She pressed back forcefully while he moved in even closer. Hawk's breathing became heavy as she eased into the couch. His hands began to travel up her thigh and over her hips. She moaned and squirmed under his touch. Then the ever-present dull pain sparked again through her body as his hand reached her ribs. Hawk pulled back and winced.

"Your ribs, still?" He said breathlessly as he sat himself up quickly.

Hawk grabbed her side and began to sit up. Caspian assisted as best he could by gingerly putting his hand on her uninjured side and pulling her up slowly.

"I forgot about your ribs for a moment." His eyes looked apologetic and bashful.

"You and me both." Hawk responded trying to sound upbeat. "It's ok, really."

"Still, I feel horrible for hurting you." His face flushed crimson with embarrassment.

Hawk reached up and put a gentle hand on his cheek. "It was worth it." He smiled back at her. She wished more than anything at that moment that she had never fallen off the treadmill.

"You know, this is all your fault anyway," she responded jokingly.

"Me?" Caspian feigned offense. "What did I do?"

"You and your smoldering eyes swooped in and distracted me while I was running."

"Hey, you can't blame me for that. The ship started shaking. I didn't make it do that."

"Yeah, but if I hadn't been stumbling over my feet while looking at you, I would have stayed upright, and instead of arguing about *this* we would be making out right now," she joked.

"But the ship shaking had nothing to do with my

'smoldering eyes.' It was altering its course to communicate with *Seeker*. Which, by the way, if it hadn't done that, then we wouldn't be together right now. So really, it was a good thing."

"A good thing?" Hawk scoffed. "That I cracked my ribs? There had to be an easier way for the two of us to get together."

Caspian smiled. "You'd think, but apparently you had to learn the hard way." He threw a pillow at her playfully. She batted it away with her free hand.

The rest of the evening was all laughs and jokes. They talked until it was late and they were both yawning.

Hawk wasn't sure when or how it happened, but she must have fallen asleep. Caspian gently rubbed her arm and pushed her hair from her face. "Hawk, wake up." She blinked in confusion, unsure of where she was. When she looked towards what would normally be the ceiling, she found Caspian peering down at her. "You fell asleep."

It was then that Hawk noticed that she had been using his lap as a pillow. "Oh, I guess I did." She sat herself up hesitantly while wiping at her mouth self-consciously, hoping she wouldn't find any drool. She wasn't so lucky. "Maybe I should be going."

She walked towards the door. Caspian walked the few steps with her, holding her hand. "I should have time to see you tomorrow morning before I leave."

"Ok." Hawk kept her response short. She didn't want to think about saying goodbye.

When the door slid open and Hawk stepped into the hallway, Caspian took a step too. He stood in the doorway, prohibiting the door from closing. He reached forward and pulled her close. "Don't worry, I'll be gentle." He laughed to himself while he very obviously positioned his hands so as to not touch her injured side. He kissed her softly on the forehead and then once on the lips. "Good night, Hawk." He said as he stepped back into the room.

"Good night, Caspian," she said as the door slid shut between them.

20

FULL-STOP

Breakfast the next morning was not as impressive as the feast she had experienced a few hours earlier, but it did have more of a selection than normal. The air remained thick with excitement and joy. As Hawk entered the cafeteria, she thought of the night before. She remembered leaving before saying goodnight to Lark, and hoped that her friend would understand.

When she sat down, Lark mentioned it immediately. "You left too early last night. The party was just getting started! Hopefully you had as much fun as we did." She indicated Rowan as the other half of 'we.'

"It was a good night." Hawk wasn't sure what else she was supposed to say. Talking to Lark about an evening with Caspian felt strange. Lark always told Hawk everything about her personal relationships; sometimes too much. Whenever Hawk so much as hinted at feelings for someone on the ship, Lark always pressed her for details. She hoped that it would be different now and that Lark wouldn't be pressing for details about her own brother.

"You missed one hell of a time." Lark continued. "It only got better as the night went on. The music was excellent, and *everybody* was out."

Rowan nodded in agreement but didn't elaborate.

"Did you find Jasper?" Hawk asked.

"He was there," she frowned when she said this, "but he was more interested in someone else."

Hawk wasn't surprised. Still, she hated that her friend always picked the same type of man. Lark had yet to be attracted to anyone that Hawk approved of.

"But no matter, I had a good time anyway. Rowan here is quite the dancer!" She sounded enthusiastic, but Rowan didn't look thrilled.

"I noticed." Hawk laughed to herself when she remembered his tense, forced movements from the night before.

"Only if by 'quite the dancer' she means 'talks with Ural Ambrose at a corner table most of the night,'" he glowered at Lark.

"Oh come on! You danced some too."

"Very little," he said again, "but she's right. There were a lot of people out celebrating. Made it a little difficult to move actually." He frowned deeply at the thought.

"I wonder what tonight will look like then. We've just been sitting around for a few days now. How happy will people be once we take off today?" Hawk turned to Lark as she spoke.

Lark responded enthusiastically. "Oh, don't you worry about that! I've been talking with the other party planners and we have something extra special planned for tonight. Haven will never be the same!"

"I thought you didn't have to work now?" Rowan questioned.

"I don't. None of the planners do but there was no way that I was going to let an opportunity like this pass me by." Lark seemed to be very proud of herself. "Of course, tonight is just a trial run really with decorations and such. We'll be working out the kinks to be extra ready for the Onsella celebration." She winked at Hawk when she finished speaking.

Suddenly, Lark's expression seemed to change as the realization of the Onsella arrival seemed to dawn on her. "Where's Caspian?" she asked Hawk.

"I'm sure he will be here soon." She responded looking towards the door, hoping to see him walk through it.

"Late night, then?" Rowan asked, making Hawk blush.

"Something like that." She noticed Caspian walking in. "There he is now."

He came over and sat down next to Hawk with very little on his plate. "Not hungry?" Hawk questioned.

"I'm a little nervous today." He confessed with a weak smile.

"Don't worry. There's food in *Seeker* too. I brought it over yesterday." Rowan responded.

That caught Hawk's attention. "*You* brought it over?" She hadn't expected that.

"While you were notifying the medics families yesterday a group from the Council brought over the food supplies. You didn't think you were the only one who got to see *Seeker*, did you?" he asked mischievously.

She shrugged. "I didn't really think about it."

Lark threw up her hands in frustration. "Hold up! You mean I am the only one from this group that hasn't seen *Seeker*? How did that happen?" She used her spoon as a baton while she moved it in a circle to indicate the group.

Caspian couldn't resist picking on his sister. "It's really nothing special, sis. I mean, it's just the *only* place outside of *Enlightenment* that anybody aboard has ever had the chance to visit. It's nothing. Really."

Lark aimed a playful kick at her brother's shin under the table and then turned to Rowan and Hawk. "What's it like?"

Hawk answered first. "Exactly like *Enlightenment*. There are just different people." Hawk couldn't blame her friend for being so interested. *Enlightenment* was all that they had ever known. The idea of something new, even another ship, was exciting.

Rowan added, "She's right. It is the exact same layout as *Enlightenment*. Some of the walls are painted a bit different and there's a little different color scheme in some of the rooms but that's all. It's *Enlightenment-Number-Two*."

Caspian joined in. "Actually, *Seeker* was made first. So really, we're in *Seeker-Number-Two*."

"Or maybe this is *Revealer III* if we want to go back that far." Rowan stated flatly.

"Good point. *Revealer I, II* and *III*. I like it." Caspian responded playfully while looking towards his sister, anticipating her reaction. Her face continued to redden.

Hawk decided it was time to soothe the conversation. "Lark, it's not a big deal. Trust me, you don't want to see it. It's better here."

Lark looked puzzled. "I thought you just said it was the same except for the people. Why is it better here?" Lark's eyes narrowed in Hawk's direction.

Hawk regretted saying anything at all. She realized too late that she had said too much. Caspian came to her rescue. "You mean because of Kit? She's a bit different that's for sure." Hawk felt instant relief for Caspian's quick thinking.

"Who's Kit?" Lark leaned in, eager for information.

All of Caspian's joking demeanor dissipated. "Kit Elderstein. She's one of *Seeker*'s leaders and she's not exactly what I would call a *cheery* person." He responded with sincerity.

Hawk jumped in. "I don't know. I like her." She couldn't explain what it was about the woman, but Hawk had felt an instant like for her even if it was clear Loris, and apparently Caspian, did not share in her opinion.

"Like her?" Rowan sounded offended. "I only talked with her for five minutes and she made me feel like a spoiled, entitled brat. There's nothing to like about that woman." He shook his head in disbelief.

"I think she's doing her best. It must be difficult for her to express herself." Hawk could relate.

"Well, she doesn't need to take it out on the rest of us then. We're there to help." Rowan sounded like the idea of anyone defending Kit was outrageous.

Lark's eyes darted from person to person as she soaked up each new piece of information. Lark turned to Caspian. "You have to spend the next two weeks with a leader like that? I see why you aren't rushing out of *Enlightenment* now."

Caspian glanced towards Hawk. "Well, that's one reason."

Lark looked as if she might swoon out of her chair. "Aww!" she cooed. "That's so sweet!"

Rowan on the other hand, rolled his eyes. "I think you have other things to worry about." Hawk thought about the illness and the mystery ship that was still unaccounted for.

Caspian nodded. "You're right about that."

Lark seemed nervous now. "Is that Kit person really that bad? You're talking like you're marching into a warzone over there." Hawk felt as if that were exactly what he was doing, but it had nothing to do with Kit.

"She's really not that bad." Caspian comforted his sister. "It's going to take me some time to get used to it. That's all."

"So, when do you leave?" Lark asked while she went back to picking at her breakfast.

"I packed my bags and said goodbye to Mom and Dad before breakfast. That's why I was running a little late. I'm supposed to report to the loading bay right after breakfast."

This was news to Hawk, but she wasn't surprised. She was certain that Loris would let her go to the loading dock to say goodbye, but Lark wouldn't have that chance.

"So, I guess this is our last meal then, isn't it?" Lark asked sheepishly.

"Our last meal *for now*. It won't be long before I join you on Onsella." Caspian countered.

Hawk felt as if she were imposing on a family moment but couldn't think up a reason to excuse herself.

Rowan met her eye and was obviously thinking the same thing. "Did you see that fruit selection today, Hawk? I was thinking about getting some more."

Hawk stood abruptly. "Me too!" She left hastily and followed Rowan to the front of the room next to the fruit table. "Thank you!" she blurted, once they were out of earshot.

"I thought they could use some time to say goodbye." he said, thoughtfully.

"I think you're right." Hawk looked back towards Lark and Caspian. Lark was slouched over her breakfast with her elbows resting on the table. By her body language, Hawk could tell she was distressed.

"Those two are pretty close, huh?" Rowan asked while he leaned forward to grab an apple.

"Very." Hawk answered as she, too, reached for a piece of fruit.

"I get it. If it were one of my siblings heading over there, I would be a wreck. Then again, we know a little bit more about the situation than she does."

Hawk felt a tinge of guilt. "I don't know if that makes it better or worse," she said thoughtfully. "Lark may seem like she doesn't care, but she always wants to be in the know. She's smart enough to know that there's something more going on. Trust me."

Rowan nodded. "I've noticed. Lark is one of the more interesting people that I've met." Hawk saw his gaze move towards Lark as well. She could see the sympathy in his eyes as he watched her agonize over the right words to say.

Suddenly, Hawk felt a vibration emitting from her wrist transmitter. She jumped in surprise. Rowan noticed. "What is it?" He leaned in to look at the screen, Hawk shifted to block his view.

"Loris needs me." Hawk frowned. "It says immediately." She glanced towards Caspian with a pained expression.

"Go. I'll let them know. You'll see him again before we leave." Rowan urged with a tinge of jealousy in his voice.

Hawk nodded in agreement before hurrying towards the helm. Loris met her at the door and escorted her in. She didn't say a word until they sat in front of the radio. "We've got a problem." Hawk put on a set of headphones and immediately knew what Loris meant.

A masculine, gruff voice speaking Onsellan sounded through the static. Although the voice was familiar, his message was not one that she had heard herself before. "This is a message to all travelers seeking safe passage to Onsella. Onsella is no longer safe. Hail our ship for safety. We promise you safety. Do not proceed to Onsella. Death awaits all who do not heed our warning."

She turned towards Loris with wide eyes. "That's him. It's Zeb." Hawk nodded. "Where are they?"

"It's a continually replaying transmission. From what we can tell, they are moving away from us. They haven't identified our position. According to our navigators, it's unlikely that they will find us unless we contact them."

Hawk felt panic rise into her chest. "What about *Seeker*'s message?"

Loris raised her hand as if to wave off her concern. "*Seeker* heard this message the same as we did. They killed their distress call right away. Even if Zeb and his crew heard the transmission, they wouldn't have been able to get an exact location."

"An exact location? So they would know generally where we are then?" Hawk did not feel calmed by this knowledge.

"They would generally know which direction we are in, yes, but there is no indication that they have altered their route."

Hawk tried to swallow down the fear that had lodged in her throat.

"The Council met this morning." Loris stated matter-of-factly.

"You what?" Hawk couldn't believe what she was hearing. "Why wasn't I included?"

"We decided it was best to exclude junior diplomats for the decision." Loris' mouth was set in a thin determined line.

"What decision?" Hawk asked despite feeling as if she already knew the answer.

"We are continuing with our original plan. We are going to Onsella."

Hawk took a deep breath trying to calm herself before she spoke again. "We are leaving behind our people in *Seeker* knowing that they are in immediate danger from the group that spread that illness?" Hawk pointed jerkily towards the direction of *Seeker*.

"We don't have a choice."

"There's always a choice." Hawk turned her back and started to walk away.

Loris' voice called after her. "You can't tell him, Hawk."

Hawk turned on her heels abruptly. "What?" she snapped.

"You can't tell him." Loris stepped forward, narrowing the distance between them. "I'm going to meet with Kit now. We have some things to discuss. You're coming with me."

Hawk stepped backwards. "I don't think I want to."

"I'm not asking Hawk. You're coming with me." Loris pushed past her. "And we need to go now if you're going to have time to say goodbye to Caspian when we get back."

———

Kit met them at the entrance. Hawk trudged along behind Loris. She wanted nothing more than to run to Caspian and warn him. Instead, she was trailing along behind the woman who was sending him into even greater danger than he had been in already.

"We need to meet in the conference area. Just us." Loris stated flatly.

Kit nodded. "I alerted the rest of the Council to be on alert. I will not keep things from the Council."

Loris chuckled. "Everything I tell and show you will be yours to do with as you see fit."

When they reached the conference area, Kit removed her helmet and sat. Loris stood. Hawk rolled her eyes and sat next to Kit, glaring up at Loris.

Loris pretended not to notice. "Was it the same message that you heard before?"

"Exactly the same." Kit confirmed.

"I know you're new to your position. Are you prepared to protect your people?" Loris asked.

"I'm always prepared." Kit straightened.

"No, I don't think you understand. Do you know *how* to protect your people? What you have in your possession to do so?" Loris said cryptically. Her eyes darted towards the wall behind the table.

Kit looked at her quizzically.

"I thought not." Loris stood and walked past Hawk and Kit. Hawk and Kit both followed hesitantly.

Loris stopped when she reached the wall and then dropped to her knees. She pushed down hard on the molding at the base of the wall. It fell away to show a small hand sized cut out. Loris looked up at Kit whose mouth hung open. "I take it nobody's ever shown you this before?"

Kit shook her head. Hawk watched intently, unsure of what to expect next.

Loris pushed her hand into the cut out and pulled up. The panel slid upward to reveal a large, dull-grey safe.

"How did you...?" Kit stammered.

"You'd be surprised what secrets a ship can hold. All of the Onsella-bound ships were built exactly the same. Only senior diplomats know about it. With so many of your council all going at the same time, I suspected you hadn't been shown this."

"But surely Pike must know." Kit sounded hurt.

Loris nodded. "That's something you will have to discuss with Pike. Right now, you need to see what's inside. What day did *Seeker* depart from Earth?"

Kit seemed confused by the question. "What does that have to do with..."

Hawk interrupted, eager to see what Loris was going to do next. "May 1, 2139."

Kit glared at Hawk while Loris turned toward the keypad on the safe's door. She typed in 01, 05, 21, 39. She hesitated for a moment and then pushed the green key at the bottom of the keypad. With a slight *click*, the door opened so that there was only the slightest crack. Loris pulled it open.

Hawk peered down as Loris picked up one of the items. Even in the dim light of *Seeker*, she could see that it was made from a shiny metal. The object was somewhat L-shaped. Loris held it from the shorter of the L-sides which was flatter and wider than the other side. The side that was not being held was cylindrical. It was hollow in the middle. By the way Loris was holding it, it must have been heavier than it looked.

Hawk searched her mind trying to remember where she had seen it before. Suddenly she remembered. It was a tool used for warfare on Earth. A gun. A pistol to be exact.

"Do you know what this is?" Loris asked Kit.

"I do, but I had no idea we had any on board. They're used to kill, am I right?" Kit's eyes were tracing every curve of the weapon in front of her.

"If used correctly, they can." Loris answered thoughtfully. "They're a very powerful tool." She reached into the base of the safe and took out a small brass colored cylinder with a grey top that came to a point. "This is a round. It contains a bullet." Loris pointed towards the grey tip. "This bullet is what shoots out of the barrel," she pointed toward the hollow cylinder on the pistol, "and hits the target. The gun is useless if you don't have any rounds loaded into it."

Loris pulled out a rectangular piece from the safe. "This is the magazine. It holds the rounds in the gun until you use them. You put it in like this," she slid it into the base of the handle, "and then it's ready to use." She pointed toward a hanging curved piece of metal in front of the handle. "You pull this trigger back when it's time." Loris waited for Kit to nod and then pushed a button and the magazine slid back out.

"I don't have time to show you everything, but you need to know it. You might need to use these." She pointed toward the other guns in the safe and handed Kit the pistol. Kit accepted it hesitantly and held it out in front of her as if she were afraid it might explode.

"It's not going to hurt you. It's not even loaded. See?" Loris took the gun again and pulled back a part on the top to reveal a hollow area on the top of the gun. "No bullets," she stated flatly before handing it back to Kit who did not look at all comforted.

Loris turned her attention back to the safe and pulled out a large book. "This will tell you everything you need to know." She threw it on the table behind them. "And this." She held up a small data chip. "There's a video on here. It will talk you through everything. Load it into one of the viewing monitors in the helm and you'll know everything that you need to. Until then," Loris reached for the gun, which Kit eagerly handed her, "keep them locked up. We don't want any accidents." She put the gun back in its spot and shut the safe's door.

Kit spoke for the first time since she had been handed the gun. "What am I supposed to do with all of those?" She pointed toward the safe which held at least a dozen weapons.

"That's up to you." Loris said flatly. "If it were me, I would want my council trained immediately. You need to be able to..."

"What? Kill people?" Kit's voice cracked as she spoke.

Loris stood. "If that's what needs to happen, yes. Your people have already been attacked once. I would think that you would be willing to do whatever was needed to protect your people. And mine."

Kit nodded, never taking her eyes off the safe. "I will do whatever needs to be done. Your people will be safe here."

"Good." Loris replied. "Now we need to get back. The medics will be boarding soon."

"And they know about the recent change in circumstances?" Kit questioned.

"I thought that would be best left for you. You will be protecting them; you should be the one to tell them what they are being protected from."

"And you want to be long gone before they find out," Kit stated firmly but did not argue. Instead, she turned toward the door. "I'll walk you out."

Hawk shook so badly with anger as she entered

Enlightenment that she struggled to wash herself and disinfect her suit.

She stepped from the shower and dressed quickly. As soon as Loris stepped out from the dressing area, Hawk pounced. "They deserve to know. Our medics deserve to know what they are getting into."

"They do. Nothing has changed." Loris replied.

"Oh really? Because I seem to remember you giving *Seeker*'s leader a vault full of deadly weapons to use against attackers. It sure seems like something has changed to me!"

Loris sat on a bench, looking exhausted. "Hawk, we don't know if they're coming back. We didn't know it before and we don't know it now. After hearing that message, I just wanted them to be protected. If anything, they're safer now than they were before."

Hawk wasn't sure she believed that. "I'm telling him," she said flatly.

To Hawk's surprise, Loris didn't argue. "I can't stop you if that's what you decide, but that is not your job to do. *Seeker* needs our medics. It is up to *Seeker* to protect them now. Not us. Not *you*."

Hawk stood stiffly as Loris walked past her toward the exit. "The medics will be here in half an hour. They're meeting as a team right now. It will be your only chance to say goodbye and tell Caspian whatever it is you decide. I'll see you then."

Hawk spent the remainder of the time locked in her living quarters arguing with herself over the right thing to do. Even as she approached the loading area, she still wasn't sure what she was going to say.

Loris met her at the docking port. When she saw Hawk, Loris moved towards her. "I'm glad you made it. We are not going to enter *Seeker* with the team. You will need to say your goodbyes before *Seeker* opens its doors."

Hawk nodded and stepped towards the hazmat suits. "You won't be needing one." Loris insisted. Hawk stepped away from the suit and moved closer to Caspian who was already putting on his hazmat suit. She risked a backwards glance at her mentor. Loris seemed to be more of a watchdog today than a leader.

Pushing the thought aside, Hawk turned her attention to Caspian. She helped him to adjust his suit and tried to hide the pain from her face. "It's only for a little while," he said as he, too, tried to smile through the heartache.

"I know," she replied. All she could think about was the illness on the other side of the doors and the people who were responsible for it. Hawk imagined Caspian running from room to room administering medication while dead bodies floated outside. Then an even worse image flashed before her mind's eye. She imagined the bodies floating around the ship and envisioned Caspian among them. A shiver went up her spine and she turned away from Caspian's face.

He reached forward and stroked her cheek. "I'm going to be fine. Next time I see you, we will be on solid ground for the first time."

His words, although encouraging, didn't make the ache in her chest feel any better. "We just started all of this and now..." Hawk let her words trail off, "I'm going to miss you."

"You were worth the wait then and you're worth the wait now," he responded with a melancholy look in his eyes. Hawk was sure he had more words to say but was equally confident that he had no intention of saying them.

"There's so much to tell you," Hawk started, "I don't even know where to begin."

Caspian looked quizzically at her face before their conversation was cut off. Loris stepped forward and began speaking in a loud, authoritative tone that suggested nobody else was to speak. She gave what Hawk was certain was a very well-worded, powerful speech. She caught the words "bravery" and "heroes" but neither Hawk nor Caspian heard it; they were too busy staring at one another. Hawk traced all of Caspian's features with her eyes and tried to memorize the feel of his hand in hers. When Loris stopped talking, she knew it was now or never.

"I can't go without you knowing..." she began, but Caspian cut her off.

"Don't. This is hard enough as it is. I've made my decision and as much as it hurts to leave you now, we both know that it's what has to happen."

Hawk nodded and swallowed back the lump in her throat. "I guess it's time then." She shifted back and forth on her feet but kept his hand in hers.

"I guess it is," he said forlornly.

"I'm not sure what to say. Good luck, I guess," Hawk said with a crooked smile.

"I'm already lucky," he said, causing Hawk to blush. She knew it was a cliché goodbye, but she couldn't help but love it anyway.

He leaned in and placed his lips on hers. The gesture was that of fleeting tenderness. Hawk was grateful that his arms were wrapped around her waist because she was not certain her legs could support her weight any longer when her knees began to shake. He pulled away and Hawk felt Loris' arm guiding her towards the exit. She didn't fight it. Instead, she looked back to see Caspian one more time. He held his helmet in front of him while he stared at her intently. She stared back. Hawk wanted to say something, anything that might show him how much she cared, but the door slid shut before she had the chance.

. . .

Hawk headed to the helm with Loris immediately. Rowan and Ural were already there. In fact, the whole Council was there. Much to Hawk's dismay, the windows were still uncovered. Hawk tried not to look at the bodies, but she couldn't help herself. She tried to focus on Loris, Rowan, her hands, the control panel; anything that would keep her eyes from drifting to the scene outside, but it was no use. Once again, she had the sudden image of Caspian's bloody body floating around in the darkness. She shook her head as if to clear her thoughts.

Enlightenment had to wait for the go ahead from *Seeker* via the radio before departing. So far, all she heard was the faint crackle of static seeping through the speakers. She looked at all the faces around her and tried to imagine what they must be feeling. To her knowledge, nobody else on the Council had a loved one staying behind on the *Seeker* other than herself. Hawk wondered if they would have thought differently about the plan if they had, then remembered that she herself had been the most insistent about helping *Seeker*. She felt guilty for what she was putting the medics through. She reminded herself repeatedly that she had done what was best... for the better good.

The better good. A phrase that Hawk would never be able to think of in the same way again. She had always uttered the phrase as if it was a given. She recalled using it during her interview for the junior diplomat position. The words were easy to repeat and even to believe. Living them proved to be much harder. Now that she was the one to make the sacrifices and watch those she loved suffer, the better good didn't sound so appealing.

A thick silence filled the room. Hawk stood stone-still along with the other council members. The helm had once again been nearly emptied of workers. A pilot scarcely older than Hawk waited at the control panel. He scanned the faces of each council member discreetly as he glanced toward the people inside the helm, the radio, the control panel and finally towards the bodies outside the window. Hawk knew that as a pilot he had probably spent more time than most with the unwelcome sight floating by.

A voice sounded from the radio causing Hawk and most of the others to startle. "*Enlightenment*, this is *Seeker*. Your medics are settled. You are clear for departure. Repeat, you are clear for departure." Kit's voice was as commanding as ever. Clearly she had brushed off her nerves from earlier in the day.

Loris reached for the microphone. "We copy, *Seeker*. Departing now." She nodded towards the young pilot. He responded instantly with the flick of a few switches and punched buttons before sitting himself in front of a steering column in the center of the ship.

Hawk felt the weight on her chest become heavier as the ship itself began to move. She walked towards the side window and watched as *Seeker* crawled into view while *Enlightenment* pulled away slowly. She had never seen the outside of a spaceship before, aside from photographs.

Seeker was long and rounded with a bubble-like domed glass towards the top-back of the ship that was filled with a bright-blue light. In the photos, *Enlightenment* had looked similar. The noticeable difference being that the metallic shine that was such a distinguishing feature in the photographs was now missing. Instead, the ship was a dull grayish-black.

Enlightenment continued to drift away. Hawk wondered if Caspian was in the helm of *Seeker* watching as they floated away. The pilot spoke over her thoughts when they had drifted far enough away to start the engines. "We are ready."

Loris spoke into the microphone once more. "*Seeker*, we are at a safe distance to depart at full speed."

Kit's voice echoed through the radio speaker. "Thank you, *Enlightenment*. We will await further assistance."

Loris took a moment before responding. "Good luck to you, *Seeker*. I will see you on Onsella." With that, she nodded towards the pilot.

Hawk felt the sickening feeling in her stomach as the artificial gravity adjusted to accommodate the speed. She watched out the side window for as long as she could. When the gravity shifted, Hawk stumbled to the side. It took her only a fraction of a second to steady herself. Still, by the time she looked back up, the ship was gone. She stepped forward until her nose was a mere inch from the glass. Her breath fogged the surface in front of her. She reached up and touched the window with her fingertips.

"Goodbye," Hawk whispered so softly that only she could hear. She waited for only a few seconds before turning to face the rest of the Council with determination etched on her face. There was no room for doubt now. They had to reach Onsella. Soon.

EPILOGUE

The only thing Hawk was absolutely certain of, was what lay beneath her feet. Onsella. She was standing on the long-awaited ground of Onsella for the first time. Deep in her chest, Hawk felt the vibration hit her from the deafening cheering that the Onsellans aimed at her and the rest of *Enlightenment*'s citizens.

Looking to her left, Loris stood tall and proud. Hawk wiped away a tear from her eye as she gazed to the sky. The first real sky she had ever seen. It was so similar to what she had seen projected on the ceiling in *Enlightenment*, and yet completely, awe strikingly different. Somewhere beyond the blue and past the clouds, Caspian was fighting for his life. Even now, experiencing what should have been the greatest joy she had ever known, Hawk wouldn't allow herself to forget.

Staring toward the heavens, Hawk shivered at the thought that she would never be happy, truly happy without Caspian standing by her side here. Hawk had always dreamt of having a home. A real home with solid ground beneath her feet. Now that she had a planet, she realized it would never be home until she shared it with Caspian.

"We'll get him back."

Hawk jumped at the sound of Loris' voice.

"We will. I promise you."

"How?" Hawk squeaked. "How do we get him back? I'll do whatever it takes, but you've seen the dangers. How do we get him back?" The trip had not been easy in the days since leaving *Seeker*.

Loris smiled down at Hawk. "I didn't know how we'd get here," Loris' eyes darted around the scene in front of them, "but here we are. I don't know how we'll get him back, but I know we will."

Hawk nodded and wiped away another tear. "We'll get him back." Hawk's voice was stronger now. "Whatever it takes. Caspian will stand on Onsella with me."

Loris wrapped Hawk's hand in her own. She gave a light squeeze before thrusting both hands into the air victoriously as the crowd yelled even louder.

RATE AND REVIEW

We hope you enjoyed *Enlightenment* by Nicole James kelley. If you did, we would ask that you please rate and review this title. Every review helps our authors.

Rate and Review: Enlightenment

MEET THE AUTHOR

Nicole James Kelley wrote and illustrated her first book as a second-grade student. Although the never-published masterpiece was lost to time, her love for writing lives on today. Nicole is an avid writer, reader, and fantasizer who writes universes that surpass anything that could exist in our known world. When she isn't writing, Nicole enjoys her career working in education. She has worked as a paraprofessional, teacher, and currently serves as an elementary principal. Nicole James Kelley lives in Wyoming with her husband and dogs.